JESSICA COLE
MODEL SPY

Also by Sarah Sky

Jessica Cole: Model Spy: Code Red Lipstick
Jessica Cole: Model Spy: Fashion Assassin

JESSICA COLE
MODEL SPY
CATWALK CRIMINAL

SARAH SKY

SCHOLASTIC

Scholastic Children's Books
An imprint of Scholastic Ltd
Euston House, 24 Eversholt Street
London, NW1 1DB, UK
Registered office: Westfield Road, Southam, Warwickshire, CV47 0RA
SCHOLASTIC and associated logos are trademarks and/or
registered trademarks of Scholastic Inc.

First published in the UK by Scholastic Ltd, 2015

ISBN 978 1407 14019 3

A CIP catalogue record for this book
is available from the British Library.

Printed by CPI Group (UK) Ltd, Croydon, CR0 4YY
Papers used by Scholastic Children's Books are made
from wood grown in sustainable forests.

1 3 5 7 9 10 8 6 4 2

www.scholastic.co.uk

For Maureen, with love.

CHAPTER
ONE

"Mission Breaking Dawn. Go, go, go!"

Jessica touched the diamond stud as the command rang through her earpiece. Drew Hopkins had made his move. Her handler quickly relayed the message: a camera had captured the Ministry of Defence boffin slipping out of the cocktail party showcasing the best of British fashion. He was heading up the stairs to the seventy-second floor of the Shard, the highest level open to the public. A few moments later, a blond man in a navy suit had followed. The meet was finally happening. According to a tip-off from a trusted MI6 informant, Hopkins planned to sell the blueprint for a driverless armoured truck he'd helped design at the MoD. An unidentified foreign buyer had taken the bait and offered twenty million pounds, with the deal happening tonight.

Typical. The timing totally sucked. Judging by the worried faces of the other models and undercover Westwood agents – Bree, Sasha and Natalia – they realized it too. They were stuck on a lower set of stairs, balancing on skyscraper Charlotte Olympia heels as they waited for their cue – the start of The Vamps track. Within minutes all the models would emerge, circuiting level sixty-nine in couture evening gowns before mingling with VIP guests, including the wives of the British prime minister and US ambassador, fashion designers and magazine editors from around the world.

"We have to get up there!" Jessica urged.

Nobody moved. Had they frozen? Surely not! It was Jessica and Natalia's first official mission for Westwood – a secret division of MI6 that recruited models and other fashionistas – but Bree and Sasha were pros. They'd both joined when they were fifteen, the same age that Natalia had recently turned. She could totally get Natalia having an attack of the jitters, but what was *their* excuse? They were twenty-one and eighteen, old enough to know better, and they were totally copping out.

Do something! Anything would be good right now.

"You have to move, Bree," Jessica pressed.

Their window to act was slipping away fast. Did she have to point out to Bree that she was supposed to be running this mission? That would go down *really* well. The raven-haired model continued to cling to the handrail, a few steps in front of her.

"You don't get to tell me what to do," Bree shot back. "This is my operation and I need time to think. We can't let everyone see us piling upstairs. Someone could follow and the mission will be scuppered."

What was she talking about? The mission would be over if they didn't get their act together.

"Only one of us has to go," Jessica reasoned. "We need a diversion and the others can come up when the coast is clear."

"Maybe we should wait for backup," Natalia chipped in. "You're the leader, Bree, not Jessica. It's your call."

"Don't you think I know that already?" Bree snapped. "Just because Nathan's our unit head it doesn't give Jessica the right to swan about acting like she's the boss."

Really? This old accusation again? Bree had a chip on her shoulder the size of Kansas after she discovered that Jessica was the god-daughter of MI6 agent Nathan Hall. She thought he routinely gave her special treatment, which couldn't be further from the truth. He was as tough on her as he was everyone else.

"We don't have time for this!" Jessica took a deep breath and pushed past the other girls to the top of the stairs. Thankfully, Mike, the event organizer who looked like he was permanently on the edge of a nervous breakdown, was distracted. The prime minister's wife had launched into a speech praising innovative British designers. It bought them a vital few seconds, long enough for her to slip past Mike and get up the next flight of stairs.

"Where are you going?" Zak, one of the three male models in the show, called after her loudly. He removed the headphones to his iPod nano and slipped the device into the top pocket of his grey Paul Smith suit. "We're not on yet. Plus you're way out of sequence. You're not opening the show, Bree is."

"Shut up!" *You idiot*, she wanted to add.

"I'm just sayin'."

Mike spun round. "I'll count you in any second now, Jessica. Get back."

She shot a daggers look at Zak as she returned to her place in the line-up. He might be a hotshot from the States, having bagged a lucrative Calvin Klein contract at the age of seventeen with his dark, rugged good looks, but he was also a total pain. Couldn't he hit on one of the other girls rather than sticking his nose into her business? For some reason he'd attached himself to her like glue all evening. Every time she turned around he was there, droning on about how many modelling gigs he'd landed and how he was being lined up to become the next big male supermodel. Mega yawn.

Bree turned around and leant towards Jessica. "Stop undermining me. I've told you before I can—"

"I repeat, Mission Breaking Dawn!"

Jessica and Bree jumped as the handler's voice boomed in their ears again. Unsurprisingly, he was panicking. The stakes couldn't be higher. If terrorists got their hands on this blueprint, they could create the ultimate weapon: a vehicle laden with explosives, which could be driven by remote and detonated anywhere.

Westwood had been given the task of stopping the deal from happening when Hopkins settled on the venue – the top of Western Europe's tallest building, in the heart of the London Bridge Quarter development. MI6 feared he'd spot their usual agents a mile off due to his MoD training, but undercover teenage models were another matter. Like most people, Hopkins didn't know they even existed. Westwood agents could identify the mystery buyer and terminate the meet, hopefully without attracting any attention.

Jessica had to think fast. No way could she let this deal happen, even if it meant letting down the red-hot British designer Ossa Cosway, who'd recently unveiled her as the face of his brand. She was wearing one of his emerald green, lace designs, together with jewellery from another Brit, Tatty Devine.

No! A guitar strummed and Bradley Simpson's voice boomed out. The Vamps track had started and they were on.

"We're out of time," Bree hissed. "It's down to you,

Jessica. It's the only option. You're last out so make sure you don't mess up."

That was rich coming from her!

Bree strode out into the photographers' flashing lights, squeezed into a corseted red taffeta Alexander McQueen number, complete with a frothy train. Natalia followed, to a chorus of gasps and applause, rocking a heavily embroidered midnight blue Stella McCartney gown. Ten seconds later, she was joined down the catwalk by Sasha, who was in a shocking pink Victoria Beckham dress. At least *she* looked embarrassed about leaving a junior operative in the lurch.

Unbelievable. They'd totally and utterly passed the buck. Were they too scared of upsetting the designers here tonight? The girls were putting their modelling careers before Westwood. Hadn't they learnt anything in training? Clearly not.

Ten, nine, eight, seven. . .

The stage manager counted in Zak. She ignored him as he attempted to catch her eye for the zillionth time that evening. She was up next. Slipping her hand into the pocket of her gown, she pulled out a secret weapon.

Her classmates back at school would never believe that the success of an MI6 mission could come down to this – a specially adapted Bobbi Brown Red Carpet lipstick – not that she'd ever be able to tell them. Her work with Westwood was top secret.

Twisting the base until she heard a tiny click, she flicked the dial to the lowest setting and slowly increased it. Too high and the electromagnetic pulse would knock out the electricity across all of East London. Too low and nothing major would happen. It had to be just right: enough to affect the whole of the Shard, from the reception upwards, to thwart any escape attempts by Hopkins and his business partner.

BANG!

Cries rang out as The Vamps' track suddenly cut and the floor was plunged into darkness. She kicked off her heels and was on the move with the help of her electronic contact lenses, which contained thermal imaging and X-ray technology. Blurry red shapes – panicking guests – loomed straight ahead. She dodged them, skirting past to the right. They didn't know where they were going, but she did.

Five, four, three, two, one. She was already taking

the stairs to the seventy-second floor, two at a time. She had no idea if the other Westwood girls were following. Had they remembered to put in their own lenses? If not, they'd be as blind as the rest of the guests until their eyes became accustomed to the lights from neighbouring buildings, and that could lose vital seconds. Jessica knew from past experience that gadgets saved lives in the field. She always carried some with her, even on photo shoots, and made sure she knew exactly how everything worked. One slip-up could be fatal, yet Bree had forgotten to do a run-through of their gear back in the hotel dressing room.

She steadied herself against the handrail and caught her breath as a sharp gust of icy wind tousled her strawberry-blonde hair. It was well below zero tonight. She caught a quick glimpse of the London skyline before the deck lurched beneath her feet. Downstairs she'd been distracted and hadn't taken in how ridiculously high up they were, as she'd avoided looking out of the windows. However, level seventy-two was open to the elements. She closed her eyes and counted to ten.

Pull yourself together.

This floor was protected by a high fence so there was no chance whatsoever of falling. Still. . .

She'd never been good with heights, particularly after a modelling shoot in Paris when she'd fallen off a six-storey building, saved only by an MI6 nano wire. Tonight had to be a piece of cake compared to that experience. There was no way she could fall. Her eyes flew open. She could do this. She ventured out further on to the deck. Where was Hopkins? Quickly, she did a circuit. She controlled her breathing and fixed her eyes straight ahead to make sure she didn't take in the views. The deck was deserted apart from a waiter having a crafty fag. Hopkins hadn't come back down so he must have gone up into the restricted area at the very top of the building. Typical. She stared up. The thought of climbing any higher made her nauseous

Keep calm. Don't think about it. Just do it.

Could she? She knew she didn't have a choice. She hitched up her skirts and climbed over the chain marked *No Entry.*

"Target's at the top of the spire. I'm in pursuit." Her diamond stud was connected to an earpiece, allowing her to receive and relay information. She'd left out the whole wanting to throw up bit. That was too much detail to give her handler.

"The Shard's sealed off," he rasped into her earpiece. "They're not going anywhere. Get a visual on the buyer and wait for backup. We have an armed unit on the ground moving in. They'll be with you in minutes."

They must have given up on the other Westwood girls. So had she, unfortunately. They were a lost cause. Nathan would rip them apart in debriefing – if they were still working for Westwood by then. A loud, whirring noise made her look up again. She watched as a dark spot in the sky drew closer.

"We've got company."

"Clarify?"

"A chopper's approaching from the west. Is it one of ours?"

The handler fell silent for a few seconds. "That's a negative. Secure the blueprint. You can't wait for backup. Go."

She hurtled up the stairs, past the dark shapes of machinery and equipment. She had to keep going, even though her knees were crumbling beneath her and her lungs were about to explode. Lunging for the handrail again and again, she hauled herself upwards. Kickboxing and ballet had helped build up her stamina, along with the karate classes she'd started at school, but this workout would test Olympic medallists. She was at the eighty-ninth level. A few more steps to go.

She paused for a split second at a clanking noise further down the stairs. Was that her backup, finally? Fingers crossed she wouldn't have to do this on her own. One last step. Panting, she stumbled out on to the deck, blinded by hair lashing her face. Pushing her locks aside, she saw a dark-haired man sprawled out in front of her. Blood poured from a gash in his forehead.

"Hopkins is down!" She felt for a pulse and found a weak one. "Assistance needed," she shouted above the whirring of helicopter blades.

"And the blueprint? Where is it now?"

Jessica looked up into the dramatic steel and glass spire towering above her. A rope dangled down from the helicopter; a blond man was already two metres off the ground. As she squinted at him, her X-ray lens picked out a small, rectangular metal object in his trouser pocket. Hopkins must have transferred his blueprint on to a USB flash drive. The MI6 informant was wrong. He'd claimed Hopkins was carrying the plans on a mini iPad.

"It's being taken by helicopter!"

She lunged forward and grabbed the man's foot. He jolted with surprise and immediately aimed a kick at her head. Dodging it, she clung on grimly as the helicopter rocked and the rope swung wildly. She couldn't let go. A glint of steel flashed above her head as the man slashed at her with a flick knife. She shifted position but wasn't quick enough to dodge the blade. White-hot pain made her gasp as blood dripped from her hand down to her armpit.

She slipped down the rope as he jabbed again, one hand hanging on while he attacked with the other. This time, the blade struck one of the planets on her Tatty Devine Saturn charm bracelet that had been adapted by MI6. That was it! She had a matter of seconds for this to work or it'd be all over. Her bracelet was decorated with five multicoloured Perspex planets, containing hidden devices including mini grapnels.

She let go, plunging three metres to the deck. She braced herself and rolled on to her back. Tugging at a pink planet, she aimed at the rope above the man's head. A mini grapnel fired out and missed.

Dammit.

Trying again, she yanked the red planet. This time the grapnel hit home. She jumped up as the embedded laser seared through the fibres and the rope snapped. The man fell to the deck, landing awkwardly on his ankle. He stared in disbelief at the severed end of the rope in his hands. Stumbling to his feet, he lunged at her with the knife again.

She sidestepped to the left, tripping him up as she twisted a green planet hanging from her wrist. The force of the hidden magnet ripped the flash drive from her attacker's pocket and attached it to her bracelet without him noticing. He cursed as he landed on his bad ankle.

"*Reviens!*" He waved his arms frantically, but the helicopter swung away.

Jessica slipped the flash drive into her pocket as he watched the chopper head towards the London Eye. She noticed panic in his eyes for the first time as he spun around and frantically weighed up possible escape routes.

"Armed officers are on their way up. You can't get away."

"You think, *petite fille*?" he snarled. His eyes fixed on a mechanical arm. He sprinted towards it. "Don't try to stop me. You'll only get hurt. Go home to mama before you catch a chill."

Her eyes narrowed. She had no intention of stopping him. He hadn't realized it yet, but she had what she wanted: the flash drive. Hopkins wasn't going anywhere either. He was still unconscious. Her side of the operation was over, as far as she was concerned. She watched as the man secured himself into a harness and climbed over the side, holding on to a rope that clipped on to an outside steel pole. Was he going to jump? She felt she should at least warn him.

"Didn't you read the guidebook? The Shard is almost three hundred and ten metres high. Do you really think you'll survive the fall?"

The man laughed. "I've no intention of falling. How do you think they clean the windows around here? *Au revoir*."

He winked, exhaled deeply and jumped. She ran over and stared as he abseiled gracefully down the glass building. That had to be *the* most hair-raising way to make an exit. She'd settle for using the lifts any day. She felt in her pocket, her fingers curling round the USB drive. Thank God that was safe.

"I've got the blueprint," she said, touching her earpiece. "You can pick up the target any minute now. He's on his way down."

"Roger that. Good work."

Suddenly, the rope ground to a halt and the man dangled helplessly about halfway down the building. Jessica waved at him. Ha ha. She knew more about window cleaning than he did after chatting to one of the Shard's employees earlier. The windows were cleaned in two separate sections, which meant the rope didn't stretch to the very bottom of the building. Another rope had to be attached at right about the point he was stuck now. He was trapped with nowhere to go – a sitting duck ready to be picked up by MI6 officers.

Phew. Tonight had almost been a total disaster, but she'd managed to pull it off without help. Where was everyone? Of course! The lifts would be out of action due to the blackout. The team would have to climb all the way to the top, carrying equipment, which would take time.

A soft humming noise made her spin around. A mini black helicopter landed nearby, its rotors whirring. She stepped closer. This wasn't a child's toy that had landed here by accident. It was some sort of drone.

"We've got another visitor. An unidentified flying object."

Silence.

"Hello? Is anyone there?"

Great. The comms were down. It could be a technical glitch, but it coincided with the arrival of the drone. She didn't believe in coincidences. The helicopter could contain some kind of jamming device. She crouched down, examining the object. GPS coordinates flashed up on a small black box. That's how it'd been programmed to land here! Someone had deliberately sent it. If she could hack into its computer system, she'd be able to trace back the coordinates to where it had come from. She fiddled with the box. This wasn't going to be easy. She wasn't a superhacker, but someone back at MI6 could break the code. Could this be the buyer's method of getting the USB drive off the building? Maybe it had already set off before the meet went wrong and couldn't be stopped.

Jessica paused. What if this were another, separate plan to steal the blueprint? The hairs on the back of her neck prickled. She glanced over her shoulder. A dark figure wearing a ski mask loomed above her. Before she could react, something was blown into her face. Eyes burning, she lurched forward blindly, trying to stand up. Gloved hands pushed her back. Her knees crumpled beneath her and her head cracked on the floor. Hard. She lay helplessly, unable to move, as someone reached into her pocket and retrieved the USB.

Her mind screamed "No!" but the word didn't come out. Her tongue was paralysed, along with the rest of her body. She couldn't open her eyelids, but sensed her attacker was nearby. She could hear him messing with the drone. He was typing in fresh coordinates. A few seconds later the helicopter took off, vibrating quietly. Her attacker hadn't taken any chances; he knew he couldn't get past the squad heading up the stairs. But the drone could.

She had to stop him. She had to warn her handler

that the USB device was being spirited away by air. He could order the drone to be shot down. Her body refused to respond. Her mind was locked in a useless shell; her mouth wouldn't open. She heard the clatter of feet and someone shouting her name. Then everything went black.

CHAPTER TWO

"Are you sure I can't get you girls any more chocolate chip cookies?" Mattie dusted an imaginary crumb from her pink Chanel suit. "They're Jessica's favourite recipe and still warm from the oven. Perfect for girls' night."

Jessica was dressed in her favourite Topshop pyjamas, curled up on the sofa next to her best friend, Becky. They'd paused the *Pitch Perfect* DVD after her head started to throb again. Instead they were quietly gossiping and looking at glossy magazines and newspapers.

"Your cookies are delicious but I couldn't eat another thing, thanks." Becky tugged at the waistband of her black skinny jeans. "I think I ate every last one. I'm fit to explode."

Mattie's blue eyes narrowed and frown marks furrowed her powdered forehead as she glanced down at Jessica. "Still no appetite?"

She shook her head, fiddling with the bandage on her hand. Sickness, uncontrollable shaking and vertigo were some of the delightful side effects of the paralysing poison she'd ingested on Sunday night. She hadn't been able to keep anything down for the last forty-eight hours apart from peppermint tea.

"Maybe toast would be better." Her grandma's diamond rings glittered as she placed her hands on her hips.

Jessica's stomach lurched. "No, I'm good."

"You need to try and eat something. You didn't have any lunch. I thought chocolate chip cookies might help get your appetite back, but they're probably too rich for your stomach. Toast will be nice and light. I'll make some in case you change your mind."

"I don't—"

"It's no trouble."

Mattie scooped up the empty plate from the table and headed out of the sitting room, her Jimmy Choos tap-tapping on the polished wooden floorboards.

"AAAAAGGGGHHH!" Jessica hurled a cushion at the closing door. "She's driving me absolutely nuts, fussing over me every second. I swear, I haven't been left alone all day. She's been checking up on me on the hour, every hour. It makes me want to scream."

Jessica shivered as she pulled the blue silk Ossa Cosway dressing gown around her shoulders. Suddenly, her pyjamas felt terribly thin. She was freezing. Had the central heating been turned off or was this a new symptom of the poison?

"Hey!" She flinched as Becky tapped her gently on the head with a rolled-up copy of the *London Evening Standard*. "What was that for exactly? I'm an invalid with a head injury, remember?"

"For being mean about your sweet, lovely grandma." Becky's long, dangly earrings shook as she ran a hand through her dark bob. "Who just so happens to make the best chocolate chip cookies I've ever tasted. Plus, she manages to bake without getting a single mark on her Chanel suit. I think she must be a superwoman or something."

"That's pushing it," Jessica said, hugging her knees tightly. "And I don't think anyone's ever called her sweet and lovely before unless it was because she was..." She managed to stop herself in time before she blurted out "undercover". No one could know about Mattie's past as a former spy. Even she sometimes found it hard to believe that her immaculate grandma had worked for Westwood when she modelled as a teenager, like Jessica's mum – a weird family tradition.

"Because what?"

"I can't remember." Jessica touched the bruise on her forehead. It totally sucked that she'd never be able to tell Becky the truth – that she'd joined the top-secret wing of MI6 to discover who'd murdered her mum when she was four. Her helicopter crash and the death of a former KGB agent were connected to something called Sargasso, according to a vital scrap of info she'd gleaned from Katyenka Ingorokva, the brattish supermodel daughter of a dodgy Russian oligarch. "Kat the Brat" had enjoyed torturing her by staying mute on the subject during their Westwood training over the last six months.

She hadn't seen her since the weekend and after-school MI6 sessions at secret venues across London had finished and was no closer to finding out more.

Her most promising lead – several anonymous text messages telling her to go to the Harry Potter landmark, platform nine and three-quarters at King's Cross station, to learn about Sargasso – had produced nothing. No one had ever turned up and after a few months the texts, from a disposable and untraceable mobile, stopped. She was desperate to learn the truth about Sargasso and becoming a member of Westwood was her only way in.

"Are you OK, Jessica? You've gone really pale."

"Yeah, I guess. My head's still muzzy, but any memory loss will be temporary, so I *will* remember you whacked me with a newspaper after eating every single one of my favourite biscuits."

"Touché." Becky sat up, causing an avalanche of magazines to fall on to the floor. "Seriously, though, Mattie's worried about you. So am I. Jamie too."

"I know, but you needn't be. I'm feeling a lot better now and the doctor said I'm going to be fine. I just need to rest for a couple of days."

Well, *a lot* better was stretching it. The doctor had warned her that she'd probably experience similar after-effects to running a marathon. What did he know? Being hit by a car felt like a more accurate comparison. She'd regained feeling in her legs in the last twenty-four hours, but they still ached like mad and she fell over if she got up too quickly. Mattie had tried to keep Becky and other visitors away, and wanted her to stay in bed. But she couldn't stand another day stuck upstairs and had insisted that an evening with her best friend would help her recover much quicker.

It had taken quite a while to get down the stairs. She'd had to stop a couple of times as the carpet seemed to leap up towards her, throwing her off balance, but she'd finally made it with Mattie hovering in the background. She knew her grandma meant well, but it sucked feeling like a tiny little kid again. She had to get her muscles working properly and the only way to do that was to be up and about, even if it hurt. A lot. Her dad was the only one who understood what she was going through. He was ex-MI6 and didn't let his MS stop him from working as a private investigator, even if it meant using a walking stick on bad days.

Jessica flicked through the newspaper. She shuddered as her eyes rested on the page twenty-six lead.

SHARD BOMB HOAX LATEST

The Shard has reopened after a bomb hoax on Sunday night disrupted a high-profile fashion evening hosted by the prime minister's wife.

Designers Victoria Beckham, Stella McCartney and Ossa Cosway were evacuated along with foreign dignitaries, including the US ambassador's wife, as armed police stormed the landmark building in London.

London Metropolitan Police received a 999 call reporting a bomb on the top level of the Shard and dispatched a helicopter as well as an armed response team. The building was searched, but no suspicious packages were found.

A man was arrested abseiling down the side of the building in what was believed to be a publicity stunt for the launch of a new website. Police said he remains in custody and is being questioned about the hoax.

The evacuation of the building was hampered by a temporary blackout, which has been blamed on the short-circuiting of the main power *transformer. Police said an unidentified assailant used the blackout to rob several guests, including top teenage model Jessica Cole. She sustained minor injuries and her condition was described as "comfortable" last night.*

Police stressed they are not connecting the muggings to the bomb hoax and are looking for an opportunistic thief.

Ha ha. Very funny, Nathan. No doubt her godfather had written the statement released to the press. She was anything but comfortable. And what website was her attacker supposed to be advertising exactly – www.trytokillyou.com? He'd been nifty with a knife and she had the stitches to prove it. Still, she had to hand it to Nathan; he'd created a plausible enough cover story for Sunday night's dramatic events. He always said you had to keep it close enough to the truth to be believed; the helicopter, blackout, armed police and a model being stretchered off the Shard could hardly be denied. Her godfather had to mould details into a story that sounded credible without confirming details that would damage Westwood's undercover operation.

"Show me." Becky craned to see the story.

Jessica silently passed the paper.

"It was such bad luck you got caught up in all that." Becky threw the paper on top of the pile of magazines after reading the article. "Have the police got any idea yet who attacked you?"

"Dad said they're still checking CCTV footage in the surrounding area for clues."

She had her own theory, though – she'd given it a lot of thought while she was stuck in bed. Their mission must have failed because it was an inside job. She couldn't come up with a more logical reason for why it had gone so drastically wrong. The attacker had used Jessica's Westwood compact to overpower her. It contained paralysing powder, something only a fellow spy would realize. Plus, a Westwood agent wouldn't have alerted the suspicions of the armed unit arriving at the Shard. Whoever it was would have had time to attack her and get down the stairs again, walking right past the armed response unit after flashing her Westwood credentials. The armed officers *must* have seen the person who'd knocked her out as they scaled the Shard. They didn't realize they had, because she was one of them – an MI6 operative, working for Westwood.

So which girl was it – Bree, Natalia or Sasha?

Bree had jeopardized the mission by being a rubbish team leader, but was her indecisiveness an act? Had she sabotaged Sunday night, deliberately delaying their ascent up the Shard to allow time for the mini helicopter to arrive? Natalia had tried to talk Bree out of acting by saying they should wait for backup and Sasha had faded into the background. She'd left Bree to dither instead of taking charge. Who had really wanted the deal to be stopped?

They both jumped as the doorbell rang. Jessica tried to stand but her legs had gone to sleep. They crumpled beneath her. Was it Nathan? She hoped so. She hadn't been formally interviewed by MI6 yet and needed to tell her godfather that a Westwood girl could have been involved at the Shard. She'd started to discuss her hunch with her dad when Becky arrived and they'd had to break off. Steadying herself against the sofa, she finally managed to get up.

"Don't go mad," Becky said, "but I think it could be Jamie."

"What? Why?"

"I mentioned to him at school that I was coming round tonight. I told him it was a girls' night only, but he said he might pop by to see how you are. He's been worrying like mad."

"No way! I'm a total wreck. I told him I'll see him in a few days' time when my face has healed up a bit more."

"Your face isn't *that* bad," Becky said. "Admittedly, you look like you've had a fight with a brick wall and come off worse, but Jamie won't mind. He can see past that into your beautiful soul."

"Very funny."

Jessica stumbled to the mirror above the fireplace and scraped her hair into a ponytail. Yikes. The bruise on her forehead was purplish and green, making her skin look even paler than usual. She looked terrible, like some kind of zombie straight from the set of *The Walking Dead*. No way could Jamie see her like this. She'd have to pile on a ton of concealer first. Where was her make-up bag?

"If it's Jamie, don't let him in. Tell him I'm too ill to see him. Please."

"You want me to barricade the door?" Becky snorted. "With cushions?"

Footsteps clattered in the hall and the door opened.

"You've got *another* visitor, Jessica." Mattie held the door open and beckoned.

It was too late to find a hiding place. Anyway, how lame would it look if her boyfriend found her crouching beneath the table? Her heart beat rapidly as a tall figure strode into the room, clad in jeans and a long black coat. He clutched the most enormous bouquet of flowers she'd ever seen – lilies, roses and sweet peas – tied with a silver ribbon. Her jaw dropped as the bouquet lowered. Her visitor had curly dark hair, not blond; green eyes and a thin, chiselled face.

"Zak!"

He looked her up and down. "Geez, you're a mess."

CHAPTER
THREE

Jessica pulled her robe tighter, her cheeks reddening. "*Geez.* Thanks for coming all the way here to tell me that. You shouldn't have bothered, especially since you're so busy, you know, with your *zillions* of modelling contracts."

"Sorry." A smile hovered on Zak's lips; his eyes glinted with amusement. "I didn't mean it to come out that way. You look gorgeous, *obviously*, because you always look absolutely drop-dead gorgeous. I was talking about the bruise on your forehead. It's hard to miss, sadly. As is your sarcasm."

He crossed the room in a few bounds, handed her the bouquet and planted a quick kiss on her cheek before she could protest. How embarrassing! She immediately flushed scarlet.

"Er, thanks, but I'm not sure. . ."

Out the corner of her eye, she could see Becky mouthing, "Ohmigod." Her blush deepened.

"We haven't been introduced." Becky almost fell over the pile of magazines as she lurched towards Zak, hand outstretched and eyes shining with excitement. "I'm Jessica's best friend and I'm single."

"Zak Dane. Also single. It must be catching." He kissed Becky's hand instead of shaking it, rendering her speechless.

He looked up at Jessica expectantly as her dad joined Mattie at the door. This was beyond excruciating.

"You've obviously met my grandma, Mattie Farr," she said through gritted teeth. "And this is my dad, Jack Cole."

"It's quite the party," her dad observed, smiling.

"Hh-mm. If you say so." Zak might be Becky's ideal party guest, but he certainly wasn't Jessica's. He'd probably want to play charades, making everyone guess which modelling contracts he'd won. She slumped back down on the sofa. Pins and needles were travelling rapidly up her legs.

Zak sprang forward to shake her dad's hand. "It's a pleasure to meet you, sir. I'm Jessica's friend."

"That's pushing it," she murmured. They'd met for the first time at the rehearsals for the fashion evening at the Shard. He'd made a point of catching her eye. Maybe it was because she was the only girl who didn't immediately swoon over him and it hurt his enormous ego. Or perhaps… Stop it! She had to stop overanalysing everything. Zak Dane wasn't worth the mental effort.

"You're a model, right?" Becky said breathlessly. "You look like a contestant on *America's Next Top Model*. Is that how you met Jessica? I don't mean on the TV show, which you'd win, of course. I mean in real life? Modelling?"

Jessica rolled her eyes at her friend. Honestly? She was practically hyperventilating after one kiss on the hand.

"I had the pleasure of working with Jessica at the gig at the top of the Shard the other night," Zak replied. "It didn't go to plan."

That was the understatement of the year. She gazed at Zak, distracted, as he undid his coat. Hello! Had she said he could stay? What was he doing here? He rubbed his jaw. Seriously, were his cheekbones for real? They looked impossibly sculpted under the crystal light fixture; his body was lean and muscular beneath his navy jumper. It wasn't hard to see why he was in such demand from designers across the world. Zak's eyes flitted to hers and the corners of his mouth twitched.

"What did you want?" she said abruptly.

Judging by his smirk, he thought she was checking him out, which she most certainly wasn't.

"To see how you are, of course. I've been worried."

"I'm good, thanks. I'd hate to keep you from whatever you're doing. Plus I'm busy. I'm expecting my boyfriend."

"Really?"

Still he didn't move.

"Yes, really. I have a boyfriend, Jamie, and he'll probably be here any minute."

"No, I mean you don't look that busy since you're in your pyjamas."

"Very funny. Now why don't you—"

Mattie took a sharp intake of breath. "Jessica's

forgotten her manners *and* forgotten to tell me that Jamie's visiting tonight too." She shot her a pointed look. "Please take a seat, Zak, and let me get you something to drink while I put these beautiful flowers into a vase. Would you like tea or coffee?"

Jessica glared at her grandma. Why did she have to prolong her misery? Couldn't she sense that she wanted him to leave, given the profiling work she'd have done during her spy training?

"Thanks." Zak flashed perfect teeth. He sat down next to Jessica on the sofa. Was it her imagination or did he deliberately brush his knee against hers? She shuffled along and placed a cushion between them.

Another smile touched his lips. "I'd love a cup of coffee, Miss Farr. Black, no sugar, please."

"Call me Mattie. Everyone else does."

"Of course. That's a beautiful necklace, Mattie. My mum loves pearls too. She says they instantly light up a woman's face."

Mattie beamed as she touched her choker. "Thank you. It's my favourite necklace." She leant in and smelt her armful of flowers. "Such a gorgeous scent. You chose well."

36

Oh no. Becky was already a lost cause. Now her grandma was falling for Zak's charm offensive too, like most women he came across. Apart from Jessica. Definitely not her.

Her dad sat next to Becky on a smaller sofa on the opposite side of the room. They stared expectantly at her. She scowled back. Didn't Dad have work to do? And what about Becky's English essay? It looked like she and Zak had become the evening's entertainment. This *so* wasn't how she'd planned tonight to go.

"I'm sorry you were hurt." Zak rearranged the cushions and shuffled round to face her. "I can't believe what happened. Neither can the other girls. Sasha was in pieces afterwards."

Jessica glanced across at her dad. This was a good place to surreptitiously pick up their earlier discussion: the possible involvement of a Westwood girl in the undercover mission. "Where did you see her? What do you remember from that night?"

Zak looked puzzled. "Er, why?"

"Jessica's memory's a bit hazy," Becky said. "She keeps forgetting things, like telling me she'd met you."

Her dad buttoned his lips to suppress a smile. "It'd

help if you could fill in the gaps from the time the lights went out."

Zak paused as Mattie returned with a large crystal vase filled with his flowers. She placed them on the table in the centre of the room and left again.

"Of course, the blackout," he continued. "That was odd. Do you think it was connected to what happened to Jessica? The newspaper said it wasn't, but I did wonder. It was quite a coincidence that so many things happened at once."

"I'm sure the police will examine every angle," her dad replied smoothly.

Zak didn't seem to notice that he'd sidestepped his awkward questions. "Yeah, sure. Well, the lights went off and everyone thought it was funny at first, but then a few people started to get nervous when they realized they weren't coming back on any time soon and we'd have to be evacuated."

Jessica flicked her ponytail behind her back as Mattie returned with Zak's coffee. "Did you see the other models?"

He flashed another winning smile at Mattie and took a slurp of his drink.

"I spotted Natalia and Sasha over on the other side of the room. There was enough light from the buildings outside to see a little bit. But Bree, no. I didn't get a glimpse of her until after the armed police had gone up into the off-limits area. That's when I followed."

"You actually went up? All the way?"

Zak smiled sheepishly. "Other people did too. We wouldn't have had another chance like that to get to the top. Plus, it was like something out of an action film: the helicopter, the armed police. It was hard to resist. The adrenaline started pumping and I followed like a sheep. Baaaa."

The doorbell rang but Jessica ignored it. "That's when you saw Bree?" she pressed. "At the very top?"

"Bree was already on her way down when we were all turned back," Zak said slowly. "She was upset and said someone had attacked you. I asked her if any other models were up there, but she said only you and she had made it to the top."

That was an interesting snippet of information. Her dad leant forward in his seat; Zak had caught his attention too. He'd placed Bree very close to the scene of the crime. Sure, they didn't get on, as Bree

39

was always crying "teacher's pet" because of her family connection to Nathan, but was there more to it than that? She'd been a total cow ever since Jessica had caught her using her mobile in the ladies' loos during a surveillance training session at an MI6 centre where phones were strictly prohibited. It was confiscated later that day, along with Kat's, during a spot check on bags, and they'd both blamed Jessica, accusing her of dobbing them in to her godfather. She hadn't, but there was no reasoning with either of them.

Was Bree really talking to a friend in the toilets at the MI6 training centre or was something more sinister going on? She'd been texting constantly in the dressing room ahead of the fashion show and seemed tense. Had she been giving away confidential information to someone on the outside on both occasions? Was that why she really hated Jessica, because she feared she could piece everything together and out her as a traitor to MI6? Bree had definitely become her number one suspect.

"Why did you and Bree go to the top of the Shard?" Zak asked. "Did you see that guy go up there? You know, the one doing the publicity stunt? Was that when you were mugged?"

Jessica ignored Zak's barrage of irritating questions. First, she needed to go over the latest development with her dad and then Nathan. Maybe she could call him later tonight after Becky had left or she could ask her dad to ring and tell him what Zak had seen.

"I could kill whoever did this to you," Zak continued. "Could you identify them? I'd feel so much better if I knew your mugger was close to being caught."

"No," she said quietly. Zak's titbit of information had made her highly suspicious, but she couldn't exactly have Bree arrested. Not yet, anyway.

"Jess?"

Geez. She hadn't seen her boyfriend walk in behind Mattie.

"Jamie!" She lost her balance as she stood up and had to touch Zak's shoulder briefly to steady herself. She felt her cheeks turn scarlet again.

Jamie frowned as he raked a hand through his tousled blond hair. "I didn't know you had another guest, sorry. I wanted to say hi and give you this."

He held up a white cake box with the name of a local baker printed on the side. "It's your favourite, you know, red velvet cupcakes. I thought you and Becky would enjoy them tonight." His eyes flickered over the huge vase of flowers that Mattie had helpfully placed centre stage.

Jessica bit her lip "That's so thoughtful, thank you. Zak called in to see how I was doing. He's leaving now, aren't you?"

Zak studiously ignored her. He took another quick sip of coffee and slowly walked over to Jamie.

"Zak Dane, Jess's friend."

The pair shook hands. "Jamie Tyler. Jess's *boy*friend."

"So she does have a boyfriend," Zak drawled. "I had no idea."

"She sure does." Jamie pulled his hand back sharply, as if he'd been stung. He glanced back at Jessica, frowning.

She glared furiously at Zak. Why was he winding up Jamie? Did he get some weird kick out of it? He knew damn well she had a boyfriend, yet he'd deliberately implied she hadn't bothered to mention that fact.

Now Jamie was acting all defensive. Not that he had anything to worry about. She wasn't even friends with Zak, let alone anything else.

Zak gently punched Jamie's arm, breaking the awkward silence. "Everything's cool, dude. I'll leave you two lovebirds alone with your cupcakes. I have to run through some Dolce & Gabbana promos tonight. Don't forget to add the flower food into the water, Jessica. It'll make the petals last longer."

He couldn't resist showing off about yet another modelling contract *and* dropping in the helpful reference to his gigantic bouquet in front of her boyfriend. She'd put it in the bin after he left.

"Fantastic," Jamie said through gritted teeth. "Knock yourself out, *dude*."

"See you later, Jessica." Zak hauled himself to the door, swinging his coat over his shoulder. "It's been a pleasure, Becky, Mr Cole, Mattie. Thanks for the coffee. Hope to see you all again soon."

"Absolutely!" Becky exclaimed. "Hopefully really soon. Jessica has my number."

He gave Becky a dazzling smile and winked at Jessica. She glared back. Who was he kidding? Their paths weren't likely to cross again. He wasn't booked on any of the shoots she had coming up, as far as she knew. Who'd given him her home address? Was it one of the other models? She'd forgotten to ask.

"He liked himself," Jamie remarked as the door closed. He handed over the cupcakes, planting a quick kiss on her lips. The smell of fresh soap made Jessica's heart quicken.

"Tell me about it. He thinks he's hot."

"Ohmigod he's *so* hot," Becky agreed. "Unbelievably, crazily out-of-this-world hot. I have to get his number from you, Jessica. I can't believe you didn't tell me about him before. How many more hot single male models do you know?"

"Erm." Why had Becky mentioned Zak's supposed hotness? Jessica would never get her off the subject now.

Jamie stared curiously at Jessica. "Do *you* think Zak's hot?"

"What? No! That's not what I think. Obviously. It's what other people say."

She glanced over her shoulder. She wanted to add that Jamie was the only boy she thought was hot, the only boy she could possibly be interested in, but Mattie, her dad and Becky were eavesdropping. It was too embarrassing to bare her soul in front of an audience.

Jamie took a step back. "Whatever. He seemed like a total jerk to me." He shrugged and turned away.

"Not to me," Becky said. "He was yummy."

"And charming," Mattie added. "Don't forget that."

Jessica sighed. They were both making this so much worse. "Jamie's right. Neither of you know him. He is a total jerk. You wouldn't believe how much he goes on and on about how wonderful he is all the time. He—"

She stopped herself. Why was she letting Zak get under her skin and, more importantly, Jamie's? Maybe the paralysing powder had affected her brain somehow. She wasn't with it tonight. She glared at Mattie and her dad as they finally said their goodbyes and left the room. Couldn't they have vanished a minute earlier? Their timing was completely off. But come to think of it, so was hers.

"Anyway, I should get going and leave you to your

girls' night in," Jamie said abruptly. "I didn't mean to crash."

"You're not crashing and you've only just got here," Jessica protested. "We haven't even had time to talk."

Becky faked a gigantic yawn. "I have to go. I'm beat already and I've got to finish my essay tonight." She kissed Jamie on the cheek and hugged Jessica, making a "call me" gesture with her fingers as she walked out.

"That wasn't obvious at all," Jessica said, rolling her eyes.

Jamie laughed, his shoulders relaxing a little. "Becky means well, even if she has terrible taste in potential future boyfriends."

"Agreed. I think this PFB—"

She lurched forward as the magazines on the floor leapt up and danced in front of her eyes. Red-hot pincers stabbed her legs.

"What's wrong?" Jamie's arms encircled her waist. She rested her head on his shoulder as the room spun wildly. He grasped her hand, which shook uncontrollably. Clasping her hand over his, she tried to steady the embarrassing tremors. She hadn't wanted him to see her like this. She felt like a *really* old woman.

"It's the after-effects..." Her voice trailed off. Like Becky, her boyfriend couldn't hear the truth about her Westwood training and assignments.

"The doctor said I might get the shakes from banging my head when I fell, but it's nothing to worry about. I'm going to be OK."

Jamie bit his lip. "There's nothing else you want to tell me?"

"What do you mean? You can't possibly think I like Zak? There's absolutely nothing going on between us. He turned up out of the blue."

"What? No, that's not what I meant."

Why did she have to bring up Zak again? "What, then?"

"I get the feeling you're holding out on me about something. You've blown me off at the last minute with loads of my gigs and you seem to be pushing me away. I had to find out from Becky that you'd been hurt."

The words stung her. He was right. She hadn't been there for him recently. She'd been gutted that some of her MI6 training sessions had overrun and she'd been forced to pull out of going to his gigs. It hadn't been easy to come up with a series of plausible reasons about why she couldn't go out on Friday nights. Sure, she should have called to tell him she'd been mugged at the Shard, but she'd already lied to Becky and couldn't face doing it again. She was such a coward. If only she could come clean with him – but MI6 had a strict rule forbidding teenage agents from disclosing their secret work to partners before years of vetting.

She was the worst girlfriend in the entire world. She took a deep breath. "I'm sorry. I don't mean to push you away, honestly I don't. I've told you absolutely everything. I promise."

CHAPTER
FOUR

"What did Nathan say?" Jessica eased herself into a chair at the breakfast table and scrutinized her dad.

He adjusted his tie even though it was knotted perfectly. That was one of his nervous tics, but what was he apprehensive about? He'd promised to ring Nathan last night; she'd felt too ill to do it herself. She'd crawled back to bed straight after Jamie left, not long after Becky.

"He asked how you're doing," her dad replied cautiously. "He's been worried, obviously."

Jessica leant forward, placing her injured hand on the table. "But you did pass on my message, right?"

Her dad shifted in his seat, reddening. He stared down at the newspaper in front of him.

"Dad?"

Finally he met her gaze. His blue eyes bored into hers. "No. I'm sorry. I didn't tell Nathan your suspicions."

"But Dad! I honestly believe it. Bree could have been involved."

"Remind me again. That's the operative you don't get on with?"

She flushed. That was putting it mildly. "This isn't personal. Zak placed her in the off-limits area. She had time to attack me and get back down the stairs."

Her dad shook his head. "I didn't want to go into this with you last night, but it's too early to start pointing the finger. It doesn't look good for you to accuse a colleague, particularly one you have issues with. It's an interesting hunch, but it's just that. MI6 will conduct its own assessment. You have to let its officers do their job."

Jessica sighed with exasperation. They were losing valuable time. They could still retrieve the blueprint if Bree confessed to her involvement and gave up the name of the buyer.

"I know I can't prove anything. I want Nathan to

at least check out my theory. The masked attacker definitely used *my* compact, right?"

"The armed response unit found it lying broken next to you. Nathan said it carried your mother's engraving."

She picked at her bandage again. Shortly after Nathan had given her the silver compact, she'd taken it to a jeweller and had it engraved with a quotation from her mum's favourite book, *Jane Eyre*.

I am no bird; and no net ensnares me; I am a free human being with an independent will.

Nathan was furious when he found out; he'd claimed she'd breached security protocols and there was a risk the jeweller could have discovered the hidden functions. Thankfully he hadn't and the quotation was useful now; it proved the attacker had stolen *her* compact, not one belonging to any of the other Westwood models, which all looked the same.

"Someone took the compact from my make-up bag. All the Westwood models had access to the hotel dressing room. Bree, or if not her, Sasha or Natalia could have swiped it before we headed to the show. Whoever it was wouldn't have wanted to risk using their own compact in case the powder contained DNA samples which could be traced back to them."

"Or someone else could have taken it," her dad pointed out. "You admitted you saw different people milling about. What about the make-up artists and the hairstylists who were coming and going? Were they legit? Had one of them been paid to swipe it? Nathan said they couldn't retrieve fingerprints off the compact, so there's no proof one of the other models knocked you out."

Jessica tapped her fingers on the table impatiently. "What about their refusal to follow orders? They didn't attempt to intercept the meet. It was left to me to tackle the buyer. Were they all really afraid of letting down Victoria Beckham and Stella McCartney or did one of them want the deal to be stopped? Where were they exactly while I was at the top of the Shard? We know for sure Bree was on her way up."

"Nathan's admitted it's a confused picture and they're still trying to piece everything together. Unfortunately, a number of guests like Zak tried to find out what was going on and went up into the off-limits area too. That's why it's been so hard to check for fingerprints. The scene wasn't sealed off and it became contaminated."

She rested her head in her hands. Sunday night had been an A to Z about how not to do a mission. Why did it have to go so horribly wrong on her first official assignment? She'd needed to prove to Nathan and his boss, Mrs T, that she was up to the job if she had any hope of staying on in Westwood beyond her six-month probation period.

Jessica flicked her hair behind her shoulders. She couldn't bear to think of the alternative. "Can't you see there's a possibility, even a slim one, that a Westwood model attacked me and programmed the drone to carry the USB device off the building?"

"Yes, but it's highly unlikely. Why would they deliberately sabotage the mission?"

"For money? Or maybe they were blackmailed?" She shoved away the plate of toast Mattie placed in front of her. "Nathan needs to check all the girls' bank accounts and maybe search their homes for potential evidence, particularly Bree's."

Her dad reached over and squeezed her arm. "I get that you feel responsible for this mission failing, but it's not your fault. You have to stop blaming yourself."

"How can I?" Her eyes filled with tears. "If this technology gets passed on to a terrorist, people could die because of me. How will I live with myself then? If I'd reacted quicker, I could have fought the attacker. I could have disabled the drone. I should have destroyed it while I had the chance."

Why hadn't she dismantled the mini helicopter? She'd been beating herself up about that ever since Sunday night. If she'd sabotaged the escape device, the USB couldn't have been flown off the building.

"Hindsight's a wonderful thing," her dad said, "and we all wish we had it. The truth is, some missions will succeed and some will fail."

"Jack's right," Mattie said, sitting down next to him. "You can't beat yourself up about what's happened. You need to learn from it and move on. It's what I had to do many, many times."

Jessica was about to argue back. She stopped herself. She hated to admit it, but spying was one thing that Mattie actually got.

"What if I can't let go?"

"Then you should quit Westwood," Mattie said bluntly, "because you'll have to make judgement calls all the time. Some will be right, others won't. You have to deal with the fallout. I did. So did your mother and father."

Leaving Westwood wasn't an option. She couldn't give up, however hard the coming months would be. It was the only way she'd find out what had happened to her mum all those years ago.

CHAPTER FIVE

"Please seek assistance."

Jessica barged into the ticket barrier, which failed to open as she swiped her Oyster card. Great. It was malfunctioning. She'd topped up her card with thirty pounds shortly before the job at the Shard and had been placed under house arrest by Mattie for the last five days, so she *obviously* had more than enough cash in her account for a return fare to Pimlico. Pressing her card against the sensor, she rolled her eyes with frustration as the message flashed up again. The barrier remained firmly shut. Typical. This wasn't a good day to be running late.

She was supposed to be at MI6 HQ in forty-five minutes for a debriefing. An MI6 agent had already visited her at home and taken a detailed statement about the Shard job. No doubt he was cross-checking to see if it tallied with the other models' versions of events. Nathan had relayed the message that she had nothing to worry about; that the case had been passed to another department and there were a few minor details to run over. Still, she'd wanted to get to the meeting early enough to catch Nathan and raise her theory about Bree's possible involvement with the mystery buyer. Face to face was far better; she hadn't wanted to do it over the phone.

Unfortunately, her dad had already delayed her; he was having trouble logging on to his online banking from his desktop. The whole system must have been down because she couldn't access his current account via his app either. After ten minutes of trying, she'd had to give up. She couldn't afford to miss today, even though it meant cancelling her usual Saturday brunch with Jamie at a local café. She'd claimed she was going round to Becky's to help run through lines for her role in a new National Youth Theatre production. He hadn't been too happy that she'd bailed on him yet again, but what could she do? She'd have to think of a way to make it up to him once all this Shard stress was over.

Checking her watch, she calculated her route as she strode over to the ticket machine. It was eleven stops from South Ealing, changing at Green Park, so she could allow three minutes per station. She'd just about do it if the trains weren't delayed. Fingers crossed. But she'd have to run like a mad thing at the other end. Hopefully she'd be up to it. She felt almost a hundred per cent – or ninety-eight per cent anyway. OK, ninety-five per cent.

She pressed "Top Up" on the screen. Her Oyster card had zero funds. What? That couldn't be right. Why didn't the thirty pounds show up? Whatever. She'd pay again and chase up her missing cash later. She sighed as she pulled out her dad's emergency credit card. She tapped in the PIN and waited.

Number invalid.

No! She tried again, but the card was rejected, as it had been at the cashpoint down the road when she'd tried to get money out a few minutes ago. This was the last thing she needed. She scraped together enough coins from the bottom of her blue Victoria Beckham handbag for a single fare to Pimlico. She'd worry about the return journey later.

She pelted down the stairs and managed to get on a train as the doors closed. Phew. That was lucky. Today had to get better.

Jessica burst into the briefing room, red-faced and out of breath. She'd spent the last twenty minutes attempting to get past reception downstairs, as her security pass wasn't working and the system had no record of her name or any of the aliases she sometimes used. What was going on today? Was this karma for lying to Jamie?

"You're late," Nathan said accusingly. "We had to start without you."

He sat at the head of the table with Natalia, Bree and Sasha on his right. Opposite were unfamiliar faces: a man with a grey goatee and a red-headed thirty-something woman with glossy scarlet lips. They didn't look too pleased to see her; the woman gave her a particularly scathing look. This wasn't a great first impression, admittedly, but surely they could cut her some slack? It wasn't exactly her fault she was horribly late. Who were they anyway?

She threw her black Ossa Cosway pea coat on to a chair and quickly slipped into a spare seat further down the table. "I'm really sorry, Nathan. You wouldn't believe the day I'm having."

He gave her a curt nod and returned his gaze to his laptop.

Jessica helped herself to a glass of water. She was dying of thirst. Thank God she'd finally made it.

Natalia shot her a sympathetic look. Her cheeks were bright red and her eyes glittered with tears. Bree and Sasha didn't look in much better shape either. Yikes. Nathan must have hauled them over the coals, or maybe it was the other MI6 agents sitting across the table who'd laid into them. He hadn't bothered to introduce them to her. Perhaps it was a blessing in disguise that she'd missed the worst of the Shard post-mortem.

Nathan tapped at his laptop keyboard without looking up. "Feeling better now, I hope? Jack's been giving me regular updates about your recovery."

"Yes, thanks." Nausea was still a problem now and then, but she'd regained all feeling in her limbs. She'd even managed to run here without getting cramps. The bruise on her face had faded and she'd have the stitches removed from her hand soon.

"Great. To fill you in, we still have this man in custody." Nathan clicked on the mouse.

A photo flashed up on the large screen on the wall. It was the Frenchman. Jessica had last seen him dangling helplessly from the window-cleaning rope at the Shard.

"Is he cooperating?" she asked. "He didn't seem the type."

"To a certain extent," he replied. "He's cut himself a deal in return for info on the underworld Chinese contacts he was acting as a go-between for. He was the middleman."

"So that's progress, I guess?" Jessica pulled out her notepad and pen from her handbag.

"Except we have an unknown player," the goatee man chipped in. "The third party who somehow knew about the deal with the Chinese and swiped the USB drive from under our noses."

She flinched. He meant *her* nose.

The woman leant forward, fixing Jessica with a hard stare. "The powder you inhaled has a temporary amnesic effect. Is there anything you've remembered since that night about your attacker? A glimpse of an identifying feature? A scent of a particular aftershave or perfume? A sound? Anything at all that can help us track him down?"

Jessica glanced at the other models. Bree glared back. Should she say something now? This could be her chance to alert MI6 to her theory, but something in the woman's eyes made her pause. Her dad was right. She couldn't throw accusations around about a colleague she had issues with in front of total strangers without proof; she'd look unprofessional or, worse still, vindictive. She'd have to grab Nathan afterwards and try to broach the subject off the record.

"I don't remember. I'm sorry."

The woman clasped her red talons together and leant forward. "Pity. We have no leads, no information and nowhere to go with this, apart from *your* account of what happened."

Her tone made Jessica catch her breath. "And you doubt that?"

The woman's lips curled into a smile, but her blue eyes were hard. "Should we?"

What was she insinuating? That she'd made the whole thing up and stolen the USB drive herself? Maybe she should have voiced her suspicions while she had the chance and landed the other models in it. Had Bree already cast doubt on her story in order to cover her back?

"I've told the truth and I'm not concealing anything."

"That's good to hear. I'm sure you'll give us your full cooperation."

The man and woman stared at her. What was going on?

"Of course," Jessica replied. "By the way, who are you both?"

"I'm sorry. I should have introduced you." Nathan gestured at the redhead. "This is Agent Clare Hatfield."

She stared back, unsmiling.

"And this is her colleague, Agent George Booth."

"I guess you're both from the unit charged with recovering the USB device?" Jessica said.

The woman laughed and exchanged looks with Agent Booth. "No, that's not our remit at all."

"Er, OK. What is it you both do?"

"We investigate colossal cock-ups like this one and determine whether a department, in this case Westwood, has been compromised by a leak," Agent Hatfield said sharply.

Jessica sat back in her seat. "So you *do* think this was an inside job?"

"If you'd managed to turn up on time, you'd have heard me say exactly that." The woman's icy blue eyes challenged her. "Someone knew we were intercepting the Frenchman at the Shard and planned ahead. They used the distraction to steal the USB flash drive."

Hello? Judging by the way she was glaring at Jessica, she must consider *her* the prime suspect. "I can assure you—"

The door banged open and a bespectacled man burst in, panting.

"I thought I said not to disturb me?" Nathan snapped. "We're in the middle of something important right now."

"Sorry, sir. But we have a breach."

Nathan was already on his feet. "Tell me."

"MI6 is under attack along with the rest of the country."

"What?"

"Sam Hewitt says to come right away."

Without uttering a word, Nathan followed him out the room. Agents Hatfield's and Booth's mobiles were vibrating.

"I've already heard," Agent Hatfield barked into her phone. "Put emergency protocols in place. Launch Operation Chaffinch."

Jessica exchanged glances with Sasha and Natalia, but Bree avoided eye contact. Did she think she'd had a lucky escape? Jessica grabbed her bag and coat and chased after the agents. Alarms sounded in the corridors and lights flickered on and off. She had to catch up; the building was going into lockdown. She sprinted after Nathan and the others, diving through a set of doors that shut and locked. Sasha and Natalia weren't as quick; they were trapped in the corridor. Nathan peeled off into a room on the right, followed by agents Hatfield and Booth. The redhead had kicked off her high heels in the sprint.

Jessica caught the door as it clicked, sealing her inside

a large open-plan comms centre. Ranks of computers lined the room. Men and women were hammering at keyboards and talking urgently into earpieces. The man who'd gatecrashed their briefing slipped into a seat and put headphones on. Another man stalked towards them. He was tall and lean, wearing green-rimmed glasses and black gloves, with a shock of curly red hair. Jessica glanced from Nathan to the other agents. None of them seemed to think his appearance was odd.

"Agents Hatfield, Booth, this is our systems analyst, Sam Hewitt," Nathan said. "Bring us up to speed, Sam."

"Our firewalls came under attack from a computer virus approximately thirteen minutes ago. It didn't appear to be anything out of the ordinary at first. We deal with cyberattacks like this hundreds if not thousands of times a day."

"Tell us something we don't know," Agent Hatfield spat out.

The analyst wiped a bead of sweat from his forehead. "This virus was different. Within seconds it had mutated and bombarded us with reams of data, which crashed our server for a few seconds. Then multiple, simultaneous attacks targeted various sites across the UK."

"Where?" Nathan asked.

Sam waved his gloved right hand. A gigantic screen suddenly appeared, cutting the room in two. "This is the current scene at Hyde Park Corner."

CCTV footage of a large roundabout appeared. Jessica gasped as cars and buses crashed into one another. The footage flashed to different cameras, showing traffic lights all flashing green.

Sam swiped the air and the image was replaced by another. "It's the same at Oxford Circus and Trafalgar Square. All the traffic lights are either out or totally malfunctioning and turning green simultaneously."

Jessica stepped forward, but Sam had already batted the image away. Now he was flicking through a video file mid-air. How was he doing that? It looked like he was operating some kind of hands-free touchscreen using those weird gloves. It reminded her of *Minority Report*, the old Tom Cruise movie she'd watched with her dad years ago.

"Whilst police were trying to deal with traffic chaos, this happened at Buckingham Palace," Sam continued.

He flicked his fingers and expanded the screen, zooming in. Police cars and ambulances surrounded the landmark building.

"A computer virus has breached the emergency services' firewall and taken control of the comms, sending police and ambulances to the palace. It's also diverted officers to Downing Street, the Home Office and every single foreign embassy in London. All have been put on a high terror alert."

Waving both hands, he brought up images of each scene and arranged them in order in front of them. All were playing real-time footage, judging by the digital time-stamp at the base of each screen.

"This must be stretching the police to breaking point," Nathan said.

"Precisely. Now this is happening."

The pictures disappeared and an image of a prison flashed up. Helicopters hovered overhead.

Sam created a split screen. "That's Belmarsh and this is Wakefield Prison."

Nathan's face went white. "Please tell me we're not looking at mass breakouts?"

"Not yet. Viruses are attacking security firewalls at

maximum security prisons. So far, every single door at Belmarsh and Wakefield has been automatically locked. Prisoners and families are trapped in waiting rooms and guards remain locked up with inmates in workshops. There's no word yet on potential casualties."

"How long before we regain control?" Agent Hatfield asked.

"A minimum of thirty minutes. The army's moving in, but we're also getting reports of hacks into the security systems of dozens of prisons across the country, including Low Newton in Durham and Long Lartin in Worcestershire."

Nathan looked startled. "We cannot afford breaches at any closed prisons. I want a maximum response, prioritizing those with Category A prisoners who are a danger to the public."

"We're on it," Sam said.

"Do you have any idea who's doing this?" Jessica asked.

Agent Hatfield swung round. "Does that girl have clearance to be in here?"

"Jessica's the least of our problems," Nathan snapped.

Agent Hatfield gave her a withering look and turned back to the screen.

"No one's claimed responsibility yet and we're still trying to trace the source of the various viruses," Sam continued. "The one attacking MI6 is most worrying. Every couple of seconds, the code mutates as it attempts to crack our firewall. We're doing everything we can to keep it out of our system. So far, it's holding up, but we can't trace the origin of the hacker. The IP address is being rerouted around hundreds of internet cafés all over the world, from India to Australia. While we try to nail it down, more virus attacks spring up elsewhere." He touched his earpiece. "Such as right now. Multiple cashpoints are ejecting money across the country. The banks' computers can't shut them down and the police won't be able to get to every site."

With a flick of his wrist, images of fighting erupted in front of them. Footage showed a man waving a wad of cash in the air. Seconds later he was wrestled to the ground by a gang of men in Manchester city centre.

"We're also getting reports that WhatsApp, Twitter and Facebook are affected," Sam continued. "Another virus is allowing people to download games, music and movies for free from several sites. Do you want me to call them up?"

"Get real," Agent Hatfield retorted. "Thousands of teenagers not being able to tweet or upload a photo of themselves is hardly a national emergency."

Jessica frowned. *That* was curious. The hacker could have raided banks, draining millions of pounds from accounts, or attacked the stock exchange, making the FTSE go into meltdown. Instead, it was giving cash and computer games away and wreaking havoc.

"It's like they're showing off," she murmured, staring at the screens.

"Pardon?" Agent Hatfield spun around again. "What did you say?"

"The hacker wants our attention. They're proving what they can do."

"They've got our attention all right," Agent Hatfield said. "But you're wrong. This isn't an exercise in showing off. It's the biggest concerted cyberattack this country has ever seen."

Jessica shrugged. "If you say so, but whoever's doing this could have toppled banks or the government.

Instead they're running rings around the emergency services and targeting online games. Why?"

"Why not?" Nathan replied. "We don't know what their agenda is, apart from causing mayhem and trying to break into MI6."

"The threat's over!" a woman shouted across the room. "We've gained control of the banks, traffic lights, emergency service comms and prison security."

"Yes!" Agent Booth punched the air with his fist.

Jessica could tell from the look on Nathan's face that celebrations were probably premature. He strode over to the woman's workstation.

"And the hacker?"

"The good news is that we've kept them out of MI6," she replied.

"And the bad news?"

"It's not the work of one hacker. It's thousands of them; a highly organized army of hackers all working simultaneously."

"How's that even possible?" Nathan pushed his glasses up his nose.

"Sam? Can you bring this up for them?" the woman said, tapping at her keyboard.

Sam nodded. "What do you have?"

"Dozens of websites demanding that hackers mobilize and attack," she replied. "We're looking at a twenty-first-century cyber flash mob. I'm sending over the details now."

The websites appeared in the air before the group.

"HackMeNow, hackus, telltheworld, uhavearite2no," Jessica read under her breath.

"All the sites went live six months ago advertising for hackers, with similar calling notices to this," the woman continued. "Sam, if you will."

The analyst waved his hand and a page from a website came into view.

ATTENTION ALL HACKERS

Prepare for the game of all games by joining The Collective. What can you hack into? Wow us with your skill. It'll take a lot to impress us. Hack into our website and you'll find the prize. LibertyCrossing

"This is a big game?" Nathan said incredulously.

"Maybe," the woman replied. "Hackers were instructed by LibertyCrossing to join The Collective by registering with untraceable email addresses. They were ordered to wait until they received the code word, 'Bluebird', to launch their best ever hacks, with the winner receiving one million dollars four days later. The code word went live at midday GMT, according to postings by LibertyCrossing on all the hacking websites. That's when everything went mad."

"The hackers waited six months to do this?" Agent Hatfield gasped. "It was all pre-planned?"

The woman nodded. "For some reason, the timing of today's attacks is highly significant."

"Please tell me you've traced LibertyCrossing?" Nathan said.

"Not yet. We're working on that and trying to track down each individual hacker, but we're talking about thousands of people, possibly from all over the world, being encouraged to attack targets in the United Kingdom and America right up until the Wednesday jackpot announcement."

Sam enlarged an image. Hackers were already

posting details of their feats on the websites. All involved hacks in both countries.

"This one claims to have hacked the federal bank," Sam said.

"I'll speak to our friends across the pond and see if they can verify that," Nathan said. "If so, it'll mean bringing the CIA on board."

Agent Hatfield folded her arms. "Great. Inter-agency collaboration with the Yanks. That always goes *so* well."

An alarm sounded again. Red lights flashed up on every computer, along with the words "Unauthorized Access". Numbers rapidly scrolled down the screens.

"No, no, no!" Sam cried. He attempted to swipe at the images in the air, but they were snatched away, one by one.

"The whole system's corrupted," the woman shouted. "The virus is inside the mainframe."

"Shut everything down now!" Nathan ordered. "Get everything offline."

"We can't," Sam replied. "They're in control, not us."

"There must be something you can do," Nathan said. "Break the connection."

"I'm trying," the woman replied.

"What are they doing now?" he asked.

"They're downloading the identities of undercover agents working active MI6 cases."

"Stop them!" Nathan yelled.

A figure suddenly appeared on every computer screen in the room as well as in a giant hologram in the air. The person's face was obscured by a green hooded top, dark sunglasses and a black scarf.

"Do we have your attention now?" a male voice boomed. "I am LibertyCrossing, leader of The Collective, dedicated to total freedom and dissemination of information across the internet. No secrets, total openness, without interference from governments and security services across the world."

"Impossible," Nathan muttered under his breath. "Is this streaming live?"

Sam nodded. "It's being uploaded into our mainframe via LibertyCrossing. We can't turn it off."

"Can he hear what we are saying?"

"No. It's a one-way transmission. You can't interact with him."

The figure started to talk again. "You've seen what

we can do and there's plenty more to come if you do not comply with The Collective's demand. Release Lee Caplin from prison in the United States and return him to the UK."

An image of a young man flashed up on the screen. Jessica recognized him instantly. He was the most notorious cyberterrorist the country had ever produced. More images followed, including one of him hugging a small blonde woman who wore a pink dress and a long gold pendant. She'd been on the news a lot; it was his mum, Louise Caplin. Next, front pages of newspapers appeared, confirming what Jessica already knew. Three years ago, the teenager from Basildon, Essex, had hacked into the Pentagon, NASA and the CIA and downloaded hundreds of top-secret files on to his home computer. The sixteen-year-old had deleted hundreds more and uploaded viruses, causing damage worth millions of dollars. Not only that, he was accused of arming American missiles and locking them on to Russian military vessels in the Black Sea.

Lee swiftly became top of the FBI's most-wanted list. He was indicted in his absence by an American federal jury for computer-related crimes and extradition proceedings were launched. The president of the United States had refused to offer clemency despite his age. Mrs Caplin, who was widowed, had tirelessly fought his extradition to the States but eventually lost the battle. The stress was believed to have contributed to her recent fatal heart attack. This week's papers revealed that Lee had been allowed to attend his mum's funeral before the start of his thirty-year jail sentence in Leavenworth Federal Penitentiary in Kansas.

"Comply with our simple request and prevent your agents' identities from being published online for the whole world to see."

"Alert every single handler and undercover agent that their cover could be compromised. Get them off the streets and to safety," Nathan said, spinning around.

Men and women started dialling and talking into their headsets.

"I speak directly to MI6 because you have the power to return Lee Caplin to the UK," the figure continued. "Refuse to meet our demands at your agents' peril. You have four days to secure the release of Lee Caplin before the confidential files we have gathered will be published on the internet. Information like this..."

The figure vanished from the screen and a photo of a dark-haired young woman appeared in its place.

"This has just been uploaded," the voice rang out from the transmission.

The screen changed again and confidential details appeared on one of the hacking websites.

Agent Andrea Lockwood, aged 21. Operating under the alias Jasmine Underwood. Location: Paris. Mission: To infiltrate jewel thief gang The Crystals.

"We're on it," Sam shouted, racing to a computer. He tapped furiously at the keyboard.

"Have we managed to warn her yet?" Jessica said, turning to Nathan.

Nathan snatched the headset off a woman. "Code name Jasmine's been exposed. Pull her out now!" He listened as the other person spoke. "Good work. Call me as soon as she's secured."

The hooded figure returned to the screen. "Your deadline is three p.m. on Wednesday. Until then, the hacks will continue and the identity of an MI6 agent will be published online each day at three p.m. as a reminder of what's to come. After the deadline has passed, we will publish your entire agent database and unleash fresh destruction that will bring this country's infrastructure to its knees. You have received The Collective's warning. From the ashes, the phoenix will rise."

He vanished.

"I've managed to crash the website and bring down Andrea's name," Sam said, breaking the stunned silence. "That's given her some breathing space at least. We'll monitor Twitter and news websites to see if it's been picked up by anyone, but so far we're in the clear."

"And our computer system?" Nathan barked.

"We're in control of the mainframe again," Sam said. "Pieces of the virus's code self-destructed, but we're working on what's left. We can't rule out the possibility that the virus could mutate and launch another attack."

"Keep me updated."

Sam nodded and fired off orders to his staff. Nathan

turned around. His face was drawn and pinched. It looked like he'd aged in the last few minutes.

"Will you meet The Collective's demands?" Jessica said quietly. "Will you release Lee Caplin?"

"It's impossible," he replied. "The US will never cave in to those demands, whatever the threat. These hackers must know that."

"Then what do we do?" Agent Hatfield asked.

"Prepare for the worst," Nathan said. "In the meantime, we need to discover the identity of LibertyCrossing and find out how his followers managed to hack MI6. Get to work, people. The countdown's begun."

It hadn't taken long for London to descend into total anarchy: ninety-six minutes, to be precise, since the first wave of attacks by The Collective. Jessica had borrowed her train fare back home from Sasha; it hadn't seemed like a good time to admit to Nathan that she might also have been a victim of the hackers. Having her Oyster card and security pass hacked and her dad's credit card frozen were small fry compared to what was going on back at MI6 HQ. Nathan had a lot more on his plate to worry about than her temporary transport and cash-flow problems.

Two youths wearing scarves over their faces fled from the supermarket up ahead, carrying boxes stacked with bottles. More youths piled in, wearing balaclavas. The cash tills of major supermarket chains had been frozen, according to the last update she'd received from MI6 before she left. Looting was taking place in cities across the country.

Jessica kept her head down, avoiding eye contact, and ran past. She couldn't intervene; she was a brown belt at kick-boxing, but there were too many thugs and not a police officer in sight. They were being kept busy elsewhere. It was going to be a long trek home across the capital. Hackers had targeted the radio communications for the Underground, causing near misses between trains at Westminster, King's Cross and Upminster. The whole network was paralysed and every tube stopped, along with planes at Heathrow, Gatwick and Stansted as a precaution. Buses were running a restricted service, which meant the queues were massive.

She hadn't wanted to risk her dad coming to fetch

her by car since roads were blocked with accidents caused by the malfunctioning traffic-light systems. She planned to walk until she came across a bus service that was, hopefully, running normally. It gave her a chance to think, anyway. She googled LibertyCrossing on her iPhone. Interesting. Liberty Crossing was the name given to the two HQs of the National Counterterrorism Center and the US Office of the Director of National Intelligence in Virginia. So the hacker had a sense of humour. He was using the name of an American spy HQ to attack a British one.

Next, she typed "phoenix rising from the ashes". According to Greek mythology, a phoenix was a bird that gains new life by rising from the ashes of its predecessor. What did that mean? Was LibertyCrossing's objective to create a new world order, rising from the one The Collective planned to destroy? She crossed the road as she spotted a brawl outside a cashpoint ahead. How could MI6 take on a cyber-army of thousands? For the first time ever, she doubted whether this was an adversary the Secret Intelligence Service could beat.

CHAPTER SIX

Jessica's silver haute couture digital gown sparkled with a thousand Swarovski crystals. Suddenly, it was lit up with over thirty-five hundred small LED lights. The extraordinary sight distracted her briefly from the fact she was cold and tired; she'd had to get up at five a.m. to cycle to the warehouse in East London for the seven-thirty a.m. shoot. She was dying for a coffee and croissant from the catering table, which was tantalizingly close.

"Testing three, two, one!" Ossa Cosway shouted from across the warehouse. "Start now!"

Jessica looked down as a text message scrolled across her floor-length evening dress: *Ossa Cosway rocks!*

"It's amazing!" she exclaimed.

The fabric flashed with more words: *#Ossa CoswayCouture.*

Ossa had certainly found a novel way to advertise his haute couture line, combining fashion with the latest digital technology. It was being launched around the world, while his ready-to-wear collection was showcased at London Fashion Week. His young assistants stood on the sidelines, busily messaging the dress, using the hashtag #OssaCosway on Twitter while he stared at the effects, mesmorized. The slightly built, fair-haired young man stroked his goatee, smiling broadly. Suddenly, he threw his arms around Christine Cooper, his chief dressmaker. The small fifty-something woman was caught off guard as she fiddled with her long gold pendant.

"Whoooaaa!" She clung on to Ossa as she lost her balance.

"You made it work, Chrissy!" her boss gushed. "You really did."

Christine smoothed her sleek black bob behind her ears, revealing purple nail polish that matched her lipstick.

"We make a good team," she said, laughing.

"Particularly with the lovely Jessica fronting your ad campaign. We chose well, Ossa. The dress looks sensational on her. I had a feeling it would. She knows how to show it off to perfection."

Jessica blushed as Ossa blew a kiss at her and Christine clapped.

"Let's get started," the photographer, Bryn, shouted over a pounding Calvin Harris track. "Work it, Jessica! I want to see what this dress can really do."

She swished the skirts from side to side and spun around. This was the best and most high-profile modelling shoot she'd done to date: the cover and an inside spread of *Teen Vogue* to highlight her collaboration with Ossa, the hot, hot, hot designer who'd been the talk of fashion editors across the world since leaving Central Saint Martin's College in London three years ago. His rise had been astronomical and the twenty-four-year-old was now the go-to designer for Hollywood actresses as well as the uber-rich who could afford to splash out tens of thousands of pounds for couture gowns.

"Keep twirling," Bryn shouted. "I love it. Give me more."

Jessica pirouetted, making sure she kept her eyes on a point on the wall between Ossa and Christine, the way she'd been taught in ballet. It prevented her from losing her balance. Well, in theory. It didn't help that her mind was wandering. When she left MI6 HQ late yesterday, Andrea, the MI6 operative outed by The Collective, had made it to a safe house, but seven other agents were uncontactable and unaware of the looming threat from The Collective.

"Again, again, again!" the photographer demanded.

How much longer could she keep this up? Her head felt like it was going to explode. Another agent's name would be published later today and Sam might not be able to remove his or her details from the web so fast. Who would it be, and had they managed to get to safety already? She hoped it wasn't one of the seven who were MIA – missing in action.

"And that's it!" Bryn said. "Let's get the close-ups in the bag next."

Jessica swayed on her feet slightly as she was surrounded by make-up artists, hair technicians and stylists, who touched up her face and fiddled with her dress. Christine knelt at her feet, pinning up the hem, which she'd accidentally caught with her spiked heel.

"The dress is stunning," Jessica said, gazing down at the sparkling lights. Another message scrolled across: *Ossa rules the world!* His assistants, clutching mobiles, applauded, and Ossa took a bow, sporting an even bigger grin.

"How long did it take you to make this?"

Christine nodded over her shoulder at members of her dressmaking team who lingered nearby; they were far younger and sported various piercings. "We spent six weeks, working day and night, to stitch all the Swarovski crystals on to it. Then we had the LED lights to deal with, which was quite tricky and time-consuming."

"You've done a fantastic job."

"Thanks. Luckily, I've got top-class backup. We've been together for years, working for different designers. We came on board for Ossa's graduation collection and have stayed ever since. He was demanding even as a student back then. You wouldn't believe some of his requests, but we haven't failed him yet. No one ever wants to let him down."

"And I'm sure you never will, Chrissy." Ossa straightened his grey waistcoat as he approached. "She's my rock, Jessica. I couldn't have launched any of my collections without her. Anything I ask, she and her team can do it just like that." He clicked his fingers. "Nothing is beyond her, including this digital technology, which would have thrown most dressmakers. The idea came to me in a dream – a dress that would light up the world – and Chrissy turned it into a reality."

"I guess your fairy godmother's in line for a nice big pay rise." Christine winked at Jessica and pushed a row of thick gold bangles up her arm. "I've been a dressmaker since I left school and have never been asked to do something as crazy as this before. But when Ossa asks, we all jump as high as we can."

Ossa blew her a kiss. "Chrissy goes above and beyond anyone I've ever known. Not only does she bring my designs to life, she juggles my diary, helps me with model castings, calms me down when I'm close to losing it and generally keeps me sane."

"Well, that's going a bit far." Christine hooted with laughter. "I don't think even I can make you *completely* sane, and I'm not sure anyone can stop you from losing your temper at least three times a day."

Ossa wagged a finger at her. "Now, now."

Jessica smiled as the pair walked away, still ribbing each other.

Bryn clapped his hands. "OK, people. Let's get this in the bag. We've still got the water shoot to go." He tapped his foot impatiently as stylists dispersed and the crew made last-minute adjustments to the lighting.

"Great. That's beautiful. Now stare directly into the camera, Jessica, and look serene."

She cupped her face in her hands, trying to ignore the raised voices in the background. It was hard to appear composed when a screaming match had erupted on set a few minutes ago. Who was having an almighty meltdown? It was really unprofessional.

"Keep it down back there!" Bryn yelled over his shoulder.

Jessica caught a glimpse of Ossa jabbing a finger in Christine's face. The photographer didn't care that the designer was at the heart of the altercation.

"For God's sake, we've got work to do," Bryn shouted. "Take it outside!"

An assistant cranked up the volume on the iPod before Ossa stormed off the set with a face as black as thunder. Jessica looked directly into the camera again. Why was he having a go at Christine? Out of the corner of her eye, she could see the dressmaker dab at her eyes with a tissue. After a couple of seconds, she disappeared out of sight. Jessica could still hear them arguing faintly in the background as the Ellie Goulding song faded out. Christine had admitted that the designer was demanding to work for and found it hard to keep his cool. That obviously wasn't an exaggeration.

But why was Ossa treating his "rock" so badly?

Half an hour later, the cover shoot had wrapped and it was apparent why Ossa and Christine were at each other's throats. The wrong gowns had been brought for the water set and Ossa was spitting blood. He'd hand-picked a deep crimson number and a midnight blue dress for Jessica to wear as she dived on to a wet Mylar sheet. Instead, Christine had picked up two very similar dresses, with slightly different hem lengths and necklines.

"It'll look virtually the same in the water shots," Christine insisted as Jessica emerged from the changing area, wearing the midnight blue gown.

"*Virtually* isn't good enough for me," Ossa said through gritted teeth. "*I'll* know the dresses are different. I don't know how you could be so careless. I put the correct dresses on the rails."

"Then someone else must have come along and swapped them," Christine shot back.

"That's impossible! Why would someone deliberately swap the dresses?"

"Enough!" Bryn said, holding up his hand. "We've gone over this a hundred times. I'm happy with the outfits. We've only got the warehouse for a few more hours, so I suggest we all get on with this. Right, Jessica?"

She nodded. To be perfectly honest, she couldn't understand why Ossa was kicking up such a fuss. He was behaving like a small child. Hadn't he noticed there were slightly more important things to worry about at the moment? MI6 had managed to keep the name of The Collective out of the news, but every bulletin carried stories about cashpoints ejecting money, planes being grounded due to technical faults and trains being derailed across the country after signal failures. Looting and even rioting were happening a few miles from here.

A man helped her up the steps on to a giant glass runway that stretched across the warehouse. Water sloshed across the mat, doused by a rubber hosepipe. Bryn was shooting from beneath, enabling him to capture interesting water patterns.

"I need you to run and dive gracefully," the photographer shouted. "No crash landings, please."

"OK, here goes," she called back.

She took a deep breath, ran and dived head first. The icy cold water almost took her breath away as she whizzed along the mat. This took her mind off things. The last time she'd done anything remotely similar, she was five years old and playing with a friend on a water slide in her back garden.

WHOOOOAAA! This was way faster and cooler.

"I'm back!" Jessica hollered as she let herself in the front door. She threw her handbag on the floor.

"I'm in here," her dad replied. "Good shoot?"

She pushed open the study door and walked in. Her dad sat at his desk, squinting at the computer screen.

"Yeah. The water was freezing, but I'm just about defrosted now. Is everything OK?" She looked over his shoulder.

"My account's working normally and no money's missing. You should be able to use the credit card again."

"That's good news. The money's miraculously appeared on my Oyster card too. I tested it at an Underground station. Pity the tubes still aren't working."

"You got a taxi back, right? I don't want you walking around London when it's so risky. There were reports of more rioting on the news."

"Yeah, of course I got a taxi. Like any buses are running today."

"Have you told Nathan that we've probably been hacked?"

Jessica shook her head. "I haven't had a chance. Anyway, like you said, everything's back to normal now. I doubt MI6 would have time to investigate something as minor as this, particularly since it happened before the launch of the midday hacking competition."

Her dad frowned. "I know it seems insignificant compared to everything else that's going on, but you should definitely record it. We don't know if anyone else at MI6 has been personally affected. You could be the only one."

"You're right. I'll let Nathan know tomorrow. There's no point trying to get hold of him now. He's got his hands full."

"Make sure you tell him." He stood up, using his walking stick, and limped to the door. "Are you hungry? Do you want a toasted sandwich?"

"Yes, please. Can I use your computer?" Her dad kept his main computer in a hidden underground bunker, accessed via the bookcase. But for day-to-day stuff, he logged on in his study.

"Sure."

She slid into his chair and checked her emails. They seemed OK. She hadn't received any spam messages, which could be a sign that the hacker was attempting to take over her account. Twitter was still down, but

Instagram and Facebook had started to work again a short time ago.

What about MI6? Had Sam managed to protect the firewalls? She logged in via a remote account and her protected PIN. She only had very limited access, but she might be able to see if the missing agents had made it to safe houses.

Blast.

Her inbox was empty. Nathan clearly didn't have time to give updates in the run-up to the release of the next undercover agent's name at three p.m.; plus it was probably beyond her security clearance. She shouldn't have been inside the comms centre when the hacking began; it was doubtful anyone else from Westwood had gained a glimpse of that hidden world.

She tried to navigate away from her home page. Six months ago, Nathan had given her a temporary password for the MI6 computer system when she was working with him in Monaco, trying to bring down a double agent called Margaret Becker. They both suspected Margaret had tampered with the helicopter that killed her mum on the orders of a notorious terrorist called Vectra. Jessica had done a secret search on "Sargasso" but it had produced nothing back then. She didn't have the clearance to search for sensitive files in more secure areas of the MI6 site. Shortly after Jessica had helped Nathan apprehend Margaret, he'd restricted her access to the computer system again.

A box flashed up, requesting a PIN again. Jessica re-entered the sequence of numbers. She opened another screen and clicked on to YouTube to check out the latest video from The Vamps while she waited for it to load. Once the clip had finished, she switched back to MI6. Ohmigod. She was in. She clicked and clicked again, navigating fully around the site. She had full, unrestricted access. This must be a mistake. Nathan would never have given her the OK to look at confidential files without supervision, probably not even back then.

What was going on?

Had MI6 experienced a security lapse while it repaired its firewalls? Sam could have temporarily changed agents' clearance levels as he rebooted the system. Or had The Collective hacked in again and deliberately widened her access, along with other members of Westwood? It could be a ruse to introduce another virus into the system if she called up confidential files.

What should she do? Sam could notice the security glitch and terminate her access within minutes. Her head was telling her to exit the site right away and ring Nathan on a secure line. But her heart was telling her something different. She would never have another chance like this to find out what files MI6 had gathered on Sargasso. Kat wasn't likely to cough up anything useful soon – she was deliberately withholding info as a bargaining chip. She'd said she might want a favour one day and wouldn't reveal more details until then.

Jessica glanced at the door. Her dad was banging around in the kitchen. She had to do this. If she noticed anything seriously wrong, she'd shut down immediately. Heart beating rapidly, she typed "Sargasso" into the file headers and pressed return. One file flashed up marked "Confidential: Restricted Access". Clicking it open revealed dozens of documents. She pulled up the first one. It was a scrambled mess of digits and letters; it had to be written in some kind of code. The second one was similarly encrypted.

She sank back in the chair as she opened the third file. A passport-style photo of her mum stared back, alongside a separate pic of a dark-haired man with glasses and a beard. He was an ex-KGB agent called Sergei Chekhova who had died in a car crash in the Ukraine. Her mum's entry was under her maiden name, Lily Matilda Farr. Both deaths were marked as suspicious.

"Here you go." Her dad kicked open the door, balancing a plate while gripping his walking stick. "Didn't you hear me hollering?"

"I'm sorry." She jumped guiltily and attempted to flick back to YouTube, but the computer was frozen. She wiggled the mouse about, unable to minimize the screen or pull it down.

Her dad put the plate down next to the keyboard and froze as he glanced at the screen.

"How did you get that man's photo?"

"You know him?"

"I used to. He was a Russian agent your mother had dealings with. She always said he was her best post–Cold War source, but he went missing."

"According to this file, he died six months after

Mum in a car accident. Their deaths must be connected somehow. They're both marked as suspicious and kept in the same MI6 file."

"Sargasso," her dad said, reading the name on the screen.

"Does that mean anything to you?"

He shook his head. "Should it? What's going on?"

She quickly recounted the barest of details – that the organization was somehow linked to her mum's death as well as Sergei's, leaving out the fact that the tip had come from Kat.

"You know this how exactly?" her dad persisted.

Jessica bit her nail. Kat had warned her that if she breathed a word about Sargasso to anyone else she'd destroy the file she'd found on the subject. She hadn't been in a position to argue back – Kat had blackmailed her into keeping quiet about a series of thefts she'd carried out using an invisibility cloak in return for the little info she'd provided on the subject.

"I can't say who told me, but I believe them."

"So Nathan's allowed you to trawl through MI6 files based on a tip-off from a source?" he said sharply.

Jessica flushed. "Well, not exactly. I was checking

my MI6 account and found that I could get in, well, you know, deeper than before."

Her dad's jaw dropped. "You mean you have total access to the MI6 computer system?"

She bit her lip, nodding.

"Are you mad? Turn off the computer. Log out."

"It's frozen."

"I can't believe you'd do something as stupid as this. It could be a trap, set by The Collective. If they hacked you yesterday, they could already know that you're working for MI6. They might want you inside the system. Can't you see that? They could be launching another hack on the back of this."

"I know. I'm sorry."

He banged the mouse up and down and tried to log out. "Aaagh!"

He reached down and pulled out the power socket. The computer screen flickered off.

"Do you have any idea what kind of trouble you'll be in if this little stunt is traced back to you?"

Tears pricked Jessica's eyes. "I have to find out what happened to Mum. I can't live with the uncertainty any longer. I want to find out if Vectra definitely ordered the hit and if Margaret sabotaged the helicopter. Don't you?"

"Not at the expense of you getting hurt," he said quietly. "If MI6 finds out you've somehow assisted the hacker, Nathan and I won't be able to protect you. You'll be thrown out of Westwood and possibly face criminal charges."

CHAPTER
SEVEN

"Seriously?" Nathan snarled. "You want to do this now?"

Jessica fiddled with her earpiece as she hid in shadows at the rear of the International High School in West Kensington. Nathan had temporarily blocked Sasha, Natalia and Bree from the comms to enable the two of them to speak in private. Her dad had warned her not to make accusations about a colleague, but she had to finally speak up. A Moscow-based academic, Andrew Docherty, had been outed on a news website as an MI6 operative hours earlier on Sunday afternoon and was now in hiding, along with his family. She couldn't let Westwood jeopardize this dawn raid on a high-ranking member of The Collective due to Bree's involvement in the mission. This was the only solid lead they had.

"I'm telling you, it's a mistake to allow Bree to take charge on the ground," she said, staring at her icy puffs of breath. "I don't trust her."

Nathan sighed with exasperation. "Is this because of the Shard job?"

"I don't have any proof, but I think she could have been involved."

"We rigorously checked all the girls, particularly Bree, after she froze that night. They're clean, understand? You can trust them. They had nothing to do with the seizure of the USB device or the attack on you. We're sure of it, so let's move on."

Jessica kicked a stone. How did Nathan know for sure that Bree wasn't a double agent? He didn't sound like he was going to budge; she had to try another tack. "What happens if Bree freezes tonight when we get inside?"

Or if she betrays me and raises the alarm, she wanted to add.

Nathan fell silent. "Fine. Change of plan. You and Natalia will go in, Bree and Sasha will keep guard at the front. Happy now?"

No. Natalia was inexperienced and hadn't exactly shone at the Shard either. She certainly hadn't backed up Jessica and had sided with Bree during that debacle. But this line-up was better than the alternative – having to rely directly on Bree for such a high-risk mission. She listened as Nathan moved the other Westwood girls into position around the perimeter. Pulling her black woollen hat further down over her ears, she leant against the wall and stamped her feet to keep warm.

MI6 had worked fast. The hacks on all the prisons across the UK, the traffic-light systems and the emergency service comms had been traced back here, to the most exclusive boarding school in London, where seriously rich expats, diplomats and some of the most powerful people in the world sent their children. They even had the laptop's exact location thanks to a trace on the IP address – room 59 in Highfield Boarding House, which was occupied by a seventeen-year-old sixth former, Henry Murray.

Henry was the only son of a Canadian diplomat. He was also spoilt, uber-bright and believed to be one of the most prolific and audacious hackers the country had seen since Lee Caplin, according to the hastily prepared MI6 file. A number of other male teenage hackers across the country had also been identified in the last few hours, but Henry was being red-flagged. Over the last nine months he'd been in regular correspondence with LibertyCrossing, the mysterious person who'd set up the hacking websites and issued the code word, "Bluebird", initiating all the cyberattacks on Saturday. With any luck, Henry could lead them directly to this shadowy leader of The Collective, who was coordinating havoc across the country.

The objective of the raid was simple: to seize Henry's laptop and persuade him to cooperate with MI6 in return for his crimes being kept secret from his dad, the police and the press. Nathan had warned Jessica that they couldn't go through official channels. As soon as the Metropolitan Police gained an official search warrant, Henry's father would claim diplomatic immunity for himself and his son. Henry would be untouchable and they wouldn't be able to discover what he knew.

It was highly dangerous. If it ever came to light that

MI6 had sanctioned a black ops mission, targeting the son of a high-ranking foreign official, it'd spark a diplomatic incident of epic proportions. That was why Westwood had been tasked to go in despite the fallout from the Shard. An adult caught on the premises would spark a 999 call and a police investigation, but a teenage girl found sneaking into a boarding house could pretend she was having a clandestine meet-up with a boyfriend.

Jessica watched as Natalia pedalled up to the far end of the wall. She too was dressed from head to toe in black, with a thick scarf knotted at her neck. They'd been given an hour's notice to cycle to the school, where they'd been briefed by another Westwood agent, Celia Tyler, in a van further down the street and fitted up with gadgets to help them get past security. Computer analyst Sam Hewitt was also here; he'd assured them that their comms were safe and the hacker couldn't access their plans for tonight's raid. He hadn't mentioned anything about Jessica's security breach earlier; hopefully he'd been so tied up with preventing further hacks he hadn't noticed that the Sargasso file had been opened and read.

"Are you OK?" Jessica said into her hidden microphone.

"I'm good, except I could have done with a full night's sleep," Natalia said. "I've got a chemistry test first thing tomorrow. If I flunk it, I'm going to be in big trouble. Bigger still if Mum and Dad discover I've gone AWOL tonight."

"I know what you mean," Jessica replied.

She'd been woken up at one a.m. by a terse call from Nathan and had left the house without waking her dad. He'd kill her if he found out she was on a dangerous night op. She was supposed to clear all Westwood jobs with him first, but he'd been feeling unwell and she hadn't wanted to disturb him. Plus, there was no way he'd sign off on something as risky as this. She had a test tomorrow too – irregular French verbs – which would be hard enough without the added sleep deprivation.

"Let's cut the social chit-chat, girls," Nathan said sharply. "Are you all in position?" He was running point from the van, alongside Sam and Celia.

The girls answered in the affirmative, one by one.

"Good. Bree and Sasha, stay where you are unless we

need backup. Jessica and Natalia will enter over the rear wall. Jessica is team leader. Go straight to the boarding house and enter Henry's room. Transfer the contents of his laptop to us immediately via the device Sam's given you in case the alarm's raised. Jessica, you stay to talk some sense into Henry while Natalia leaves with the laptop. Do not deviate from the plan. Understood?"

"Yes," Jessica replied.

"Natalia?"

"I guess. If you say so."

"I do say so," Nathan snapped. "Jessica has more experience than you in the field. You're to follow her lead. Understood?"

"Of course. I'll follow your god-daughter's lead."

Jessica flinched. That was low. They got on most of the time, but Natalia obviously felt snubbed. She was following Bree's lead by insinuating that Jessica was getting preferential treatment due to her family connections. Was she going to be a problem tonight? They couldn't afford for egos or petty gripes to jeopardize the operation. Natalia had no idea about the dangerous MI6 missions she'd embarked on before officially joining Westwood.

"OK, girls, now that's sorted, let's move in," Nathan said. "Good luck."

Jessica and Natalia pulled out specially adapted bicycle pumps from their rucksacks and aimed at the top of the wall. Grapnels shot out, sinking into the brick. A few seconds later, fine ropes swung down. Together they scaled the wall, pulling themselves up hand over hand. Natalia got to the top first; Jessica was a few seconds behind. She swung her legs over the wall, retrieved the rope and pointed her watch at the security light. A high-powered dart pierced the glass.

"Good shot," Natalia muttered.

"Thanks. Three, two, one. Go."

They dropped on to the gravel below and sprinted towards a tall red-brick house on the right of the main building. Highfield Boarding House was home to sixty boys aged thirteen to eighteen, along with their housemaster and matron. If any of them woke up and stumbled across them, their mission would be a write-off. The entrances were at the front and rear, but both were locked at night and only accessed with a security code via the keypad.

Jessica already had her diamanté key ring ready; it

contained a scanner that would identify the numbers she needed to punch in. As she reached the door, Natalia overtook her.

"Something's wrong," she breathed.

Jessica stared over Natalia's shoulder. The door was slightly ajar. This didn't look right. There was no way the school would allow a security lapse like this; anyone could walk in or out, which would put the safety of all the pupils at risk.

"What do you want us to do, Nathan?" Jessica said, examining the keypad. "The door's open. Someone's tampered with it."

"Proceed with extreme caution."

They'd been warned that all the corridors would be fitted with night lights, but the boarding house was shrouded in darkness, another bad sign.

"We need night vision." Jessica rummaged in her rucksack.

They fixed glasses on their faces and stepped into the pitch-black entrance hall. Henry's room was three flights up. According to the plans Sam had accessed, the housemaster and his family occupied the entire ground floor. They had two Labradors, Silky and

Sabba, that needed to be subdued. Natalia held out a small aerosol can of MI6 adapted hairspray; a few squirts and the dogs would fall asleep instantly. They'd wake up in a few hours, unhurt.

"Stop," Jessica whispered, catching Natalia's hand. "Look over there!" Both dogs lay a short distance away from each other.

Natalia tiptoed over and stroked their fur. "They're drugged. Someone got here first."

"The Collective's here, Nathan!" Jessica hissed.

"Affirmative. Bree and Sasha, go in. I'm calling for further backup."

Jessica took the stairs two at a time, followed by Natalia. They cleared a floor without disturbing anyone. As they reached the second floor, a door banged. The girls pressed their backs against the wall on the landing. They waited a few seconds before climbing up to the third floor.

"Let me go ahead and assess the situation," Jessica whispered. "You wait here until my signal."

"No. I can do this. I don't have a relative in MI6 but I'm as good as you!" Natalia darted away before she could stop her. An explosion of bright white light in the corridor lit up the landing. There was a loud scream, followed by a bang.

"We're under attack!" Jessica ran into the corridor after Natalia, who lay on the floor, motionless. Another flash of light erupted, blinding her. As she ripped off her glasses, something solid smashed into her. Spinning around, she could make out a dark figure sprinting away. She ran after the intruder, gripping her side. Glass exploded from the window at the bottom of the corridor. The figure leapt through the gap without slowing down. A torch, emitting a pulsating white light, clattered to the floor.

"The intruder's jumped out of a window on the west side of the building," Jessica wheezed.

"We're on it," Nathan replied.

She squinted as she picked up the torch. She'd only ever seen one of these devices in training; it was designed to obliterate night vision. The attacker had come prepared with a military-style gadget.

She ran over to Natalia and felt for a pulse. She was out cold, but still breathing. As Jessica shone the torch on her neck, she noticed a two-pronged burn mark. The attacker had used some kind of electrical stun gun to knock her out. She shone her torch up and down the corridor. She could smell smoke. Where was it coming from?

A door swung open and a boy peered out, squinting at the torch.

"What's going on?" he mumbled. "Who are you?"

She ignored him as Nathan's voice rang in her ear again. "Secure the laptop and find Henry Murray. Move before you're discovered!"

Too late. She jumped to her feet as a fire alarm screeched. More boys spilled out of their rooms, rubbing their eyes.

"OK, listen up, everyone," she yelled above the alarm. "This isn't a drill. You need to evacuate. Don't go back to your rooms." She handed the torch to one of the older-looking boys. "Take this and lead the others." She nodded at his friends. "Help carry this girl – she's passed out."

The pupils hoisted Natalia up and joined the evacuation.

Jessica ran back towards Henry's room. As she flung the door open, she was hit by a smothering blanket of smoke and heat. She fell back a step. Flames flickered up the wall from a wastepaper basket, setting the curtains ablaze. Nearby was a bloodstained baseball bat. A blond boy clad in jeans, a sweater and trainers lay on the carpet, blood trickling from his forehead. He was attempting to pull himself towards the door, commando-style, on his elbows.

"Henry!" Jessica lunged forward, protecting her mouth and nostrils with the sleeve of her jumper. She grabbed the boy under the armpits and pulled him to his feet. "Here. Let me take your weight."

"Can't breathe." Henry coughed violently as he slung an arm over her shoulder.

"Let's go," she cried.

They stumbled out of the door. Jessica pulled it shut and helped him further along the corridor. Henry's legs collapsed beneath him and he sank to the floor. He touched his forehead, which was wet with a slick of blood. The gash was about five inches long and deep.

"My laptop's on fire," he spluttered. "It's in the bin. It's my insurance policy. Without it, I'm dead."

"I'll get it." She grabbed a fire extinguisher and kicked open the bedroom door. She gasped as she stepped into the choking wall of flames and acrid smoke. Eyes stinging, she edged closer and blasted the bin again and again. She could barely breathe. Suddenly, she felt someone grab her arm and pull her back.

"We have to leave before we're caught," Bree insisted. "The mission's aborted."

"Get off me! I can get the laptop!" Jessica struggled against her grip.

"It's gone."

Jessica pushed her away. "It's not! Who the hell are you working for tonight, anyway?"

Why hadn't Nathan listened to her? This was the second mission Bree had been tasked to that had gone horribly wrong. The Collective knew they were coming and had moved faster. Had Bree leaked their plans to a third party?

Bree frowned. "What are you talking about?"

"She's working for me," Nathan said through the comms. "I sent Bree in to get you. She's following orders. Abort the mission and make yourselves scarce before you're apprehended. Move now!"

Jessica staggered backwards. The fire had spread to the bed and ceiling. She couldn't fight this with a single extinguisher. Within minutes, the room would be totally engulfed in flames. She slammed the door and looked up and down the corridor. "Where did Henry go? He was right here!"

"Sasha's helping him downstairs. Nathan's waiting for them at the bottom. He's taking him to hospital, along with Natalia." Bree paused at the sound of sirens. "The fire brigade's almost here. We have to leave."

"Wait one minute."

Jessica ran up and down the corridor, checking all the boys had evacuated. "It's clear."

"What are you doing here?" a voice shouted. "Did you start this fire?"

A middle-aged man wearing a red dressing gown stood at the end of the corridor. Jessica recognized him from his photo in the MI6 file. It was the housemaster, Sean Hughes.

"We have nothing to do with this," she yelled back. "We saw the flames from the street and came to help. The downstairs door was open. All the boys are out. Check the other floors!"

Mr Hughes hesitated and then stumbled away,

covering his mouth with the sleeve of his dressing gown. A couple of sirens blared loudly outside. The fire engines must have pulled up in the grounds.

"The crew will be up here any second. How are we going to get out?" Bree's face was panic-stricken.

She'd frozen yet again in the middle of a mission. What was going on with her?

"Follow me." Jessica ran towards the window. The intruder had left this way; they could follow. She peered out. The fire engines and evacuation point must be at the front. They could escape, unobserved, and regroup at the bottom. She climbed out, careful not to cut herself: a shard of glass jutted out from the bottom of the window frame. A grapnel was still attached to the wood, with a rope hanging down. The person who'd attacked Henry and set fire to his laptop must have shot it at the window as they ran; it looked slimmer and lighter than the one MI6 used, yet it had totally disintegrated the glass. Did it have some kind of pulsating mechanism? If so, it was far more advanced than MI6's technology.

She shone her torch on to the frame as Bree followed her.

"Hold on!" Jessica pulled a fine silver thread from the wood and carefully placed it in the small plastic bag she'd retrieved from her pocket.

"What's that?"

"The intruder left it behind. It must be from their clothing."

"Interesting, but let's go."

Jessica gripped the rope and abseiled down the building. She jumped the last few feet on to the gravel.

"Nathan? Are you there? Do you have Henry?" She touched her ear.

"He's already in the ambulance with Natalia," Nathan replied. "Get off the property. We're all exposed. At least two police cars are on their way."

Jessica looked up. Bree was still dangling from the window sill.

"Get a move on!" she hissed.

Bree carefully lowered herself down.

"Jump!" Jessica urged. "Now!"

Bree looked down. Her face was etched with terror. Finally, she let go.

"We'll leave the way Natalia and I came in."

Jessica darted to the wall and grabbed her rope.

She pulled herself up, hand over hand, with Bree a few seconds behind. They dropped on to the street. Bree sank down, putting her head between her knees.

"Come on. We don't have time to stop." Jessica grabbed Bree's arm and pulled her to her feet.

Bree shook off her hand. "I don't need your help. What did you mean back there when you asked who I worked for? Does this have something to do with Nathan switching Natalia with me at the last minute? I bet you asked your godfather to do that, didn't you? Why?"

"You tell me. How did The Collective know we were coming tonight?"

Bree's eyes narrowed. "They must have hacked into our comms or the computer system. It's the only explanation."

"If you say so." It wasn't the only theory she could think of.

"What are you insinuating? What have you been saying to Nathan behind my back yet again?"

Jessica shook her head. Bree was trembling with rage. There was no point getting into this now. She'd only deny being a double agent.

"We could be caught. Natalia's bike is over there. Grab it and go!" Jessica pointed to the bushes. She raced to get her own; it was still where she'd left it nearby. As she climbed on, the bike wobbled beneath her.

The tyre was flat.

Bree doubled back on her bike. "Use this one. I can make it on foot."

Jessica glanced up, surprised. "No, you go. I'll be OK."

Bree hesitated. "I don't know what you've been secretly reporting to Nathan about me, but you're way off the mark. Some of us actually had to earn a place on this team." She pedalled away without looking back.

Jessica threw the bike down. Was she mistaken about Bree? Maybe. Maybe not. Bree could have offered to help to try and throw her off the scent. She ran around the side of the wall and peered out. Dozens of boys clad in pyjamas and dressing gowns stood huddled in groups. Their housemaster was a little distance away, holding a clipboard and shouting out names. He broke off from the roll-call as two ambulances pulled away, sirens blaring.

"Natalia and Henry are en route to hospital," Nathan said in her ear. "I'm following in the van. Go home, Jessica. That's enough for now. You'll need to come to a debriefing later this morning. I'll message you the details. Ask your dad to write a note for school."

"Will do."

Great. Jamie would notice her absence and want to know what was wrong. She'd have to come up with yet another lie. As she turned away, she noticed a tall boy slip away from the others. He wore a blue dressing gown with a hood that covered his face. That was odd. He wasn't barefoot or in slippers like the others. Trainers and jeans poked out beneath his dressing gown.

"Henry!" Jessica broke cover and charged towards him.

The boy jumped and turned around. Fear flickered over his blood-splattered face.

"Keep away from me!" he screeched.

He sprinted away, ditching his dressing gown. Boys stared and pointed.

"Nathan! Come in!" Jessica shouted as she ran.

Silence.

Nathan had turned off his comms. "Sasha? Bree? Are you there? Talk to me!"

Henry had tricked them. He must have persuaded a friend to take his place in the ambulance. Jessica rounded the corner in time to see him scaling a high wall into a park. "Stop!"

The boy paused and looked over his shoulder, his legs astride the wall. "Who are you? What do you want with me?"

No way could she risk giving him her real name. "I'm Jenny. I've been sent by MI6."

"This is about LibertyCrossing, isn't it?"

Jessica nodded. "We've come to help you. We can protect you. I need to bring you in."

"You don't get it, do you? You can't protect me from LibertyCrossing or the rest of The Collective. No one can."

"We can. I promise. Who's the leader of The Collective? Who tried to kill you tonight?"

Henry hesitated. "Someone far more powerful than the whole of MI6." He swung his other leg over the wall and jumped.

CHAPTER
EIGHT

"I'm afraid your daughter's in big trouble, Mr Cole."

Jessica and her dad sat on uncomfortable plastic chairs in the head teacher's office. Richard Reynolds must have adjusted his chair to be deliberately high, as he towered above them even though her dad was six foot two. She glanced at the clock. It was nine a.m. and so far, the worst Monday morning *ever*. She'd only managed to grab a few hours' sleep after returning home from the mission before her dad had woken her with the bad news – they'd been summoned to school for an urgent disciplinary meeting.

"Perhaps you could enlighten us about what's going on," her dad asked pleasantly.

"Shall I tell him or will you?" The grey-haired man glared fiercely at Jessica.

"I have absolutely no idea what you're talking about."

Mr Reynolds slammed his hand on the desk. "Do not take me for a fool. There will be extremely serious consequences for your actions this weekend. It'd be far better if you confessed to hacking the school computer system now."

Oh no. She exchanged worried glances with her dad. Her hands trembled slightly as she gripped the chair. "I don't know what you're referring to, Mr Reynolds. Tell us."

"Fine. Have it your way. At precisely 1.26 p.m. yesterday you hacked into the school computer and—"

"No, I didn't!"

"Let me finish uninterrupted, please." The head teacher glared furiously at her. "As I was saying, you hacked in and retrieved confidential information on every single member of staff – dates of birth, home addresses, telephone numbers, etc – and uploaded them to a dating website, www.oapsneedlove2."

Jessica's jaw dropped. "I can assure you..."

"Immediately afterwards, the IT department tells me you placed the entire school and its contents – including personal information about every pupil in year eleven – on eBay with an opening bid of one pence."

She stared at her dad in stunned silence. The hack on the school was about the time she'd used his computer to log on to the MI6 account. This had to be the work of The Collective. The hackers had seized the opportunity to attack their home software and get her into trouble.

"Did you find your exploits amusing?" Mr Reynolds continued. "Because I can assure you I didn't. Neither did any members of my staff. Teachers have already received telephone calls and email correspondence from the dating website."

"I can personally assure you that Jessica had nothing to do with this," her dad began.

"Our IT department traced the thread to her Facebook account, where she also posted about her exploits. For example, I'm told this went up at four a.m. today." Mr Reynolds picked up a piece of paper from his desk. "'Check out the website www.oapsneedlove2 – Hatchet Hatcham might find his soul mate. Not. Jessica ;)'.' "

She barely used Facebook now she had WhatsApp and Snapchat and she definitely hadn't targeted her least favourite teacher at school. The message had been posted shortly after she'd returned from the botched raid at the International High School. Was LibertyCrossing exacting revenge after she'd rescued Henry Murray from the blaze? His attacker must have hoped he'd succumb to smoke inhalation after clobbering him with the baseball bat.

"I didn't write that."

"Really?" Mr Reynolds continued. "How about this letter, which was sent to the parents of every pupil at this school from your email account at four thirty a.m.?"

Jessica groaned inwardly. "What did it say?"

"You're insisting on keeping up with this pretence?" He gave her a withering look and read from the piece of paper.

"*Dear Parent,*
I wish to inform you that school is shut

127

today. Don't bother sending your little brats
because I won't let them in.
   Yours insincerely,
   your miserable head teacher,
   Richard Reynolds'."

"Again, it wasn't me." Jessica felt her face redden further. She must be puce by now.

"Then how do you explain what's happened?"

"I think someone hacked into my dad's home computer yesterday. They must have gained control of my email and Facebook accounts and set me up."

"Do you really expect me to believe that someone would go to such great lengths to get you into trouble?"

"Yes, I do," she said simply. "And it's—"

"Jessica!" her dad barked.

She glared at him. Did he think she was that stupid? She wasn't going to blurt out about the latest Westwood case.

"Jessica's telling the truth about problems we've been having with our home computer," her dad said. "I've checked with my bank. My account was definitely hacked into and funds frozen. I can get you a statement from their internet fraud department, which will verify that. I'd also like to employ the services of an independent IT professional who can examine the school's equipment and our home computer. That way, we can get to the bottom of this unfortunate matter."

"Thank you," Mr Reynolds said stiffly. "That sounds like the most reasonable course of action to take. In the meantime, though, I'm afraid I have no option but to suspend Jessica until this incident has been thoroughly investigated."

"Is that necessary? I'm confident my daughter will be cleared within days."

"If so, she will be welcomed back. Until then, I cannot have her on the premises. No member of staff will agree to teach her after what's happened and I can't say I blame them."

"It's OK," Jessica said, standing up. "I understand. Don't worry, Dad. I'll be back in school before the end of the week."

Her dad rose to his feet unsteadily. "You're making a big mistake, Mr Reynolds. I'll expect a personal apology to Jessica and me when this is all over."

"Which you shall have, if and when your daughter's name is cleared. However, I'm about to deal with some very unhappy teachers and parents. I have the feeling it's going to be a very long day."

He had no idea. If members of The Collective had managed to wreak this kind of havoc at school by hijacking her identity, what damage had they unleashed on MI6?

"There's good news and bad news," Nathan said, kicking off the emergency Westwood meeting.

Jessica held her breath. Had MI6 systems analyst Sam Hewitt finally discovered her Sargasso security breach? She'd been summoned by text to an urgent debriefing at MI6 HQ shortly after the showdown with Mr Reynolds and had been on tenterhooks ever since. Bree had refused to make eye contact when she walked in, which could also be a bad sign, but Celia had glanced up and smiled briefly.

The door banged open and Sasha flew in, red-faced and panting. She threw herself into a seat. "Sorry I'm late. I had to pretend I'd got a migraine in A-level maths. It took a while to persuade the school nurse that I needed to go home."

Poor Sasha. Having a suspension on Jessica's school record was bad news, but it had made getting here at short notice much easier than usual.

"You're here now, Sasha, which is what's important," Nathan said briskly. "The good news is that Natalia is expected to make a full recovery. She's in hospital recovering from a severe electric shock but won't have any lasting injuries. We're still trying to determine the weapon used to attack her last night."

Jessica shuddered at the thought of Natalia's burn mark. If only she had remembered her training – always be prepared for the risk of attack when moving into a hostile environment. Instead, she was just trying to make a juvenile point that having a family member in MI6 didn't give Jessica the right to issue orders.

"Further good news is that we don't think The Collective has found Henry Murray yet." Nathan cracked his knuckles. "Members are currently posting about looking for him."

"And the bad news?" Jessica asked tentatively.

"We've had forty-eight hours of hacking and are still no closer to finding the leader of The Collective. In addition, we have no idea where Henry is either. He didn't return to school this morning and has officially been reported as missing by his head teacher and father. He hasn't made any attempt to contact his family in Canada or friends in this country. He's gone completely off-grid – no phone calls or texts, money withdrawals from his credit card, email use, sightings on CCTV cameras across London. Nothing."

Phew. Nathan didn't know about her computer activity after all. She cleared her throat. "Henry didn't think MI6 could protect him from The Collective. He was absolutely terrified last night. He's lying low somewhere until he figures out his next move. Henry must know the only chance he has to remain undetected is to avoid using his mobile or any electrical device."

Nathan nodded. "He's right to be afraid. A few hours ago, LibertyCrossing posted an alert, telling hackers to track Henry Murray through his credit card, Oyster card, phone and any electronic equipment. As soon as he uses anything, members of The Collective will find him."

"We have to get to Henry first," Celia said. "But how?"

Jessica glanced across the table. The stunning twenty-three-year-old redhead had led one of the seminars during her training about how to keep up a double life. Celia should know; she'd recently been announced as the new face of Burberry and Thierry Mugler perfume while rising up the ranks of Westwood.

"We're examining Henry's text messages and emails over the last week." Nathan pushed his glasses up his nose and cracked his knuckles again. He had dark circles under his eyes. When was the last time he'd slept? Probably Friday night, before the hacks started.

"Westwood agents are being drafted in to speak to Henry's friends under the guise of being volunteers from an anti-bullying charity," he continued. "His year group's already been told it's suspected he was being bullied. You'll quiz his friends about possible harassment while tapping them for info at the same time."

Jessica nodded. It sounded like believable cover, plus her whole day was free now she was banned from lessons. She'd need to fill Nathan in on what had happened at school as soon as the briefing wrapped up.

"We need to concentrate our efforts on identifying LibertyCrossing and the person who attacked Henry last night," Nathan said.

"They could be the same person," Celia pointed out.

"It's possible," Nathan said. "But why did LibertyCrossing turn on Henry? He's one of The Collective's best hackers and most loyal followers. He's been in direct contact with LibertyCrossing for a considerable period of time."

"Henry talked about the laptop being his insurance policy," Jessica said. "He seemed to think it was the only thing that could keep him alive. Perhaps he fell out with the leader of The Collective, or he could have been blackmailing him."

"It's possible LibertyCrossing realized Henry knew too much and would inevitably blab if caught by MI6," Celia reasoned. "He had to silence him for good and destroy the evidence."

"We need to work out what Henry knows ASAP.

It's going to be all hands on deck across MI6. We only have two more days until The Collective's deadline."

Nathan picked up his mobile as it vibrated. "Show him up," he told the caller. "We're in briefing room 304D."

Jessica raised an eyebrow. "We have company?"

"The CIA has agreed to help since the US has also been targeted. It's come across The Collective before. We've been loaned an operative who can provide us with further insight into the hacking organization."

Nathan was in no mood to wait for the visitor. He scribbled notes as Bree and Sasha ran through their accounts of last night's mission. Bree conveniently left out the part about how she froze when they were outside Henry's room and couldn't come up with an escape plan. Typical. Jessica nibbled her nails; if only she'd managed to stop the attacker or get a proper glimpse of their face. She had only a vague description: five feet and seven or eight inches tall with a slim build, wearing dark clothing and a balaclava. The thread she'd found trapped in the window frame might give a clue, but she hadn't had chance to hand it in to forensics. She'd meant to ring Lucas, a mate in that department, first thing but had been thrown by the early school meeting. Lucas was cool; he'd arrange for the thread to be picked up from her home and have it analysed by close of play today. With any luck, it came from an unusual material that wasn't mass-produced. That could help track down its owner.

Jessica glanced up at the sharp rap on the door. A blonde woman poked her head round.

Nathan put down his gold fountain pen. "Show him in, Lucy."

A dark-haired figure brushed past her, a black rucksack slung over his shoulder. Jessica's jaw dropped. What on earth...?

"Thank you for coming at such short notice," Nathan said. "Let me introduce you to the team."

Zak scanned the room. His eyes lingered on Jessica. "Hello again."

CHAPTER
NINE

To Jessica's annoyance, she felt her cheeks colour up. "What are *you* doing here?"

A smile hovered on Zak's lips. "I've come to save your butts. You can thank me later."

"What's he talking about?" She stared at Nathan, horrified. This could *not* be happening.

"Of course, I forgot. You met Zak at the Shard, didn't you, Jessica? As did Bree and Sasha." Nathan gestured to the other Westwood girls. "Celia Tyler, this is Zak Dane. Please take a seat."

"Er, I mean, well, yes," Jessica stuttered. "I kind of know Zak, but that doesn't explain what he's doing here."

He slumped into a seat opposite. "It's good to see

you again too, Jessica. You look in better shape than the last time I saw you."

She scowled back.

"Zak works for Rodarte, the CIA version of Westwood," Nathan said.

"You see, I'm a model and a spy, just like you." Zak smiled as he ripped off his dark grey coat and pullover, revealing a crisp white shirt underneath. "Who'd have thought we'd have so much in common?"

"You have to be kidding," Jessica snorted.

"Do I look like I am?"

"Hmm. I don't see it. You know, you being a spy. A really vain model, yes."

A look of annoyance flickered over Zak's face. "Why? Because you think I'm empty-headed and shallow, banging on about Calvin Klein and my other modelling contracts all the time? Good. Because that means I'm doing my job well. You didn't suspect a thing. But I guessed you were up to something that night at the Shard. I didn't know what had gone down until Nathan filled me in on the *failed* mission yesterday morning."

Jessica glared at him. "Yes, thanks for that night.

You know, alerting Mike to the fact that I was trying to get up the stairs. It was massively helpful. You're a great undercover spy, Zak."

"I had no idea you were on a Westwood mission, otherwise I'd have kept my mouth shut and helped you," he drawled. "It's a pity your people didn't let Rodarte into the loop. I hate to say it, but if Westwood had asked me to come on board, I'd have handled the Shard job completely differently. Likewise, last night. I hear you managed to let your best lead escape, Jessica. That was careless of you, if you don't mind me saying. Tsk, tsk, tsk."

Her eyes narrowed. "Actually, I do mind. I've no idea why Nathan thinks we need you here. Frankly, I'm amazed you managed to make it through the door, considering the size of your colossal ego."

"Ditto. Why do you seem to think you're the only one who can do this job?"

"What? How dare you?"

"That's enough, you two!" Nathan snapped. "We've established you're both government agents. Now start acting like them. We've got bigger things to worry about than wounded egos, if you hadn't

139

noticed, like finding Henry before The Collective and protecting our agents out in the field. We have less than three hours until the next MI6 operative is named on the web."

Jessica glowered at Zak. Who did he think he was, marching in here, acting as if he were her boss? She didn't answer to him. No way.

"Zak is one of Rodarte's best operatives, which is why he's coming on board with Westwood," Nathan continued. "You're all to cooperate with him. He has full security clearance on The Collective brief."

Jessica's jaw dropped. This was unbelievable. She knew The Collective had to be their top priority, but she couldn't let the incident at the Shard go. Not yet.

"So let me get this straight, Zak. When you came to my house that evening, wanting to know if I recognized the person who attacked me, you were investigating what had happened for Rodarte?"

Zak nodded. "My bosses demanded a report, seeing that the US ambassador's wife had been caught up in an armed siege. They smelt a rat from the official reports about a publicity stunt gone wrong. We didn't know at that stage it was a Westwood operation.

Correction. A ballsed-up Westwood operation."

She sucked in her breath, remembering the huge bunch of flowers he'd given her, along with the kiss on the cheek, and his general flirting, which had annoyed Jamie. And her.

"Why? You didn't actually think..." Zak's voice trailed off as he grinned at her.

"No, I did not!" Jessica retorted. She could feel her cheeks reddening again. Why did she have to blush so easily?

"Think what?" Sasha asked. "I'm confused."

"Forget it," Jessica growled. She felt stupid enough already for thinking Zak might be interested in her without having to admit her infuriating mistake to everyone present. "Why are you really in London?"

Zak pushed his chair back abruptly. For some reason, his cheeks were flushed too. "In a week's time, the president of the United States is scheduled to visit for a trade meeting with your prime minister. I joined the secret service team sent ahead to assess active risks in the capital. As of this weekend, our main concern is The Collective. The hackers' leader has been active in the States for years – attacking personal bank accounts – but has only chosen to reveal himself in the UK days before the president's arrival. That worries us."

"I get the secret service being involved in a security visit, but why Rodarte?" Jessica asked.

"The president wants to meet with representatives from the British fashion industry while he's over here," Zak said shortly. "Plus, his eldest daughter, Lydia, is scheduled to join him for the trip. She's opening for Mulberry at London Fashion Week and also giving a talk to young diabetes sufferers at a conference."

Of course! Lydia Eastwood was huge in the States, landing lucrative contracts with Mulberry, Coach, Michael Kors and Estée Lauder. She'd also featured in an exclusive spread for *Vanity Fair*, revealing how she'd volunteered to become the goodwill ambassador for a charity helping people with diabetes. This was shortly after her father, Robert Eastwood, made headlines across the world with the news that he had the lifelong condition, which means the amount of glucose in the blood is too high for the body to manage.

"Working London Fashion Week gives me a handy cover *if* the visit takes place," Zak said. "I'll be a member of Lydia's protective detail at the show, although she'll never know that. I don't stand out as much as the secret service. They're hard to miss – you know, dark shoes, dark glasses, etc. They're what you'd expect from the movies. I'm not. People don't notice me. Well, not in that way."

He leant back in his seat and stretched his hands behind his neck. Muscles rippled beneath his shirt sleeves. Bree, Celia and Sasha shot him admiring glances. Could Zak *be* more full of himself? Why did the Rodarte agent have to be him, of all people?

"Zak's boss has offered us their full assistance, including access to CIA files on The Collective." Nathan checked his watch. "Perhaps you can crack on."

Zak pulled out a folder from his rucksack. "LibertyCrossing started targeting the US about five years ago. We have every reason to believe this person is based here in the UK."

"Why?" Jessica asked. "What evidence do you have?"

"Phishing emails that were traced to IP addresses in the UK, under the name LibertyCrossing. The scam back then worked by hacking into thousands of people's email accounts in the States and vacuuming up passwords to things like online banking. Money was siphoned off into offshore bank accounts while the hacker also sent out fake emails under the guise of the people he'd hacked, begging for cash. He came up with heart-rending stories, like they'd had their credit card stolen while travelling abroad and needed urgent help. Unfortunately, a lot of people believed their friends or family members were in trouble and immediately transferred cash, again to what were actually offshore bank accounts. We believe the hacker has made millions of pounds over the years through these scams."

Jessica had been doodling on her notepad. She looked up. "Were the hacks ever linked to Lee Caplin? He'd have been fourteen back then."

"His computer, mobile phone and iPad were seized after the attacks on the Pentagon and the CIA three years ago and they contained no trace whatsoever of the phishing emails or any evidence of LibertyCrossing. Plus, LibertyCrossing remained active even though Lee's computer equipment had been confiscated during the extradition battle." Zak sifted through the file. "The hacking method suddenly became more sophisticated eighteen months ago. Instead of a scattergun approach, LibertyCrossing started to pick high-profile US victims, which really caught our attention." He tossed a selection of photos across the table. "Politicians, diplomats, Hollywood actors and actresses, the chief executives of major companies and multimillionaire businessmen."

Jessica stared at pictures of some of the most famous people in the United States. "What happened to them?"

"The victims were all hacked, but not through the use of spam or phishing emails like before. We've been unable to discover how the hacker actually got into their computers. Most had their bank accounts totally drained, with funds diverted to untraceable offshore accounts. However, others had photos and personal details stolen. They faced having lurid allegations about their private lives posted on the web and were blackmailed for substantial amounts of money to stop that from happening. The cyberattacks were all traced back to LibertyCrossing."

"Why these people? What do they have in common?"

"Duh," Zak sneered. "Apart from being massively wealthy, famous and, er, obvious targets?"

Jessica glared at him. "There could be something else that *you* haven't spotted yet."

It was Zak's turn to scowl.

Nathan ignored them both and leafed through the photos. "It's strange that LibertyCrossing's modus operandi changed again with the attacks in the UK this weekend. He went from being a thief, stealing millions of pounds using different cyber-methods, to recruiting a hacking army, wreaking havoc and declaring the need for total freedom of information across the internet. Thoughts, anyone?"

The door banged open, making everyone jump. Agent Hatfield strode into the room in a black suit and high heels, followed by Agent Booth, Sam the computer analyst, and three security guards. Agent Hatfield shot Jessica a furious look. She blushed guiltily. Oh God. They *had* found out about the Sargasso file. She should have come clean to Nathan right away instead of waiting to be discovered.

"Close this briefing down now!" Agent Hatfield barked.

"What's going on?" Nathan demanded.

"Sam's traced the source of Saturday's hack on MI6," Agent Hatfield said.

Nathan walked towards them. "And?"

"It came from Jessica."

She pushed her chair back and stood up. "That's impossible."

"It's true," Sam said. "The first attack came from *your* iPhone in this exact room. It hacked into Nathan's laptop and launched a virus to attack our computer system's mainframe. It was definitely an internal hack, originating from you. The second attack also came from inside the comms room. Again, your phone is the likely culprit."

"I didn't do this. I'm pretty sure I was hacked over the weekend too. I think my Oyster card, MI6 security pass and my dad's bank account and credit card were targeted by The Collective on Saturday morning."

Zak took a sharp intake of breath.

"Why am I only hearing about that now?" Nathan

demanded. "Didn't you think that might be relevant to our investigation?"

Jessica picked her finger behind her back. "I didn't want to bother you when Armageddon was breaking out across the country – you had bigger things to worry about. But I was going to tell you everything once this briefing wrapped today."

"Is that the cover story you're actually going with?" Agent Hatfield snapped.

"It's not a cover story. It's the truth."

"As soon as the hack started, I launched Operation Chaffinch – a separate internal investigation monitoring the computer accounts of every single MI6 employee, from agents out in the field to secretaries and technicians. So tell me the truth, Jessica. Did you or did you not hack into confidential MI6 files at one fifteen p.m. on Sunday and access a restricted document entitled Sargasso?"

Jessica felt the room lurch. "Yes, I did. But that's all."

"What?" Nathan stared at her.

"I didn't hack in. You have to believe me. I logged on to my MI6 account and discovered I had unrestricted access. I admit I took advantage of the security lapse. You see, I had to find out about my mum's death. I've been investigating it for the last six months. I know it's connected to something called Sargasso. This was the only chance I had to see what MI6 had on it."

Nathan looked stunned. He held up a hand to silence her. "I'd advise you not to say anything that will incriminate you further."

"But—"

"You're working with The Collective, which explains why last night's mission failed," Agent Hatfield said. "You helped the group hack in on Saturday and then tipped off someone that we were coming for Henry. You insisted that your godfather swap a senior agent, Bree, for Natalia, a far less experienced operative, who you knew would be easier to handle and let Henry escape to prevent us from taking him into custody."

"You've got it all wrong. I wanted Natalia with me because I didn't trust Bree after the Shard job."

"Another mission you took part in that we suspect involved a leak to a third party," Agent Hatfield snarled. "Funny, that."

Jessica glanced at Bree, who scowled back. She'd definitely made an enemy of her. Possibly a very dangerous one, who'd incriminated Jessica before she'd had chance to expose *her*.

"I had nothing to do with the leaks on either job," she insisted. "If it wasn't for me, you'd never have caught the Frenchman at the Shard or discovered Henry was missing until the ambulance arrived at the hospital."

Agent Hatfield shook her head. "You've jeopardized the whole of MI6 and put countless agents at risk. How long have you been involved with The Collective?"

"I'm not. Can't you see what they're doing? They're trying to frame me. They hacked my dad's home computer yesterday and used it to get into my Facebook account and my school's database. They posted teachers' names on a dating website and sent emails out under my name."

She paused. Why hadn't she thought about this before? The Collective had posted about Hatchett Hatcham on her Facebook account. How had the hackers known her nickname for him? They must have read text messages and email exchanges between her and Becky and Jamie. That was the only time she might have referred to the most loathed teacher in her school.

Cyberstalkers had been secretly studying her life.

"You should have reported all of this to me as soon as it happened," Nathan pointed out. "You must realize that."

"I only found out about the hack at school this morning when the head teacher called me and Dad in for a disciplinary meeting. I've been suspended while Dad gets an IT expert to examine all the computer software."

Agent Hatfield's lips curled into a snarl. "Presumably they'll find what we did – a secret back-door password that you used to access the MI6 system. 'Lily'."

Jessica stared at her, stunned. It was her mum's name.

"I'm being set up by someone who knows me. Someone who knows how to press my buttons."

"Really? By whom?" Agent Hatfield looked unconvinced.

There was only one person who'd pull a stunt like this. "Margaret Becker."

Agent Hatfield frowned. "The ex-MI6 agent?"

Jessica nodded. She'd given evidence against Margaret in a closed court six months ago and the double agent had been jailed for life for treason. She'd worked alongside villains including deranged former supermodel Allegra Knight and the terrorist Vectra before she'd finally been brought to justice.

"Margaret's locked up in a maximum security prison with very limited access to computers," Nathan said. "She can't be involved in this."

"I'm telling you, it has to be her. She's using my mum against me again. She's done it before. She told Allegra details about Mum back in Paris. She could have told LibertyCrossing stuff about me. This is personal. Margaret's still trying to attack me from behind bars as revenge for helping to put her away."

She closed her eyes. How could this be happening all over again? She thought she'd heard the last from Margaret Becker, but it was possible she'd found another way to get at her even from prison.

"You're clutching at straws," Agent Hatfield said.

Jessica's eyes flew open. "I'm not. You have to investigate this, Nathan."

"We're under immense time pressure, which means

I have to prioritize what leads need chasing," he replied. "I can tell you that Margaret's subject to the highest level of monitoring, both online and off. Staff double-check all material she has access to and red flag anything of concern. So far, I can tell you there's been nothing. I should know; I get regular updates from Low Newton prison."

Jessica blinked. She'd heard that name before. "Low Newton. Wasn't that one of the prisons hacked by The Collective on Saturday?"

"Along with virtually every prison across the country," Agent Hatfield said quickly. "It's hardly significant considering the fact that Belmarsh and Wakefield, which house some of the most violent criminals in the country, suffered much more serious hacks."

"It's true," Nathan said, pushing his glasses up his nose again. "Members of The Collective did us one small favour. They exposed huge loopholes in the security systems of many prisons around the country, which need to be fixed. However, Low Newton's firewalls were among the strongest. No one from The Collective managed to open or lock a single door."

Jessica bit her lip. She was sure Nathan was wrong

about Margaret; she could have found a way past the security checks in prison to contact LibertyCrossing. She may even have been involved in the attack on her own prison.

"I'm going to prove to you that—"

"You won't be doing anything," Agent Hatfield interrupted. "You're no longer a member of Westwood."

Out of the corner of her eye, Jessica saw Bree cover her mouth with her hands. Was that a smirk she was concealing? Had she helped Margaret and The Collective to set her up?

"Haven't you heard of innocent until proven guilty?" she said, clenching her fists.

"Have you ever heard of a twenty-year jail sentence for assisting in the hacking of MI6?" Agent Hatfield shot back.

"For God's sake!" Nathan exclaimed. "It's not going to come to that."

"This is what's going to happen, Jessica," Agent Hatfield said quietly. "You will hand over your security pass, along with your iPhone. These guards will escort you home and you will give back every single MI6 gadget you possess. Nathan will provide us with a list and the guards will not leave until every item is accounted for."

Jessica steadied herself against the table, hands trembling.

"We will also take whatever electronic equipment we find in your home – iPads, computers, laptops," Agent Hatfield continued. "Everything will be subjected to a thorough forensic examination while we investigate the extent of your connection to The Collective. After that, we'll consider what action to take. But Nathan's right, this can't go through the courts. What's happened can never be made public."

Had it even crossed Agent Hatfield's mind that she could be innocent? The MI6 operative was building a case around the single fact she believed to be true: that Jessica was The Collective's mole at MI6. Was everyone else thinking that too? No one was going to help her, not even Nathan.

Bree broke the silence. "What happened to the thread we collected last night, Jessica? Have you handed it in to MI6 or are you covering for your co-conspirator?"

Jessica reeled. Bree had stuck the knife well and

truly in her back as revenge for the whole mobile phone incident months ago. Not handing the evidence in straight away looked bad when she was already under a cloud of suspicion. "It's in a sealed bag at home. I was going to hand it over to forensics later today."

"Jessica!" Nathan remonstrated. "What were you thinking?"

"It's over for you," Agent Hatfield said witheringly. "The guards will retrieve the forensic evidence, *our* evidence, as well as all the equipment. You're lucky I don't throw you into a prison cell for obstructing our inquiry. If it wasn't for the fact you're Nathan's god-daughter, I would."

Bang! Zak threw his rucksack down on the table.

"Seriously? You're actually naive enough to believe that Jessica is involved with these hackers? It makes no sense whatsoever. Sure, she's made a few bad choices. She should have reported the hacks immediately, but she didn't. It's obvious she's been set up. As for the thread, we're talking about a delay of a few hours. Big deal." He turned to Nathan. "Come on. You have to stop this lunacy before it's too late."

Jessica stared at him, stunned. Seriously, Zak was the last person she expected to fight her corner. Hadn't he accused her of screwing up the job at the Shard and last night's mission, claiming he could have done better?

"The rules under Operation Chaffinch are clear," Agent Hatfield said coldly. "Immediate suspension followed by investigation, expulsion and punishment. Jessica's out and won't be coming back."

"Oh shut up, will you!" Zak snapped. "I don't know what kind of power kick you're on, lady, but give it a rest. You need Jessica on the inside of this investigation, not the outside. She's the best you've got."

The words rang in her ears. She had no idea what had got into Zak. It was as if he'd been replaced by his far nicer identical twin.

"Be very careful how you speak to me, young man," Agent Hatfield hissed. "You're in this country by invitation only. That can be revoked at any time, and you'll find yourself on the first plane back to Washington."

"I'll handle this, Zak." Nathan strode over to Jessica and placed his hand on her shoulder. "I'm sorry.

I'll do everything I can to help clear your name, but you'll need to go with them now."

"That's it?" Zak's tone was outraged. "That's all you're going to do for your own god-daughter?"

"That's all I can do at present."

Zak clenched his fists, his green eyes sparking with anger.

"No, Zak. Stop!" She stepped forward, blocking him as he approached Nathan. He looked as if he were about to throw a punch. "It's OK. I'll go with them. I can clear my name, I know I can."

She turned to face Nathan. "I did access the Sargasso file, but I swear that's it. I had nothing to do with the hack on MI6. Please look into Margaret for me. I know she's connected to this somehow."

Nathan didn't reply.

Zak caught Jessica's hand as she walked past. "This isn't over by a long shot. I'll make sure of that."

She managed a small smile. Had she been wrong about him? He'd come into the briefing all guns blazing and dissing her in spectacular fashion. Now he was fighting tooth and nail to protect her from her accuser, Agent Hatfield.

"Thanks, Zak. I appreciate it."

Before she could protest, he pulled her towards him in a tight embrace. She inhaled the woody scent of his aftershave and felt something heavy drop into her pocket as she broke away.

"This way, please, Miss Cole," one of the guards said.

As she followed him out, she felt in her pocket. Her fingers curled around a mobile phone. Zak was going out of his way to help her, but why?

CHAPTER
TEN

"So how does it feel to be the muse of the most talked-about fashion designer in the world right now?" Hillary St Joseph asked.

The *Teen Vogue* journalist smoothed a wrinkle from her red Ossa Cosway shift dress and flashed a smile at Jessica. She was doing an interview alongside Ossa to go with her front cover and photo shoot from the other day. Normally, she'd have tucked into the delicious pastries and cakes served with afternoon tea at Claridge's, but she didn't have any appetite today. She'd been booted out of school and Westwood, and her iPad, computers, gadgets and MI6 phone had been confiscated. That had only happened yesterday, yet it felt like a lifetime ago. Somehow she had to clear her name, but how?

"Sorry, what was the question again?"

Hillary rolled her eyes. Jessica could feel the journalist's patience beginning to wear thin. She had to admit, she wasn't a dream to interview.

"I asked what it feels like to be Ossa's muse," she repeated.

"It's a huge honour," Jessica said, pushing her plate to one side. "I never expected to be picked by Ossa. I love his clothes."

"I have to ask, Ossa, do you give Jessica lots of freebies?" Hillary said. "I couldn't believe it when I was given this dress. I'm so grateful."

"Jessica receives items from each collection I launch," Ossa said, stabbing a profiterole. He watched the cream ooze out, suddenly distracted.

"Lucky you!" The journalist sighed enviously.

Jessica smiled dutifully. Would Hillary still be jealous if she knew the truth? Her contract stipulated she had to wear Ossa Cosway clothes any time she wasn't at school in case she was snapped by the paparazzi. It was another way to advertise the designer's clothing range since the pictures could get picked up by newspapers and magazines across the world.

Sure, she liked Ossa's clothes, but sometimes it'd be cool to pull on a pair of old trackie bottoms and her favourite Topshop sweatshirt to run to the corner shop for a bag of crisps, instead of having to promote something posh and branded. Still, she shouldn't complain. She was unlikely to get any sympathy from this journalist who was coveting the navy pea coat and grey sweater dress she'd been instructed to wear for today's interview.

Hillary nodded encouragingly at Ossa. "Can I get more background detail about how you made it to the top? You said you graduated from Central Saint Martin's College three years ago, right?"

Ossa smiled. "That's correct." He fiddled with his watch, which was attached to his waistcoat with a gold chain. He was wearing his trademark three-piece suit, which had recently been stocked in Macy's department store in New York.

"How did you manage to launch your collections so quickly?" Hillary persisted. "Usually that takes years to pull off. No one from your graduating class has had anywhere near your amount of success so quickly."

"I was very lucky," Ossa explained. "I recruited

an amazing team of dressmakers, who are all expert seamstresses and work very fast. Plus, my financial backer has been very generous. The cash enabled me to launch Ossa Cosway Ltd in my final year at college."

"Who is your backer?" the journalist pressed.

"I'd love to tell you, but he's a very private person. He doesn't want any publicity."

"You're still with him?"

"Yes, his funds enable me to continually expand the global brand. We now have branches in Paris, Tokyo and New York. I can also afford to experiment with innovative ways to create outfits, such as the hashtag dress that promotes the latest digital technology."

"Brilliant!" Hillary exclaimed. "I need one more thing from you, Jessica. How do you manage to juggle your schoolwork with modelling? Are your teachers very understanding?"

Her teachers hated her guts right now, as they thought she'd posted their personal details on a dating website. If they saw her, they'd probably string her up. She had plenty of time to model since she was kicking about at home with absolutely nothing to do.

"School's been great," she said through gritted

teeth. "My teachers have been really accommodating. Obviously, I try not to let modelling interfere with my schoolwork too much. I want to get good grades and eventually go to university."

The journalist nodded. "Anything else you'd like to add, Ossa?"

"Jessica is strong, intelligent and beautiful – an inspiration to girls and women all over the world. She's a true role model."

It was a good job he didn't know what else she was – an ex-Westwood agent and suspected member of a sinister group of hackers, The Collective. That would definitely damage the Ossa Cosway brand.

Jessica's new mobile buzzed as she left Claridge's a short time later.

"Meet me at Café Panorama. Heading there now."

Zak had picked a venue close to her home in Ealing, West London; he must have done it for convenience. He couldn't have known that was where she usually met Jamie after school. She checked her watch. She had time to grab a quick drink with Zak; Jamie had football practice today. It was the least she could do considering Zak was the only person who'd stood up to Agent Hatfield yesterday. He'd given her this disposable mobile and was her only contact with Westwood now. She had no way of monitoring developments without his help.

The Underground was hit with signal failures again; the Piccadilly and Central lines weren't running, no doubt due to another hack from The Collective. Despite a long-winded route back to Ealing, Jessica still managed to arrive first at the café and grab a table. She texted Jamie to say she was running late, which would hopefully delay him. As she sipped a camomile tea, she picked up the newspaper lying on the table.

MI6 LEAK: AGENT ALMOST KILLED BY LYNCH MOB

MI6 operative Aarash Sadai was airlifted from Afghanistan yesterday after his identity was mysteriously leaked to a news website.

Sources in Afghanistan say that Mr Sadai narrowly escaped with his life when his home was firebombed by an angry mob.

On Sunday, another MI6 agent working in Iran, Annette Oderra, was named by a different news website. Sources say she is now in a safe location.

MI6 has refused to comment, but insiders claim that an internal investigation has been launched to discover the source of the catastrophic security leak.

Jessica pushed the paper aside. What a nightmare, but at least the agents were safe. That was something. Plus, it didn't look as though The Collective had approached the press, claiming responsibility for the hacks, so MI6 could keep a lid on what was happening. However, another agent's identity would already have been leaked this afternoon, and their life would be in jeopardy. Had they been as lucky as the others?

Jessica glanced over her shoulder, wondering whether to order another tea. She spotted Zak stride in and place an order at the counter. For some reason, she had butterflies in her stomach and her throat felt dry. She took a last gulp of tea and knotted her fingers.

What did she have to be nervous about?

He flung himself down across the table from her and ran a hand through his curls. His chin was covered with stubble and dark shadows circled his eyes.

"I guess you didn't get much sleep either?" Jessica had resorted to piling on bucketloads of under-eye concealer ahead of her magazine interview after a night spent on the sofa, channel hopping with the TV remote control.

"I pulled an all-nighter. So did Nathan. It's been intense with the whole list thing, plus the general hacking problems."

"They targeted the Underground again today."

"Along with Manchester airport, eBay and the *Guardian* and *Wall Street Journal*'s Twitter accounts. Hackers are flooding websites with demands for the million-dollar jackpot. They're desperately trying to get LibertyCrossing's attention in a bid to win his hacking contest."

"And have they?"

"Who knows? There's no news about the jackpot. In the meantime, LibertyCrossing's troops are getting careless. MI6 has made some arrests already. More hackers will be detained this week." He flashed the attractive waitress a dazzling smile as she delivered his chocolate chip muffin and hot chocolate. Jessica watched as he devoured the muffin in a few mouthfuls.

Zak wiped his mouth with a paper napkin. "Sorry. No time for lunch today." He glanced down at the newspaper and pointed to the story on the exposed agents. "Have you ever worked with either of them?"

Jessica shook her head. "I haven't done a foreign mission before. Well, not officially." Sure, she'd spied in Paris and Monaco, but she hadn't been part of Westwood back then. She dug out the mobile and placed it on the table. "Do you make a habit of carrying around spare disposable phones?"

"I do, as a matter of fact. They're an essential tool of the job. You should stock up too."

Jessica bit her nail. She was usually good at getting the size of people, but Zak was a hard one to figure out. She still didn't know what to think.

"Why are you helping me? You seemed to think I did a rubbish job at the Shard and at the boarding school."

"I thought your Westwood backup was rubbish, but not you. From what Nathan told me, you were the only one to show any real initiative. You were fearless that night on the Shard. You weren't to know…" His voice trailed off.

"That I was going to be ambushed and attacked?"

Zak's cheeks coloured. "Yes. Anyway, that's not why we're here. It's D-Day tomorrow afternoon. The US won't release Lee Caplin, so the entire agent database will go up online unless we can stop The Collective."

Jessica shivered. How many agents would lose their lives if that happened?

"What are you doing about it?" she asked.

"Now you're out of the picture, I'm supposed to liaise with Bree." Zak raised an eyebrow. "Which I'm thrilled about, naturally. She's not exactly Miss Super Spy."

"It could be worse than that. She could be a double agent."

"Really? Go on."

"Nathan says she's good, but I don't trust her. You saw her coming down the stairs that night at the Shard. She could have attacked me and stolen the USB flash drive. It's possible she helped The Collective find a way to hack MI6 and tipped them off about the raid on

Henry's boarding house."

"I'll get Rodarte to run its own background checks on her," Zak said, stroking his stubble. "But to be honest, I'm not sure I trust anyone at MI6. Neither should you."

"Nathan's my godfather. I can trust him."

"Are you sure? From where I was standing yesterday, he rolled over when Hatfield went for you."

Jessica nibbled another nail. She wanted to disagree but couldn't. He was right. Nathan hadn't put up much of a fight against Agent Hatfield. Maybe he was worried that she could drag him down with her and was trying to protect his own career with MI6.

"Why are we really here, Zak?"

"I want your help." He fiddled with the sugar sachets in the bowl without looking up. "Work with me to bring down The Collective."

"I've been thrown out of Westwood, remember? I'm not much good to anyone."

"Officially you're out, but you can assist me off the books."

"I'm flattered you're asking, but what can I do? I no longer have access to Westwood info. I have no idea what's going on with the investigation. I'm completely out of the loop."

"I can regularly update you on everything that's going on at Westwood and Rodarte to do with The Collective in return for a favour."

Jessica's mind whirred. She couldn't think what he was after. "Which is?"

"Help me get to Margaret Becker."

She sat forward in her chair. "I'm listening."

"My bosses are interested in your theory that she's involved in this somehow. They believe she's a lead worth pursuing, yet MI6, which has the jurisdiction to organize a prison interview, has ruled out the possibility, as it's concentrating on other clues. We believe that's a mistake." Zak rubbed his forehead. "That makes things difficult for us. Time's running out for Britain and America. When that list goes live tomorrow, British agents working in hostile countries overseas could be captured and tortured; undercover US operatives could be endangered by association too. Plus, we have the president's visit to worry about. He's insisting upon going ahead, against the advice of the National Security Council, because his daughter won't pull out of London

Fashion Week. The CIA has to act. Rodarte wants me to visit Margaret, but I can't do that alone."

Jessica's mouth fell open. "You want me to come with you?" Helping Zak get to Margaret in prison was one thing, but actually having to see the traitor who'd repeatedly tried to kill her was another.

"You know Margaret," Zak said. "She'd never agree to speak to me, but the two of you have history. She could open up to you."

"Why on earth would she ever want to talk to me? She gained a life sentence because of my evidence against her in court. She hates me. She wants me dead."

"Isn't it worth a shot? Shouldn't we try to save all those agents before it's too late? They might not be as lucky as Aarash and Annette." He jabbed a finger at the newspaper story.

"You must have read the file on Margaret by now. You know it's possible there's a link between her and the death of my mum in a helicopter crash? My dad and Nathan think she was paid by a terrorist called Vectra to sabotage the chopper."

"Surely that's even more reason to confront her? As I said, you have personal history with her. You know which buttons to hit. I don't."

Jessica picked her finger. The skin around her nail was ragged and bleeding. Zak had no idea who he was dealing with. Even behind bars, Margaret was manipulative and highly dangerous.

"Margaret won't even consider helping us unless there's something in it for her," she said finally.

"We've already anticipated that."

"So what are you offering her? A get out of jail free card in return for her full cooperation? I won't be part of any deal like that. I want Margaret kept behind bars where she belongs, whatever happens tomorrow. She's a psychopath."

Zak shook his head. "It'd be nothing like that, I promise. There's always something a prisoner wants – a better cell, more privileges, and a higher paid job on the inside. What do you think? Will you help me if I can set up a visit? It could be our only chance to stop that list from being made public."

Jessica closed her eyes. She felt sick at the thought of seeing Margaret again and having to listen to her taunts. She'd enjoy torturing her by mentioning her mum and then refusing to help them. "OK. I guess."

"Brilliant. Thank you. It's going to take some organizing our end to ensure the prison authorities cooperate. I'll text you when it's sorted. We'll need to leave early tomorrow to get to Durham, so come up with a cover story. You can't tell anyone, including your dad or Mattie, in case they tip off Nathan."

Spilling the beans about visiting Margaret wasn't something she was keen to do with anyone in her family. She could pretend she had another modelling shoot with Ossa; it was believable. This contract was taking up a lot of her time.

"I promised I'd keep you up to speed with everything in return. So here goes. I can tell you that Henry's still missing."

He handed over a brown file marked "Henry Murray". She flicked it open and stared at the first document – a photo of the blond, blue-eyed teenage boy.

"Are you any closer to finding him?"

"Not really, but he has resurfaced." Zak leant over and fished out a grainy picture from the file.

"This was snatched from CCTV cameras late

yesterday – a young man begging near Notting Hill Gate. We ran it through facial recognition technology. It's definitely Henry."

"Which suggests he's still not risking using his credit cards," Jessica said. "He could be sleeping rough or dossing down in a squat somewhere."

"It's the most logical explanation. We've questioned his friends and examined his texts and emails going back months. He's not visiting familiar haunts or getting in touch with anyone he knows."

"The Collective could have hacked CCTV cameras in central London and found this footage too," she pointed out. "If Henry's got any sense, he'll stay away from built-up areas as much as possible."

"He won't be able to if he can't find food from soup kitchens," Zak said. "He has to eat and keep warm. He can't sleep rough for long in these temperatures. February's brutal."

"The Collective will find Henry sooner or later, particularly if the hackers think that could be a way to win the jackpot."

"That's our worry. MI6 has agents out looking for Henry too. But it's pounding-the-street kind of work; a lot of manpower for negligible results so far."

"I could help. I modelled for *The Big Issue* a few months ago and I'm still in contact with Lucy, one of the vendors I met on the shoot. I could print off some copies of Henry's photo and ask her to tell other vendors to keep a lookout for him."

Zak stuck a muffin crumb on to his thumb and licked it off. "That's why I knew MI6 should keep you on board. But be vigilant. You have to assume that The Collective has hacked everything you own." He nodded at the mobile. "You need to be careful what you say even on your new phone."

"I know Lucy's spot in Kensington," she said, tucking Henry's photo into her handbag. "I'll visit her later and ask her to put the word out on the street."

"Brilliant." Zak reached out and squeezed her hand. "Thanks, Jessica. I mean, for everything." Before she could reply, he'd snatched his hand back. "I'm really sorry." His face was beetroot red.

"What do you mean?"

Zak jerked his head towards the door. Jessica looked over her shoulder. Jamie stood watching them, a look of disgust etched on his face.

"Oh God." Why hadn't she kept a better eye on the time? Football had finished already. Hadn't he got her text?

"You can talk Jamie round," Zak said softly. "I'll be in touch later. Remember, find a cover story for all day tomorrow. I will too. It's a long drive to Durham. Good luck." He stuffed the file in his rucksack and strode out the café.

Jamie didn't take his eyes off Jessica as he weaved through the tables, knocking into chairs with his sports bag. He flung himself down into a seat and kicked the bag under the table.

"What was *he* doing here? Why were you holding hands?"

"We weren't holding hands."

"It looked like you were from where I was standing."

Jessica shook her head. "I told him about being kicked out of school and he was commiserating with me. He was being a friend."

"So he's a friend now?" Jamie stared at her in disbelief. "I thought you couldn't stand him. I distinctly remember you calling him a jerk. Times *have* changed."

Jessica flinched at the bitterness in his voice. This wasn't like him at all. "I know what I said, but I was wrong about Zak. I've given him a second chance. He's actually quite a good guy. I think you'd like him if you got to know him."

"I really don't think so. You haven't explained what he was doing here. Your text said you'd be running late because of an interview across town, but here you were entertaining Mr I Think I'm So Wonderful."

She took a deep breath. She couldn't remember the last time she'd been totally honest with him. "Zak wanted to discuss London Fashion Week. You know, it's coming up. We're modelling for the designer Ossa Cosway. He needed some tips, as he hasn't done the London show before."

Jamie eyed her suspiciously.

"That's it," she insisted. "You don't have any reason to be jealous. It's you I want to be with, not him."

The muscles in his face relaxed a little as she reached out and clasped his hand.

"I mean it." She leant forward and kissed him. His lips were amazingly soft. Her whole body seemed to melt as he kissed her back. But he pulled away first, running a hand through his hair.

"I was standing there a while, you know," he said quietly. "You two looked intense, the way you were talking. We haven't talked properly like that in ages."

"It was business." At least that wasn't a lie.

Jamie sighed. "I trust you, Jess. I really want to. It's just. . ."

"What?"

"Everything's so messed up at the moment. You haven't been the same since the summer. You're here, but it's like you're a million miles away."

"I don't—"

"No, hear me out. It's true. You're different somehow, like right now. I don't get how you can be so wrapped up in modelling when you've been suspended from school. This is serious, Jess. If you're permanently expelled, we won't be able to see each other every day. You could end up in another school, the other side of London. You'll make new friends and we'll drift apart. It's inevitable."

"That's not going to happen. I told you, my dad's going to sort this mess out. He's getting my computers and iPad examined." She bit her lip. Well, he would have had them analysed if MI6 hadn't confiscated them first. "I'll clear my name, I promise. I'll be back at school before you know it. You'll be sick of the sight of me before long."

Jamie ignored her feeble attempt at a joke. "Not if Hatchett Hatcham has anything to do with it. He's been telling kids today that you're history, that Mr Reynolds has already decided that you're never coming back and he's been approaching head teachers at other London schools about taking you off the roll."

She stared at him, aghast. Surely Mr Reynolds couldn't do that? He'd promised she'd be reinstated if her name was cleared. She shook her head violently; it had to be a lie.

"Hatcham's always had it in for me. You know that. He doesn't want me back, but he won't have a choice. Mr Reynolds will have to reinstate me when I've proved my innocence."

"I hope you're right."

Jessica did too. She wasn't sure their relationship could survive her expulsion from school. It felt as though it was hanging on by the most delicate of threads. She didn't want it to finally break.

CHAPTER ELEVEN

"Are you sure this is going to work?" Jessica squinted up at Low Newton prison, shielding her eyes from the bright morning sun. Her stomach had churned horribly all the way up the motorway. Most of her fingernails were chewed down and her cuticles were bleeding by the time Zak had found a space in the prison car park. They walked slowly towards the main entrance.

"Run it by me one more time. How are we going to pull this off?"

Zak shot her a quick look. Was he worried she was going to screw up big time?

"Rodarte's told MI6 that I'm working on security detail for the president's visit, so Nathan's not expecting me at HQ today. My bosses have given us fake IDs, which will get us in and out, no problem. Your suggestion for our aliases should work – Ben and Matilda Becker will make Margaret curious. She'll want to know who dared take her grandchildren's names. She won't refuse to see us."

Jessica noticed the security cameras panning down on visitors streaming towards the first checkpoint. "And those? What if they use facial technology and run a check on us? They could find our real identities and alert MI6."

"Again, it's taken care of."

"How?"

"Let's just say, Rodarte has taken advantage of the current security situation with The Collective."

Jessica's mouth fell open. "Please tell me you haven't hacked into the prison's security system. Are you crazy?"

"Not here." Zak grabbed her arm, pulling her to one side. "You know The Collective exposed loopholes in the security of prisons in this country. We're briefly exploiting that to access the CCTV here. My team plans to take over the camera system temporarily.

They'll either block cameras or redirect them to prevent us from being filmed."

"Zak!"

"Once we're gone, everything will go back to normal. There's no risk involved. The guards won't be alarmed if certain cameras go offline for a few minutes. Any longer and they could run a diagnostics check, but it'll never get to that stage. It's a quick hack, in and out, before they know what's hit them. It's the only way to protect our identities."

Jessica shook her head. "This makes us no better than The Collective. As government agents, aren't we supposed to be above that sort of thing?"

"We have to be prepared to do unpleasant things to protect our countries. Do you want to find out if Margaret has any connection with The Collective? Do you want to try and protect all those undercover agents?"

"Of course I do."

The latest agent to be outed yesterday was twenty-four-year-old Veronica Furrows, who was spying on the Kremlin while studying for a PhD at Moscow University. The radio bulletin they'd heard in the car had described her arrest as a "diplomatic nightmare" for Britain.

"Then let's get going," he said. "The last thing we need is MI6 discovering we've visited Margaret. We need to keep this under wraps for everyone's sake, yours in particular."

She didn't need him to spell out how vulnerable she was. If Agent Hatfield or Nathan discovered she was still working the case, she might find herself in a young offenders' institution that looked very similar to this prison.

Zak was right; they sailed through the security checks even though they were visiting a high-risk prisoner. Rodarte had submitted the visitor applications and secretly managed to get them fast-tracked without notifying MI6. It was strictly against protocols, which was why he stressed yet again that their real identities mustn't come to light. The fact that he was beginning to freak out made her even more nervous.

Her heart was beating rapidly as they approached Margaret's wing. She rubbed her damp palms on her Ossa Cosway light blue trench coat. The smell of disinfectant made her feel nauseous. Now they were here, she wanted to get it over with and leave. The atmosphere inside was claustrophobic and noisy; shouts and screams rang out from cells. The prison guard took them through a maze of corridors, opening each door with his thumbprint and a security code. She didn't want to lose sight of him on the way out. Even if she could crack the code with her gadget key ring, she still wouldn't be able to get out, as the lock was only activated with an approved thumbprint.

"Here we go," the moustached man said sternly. "We're in the maximum security area, which has strict rules you both must abide by." The guard cocked his head down the corridor at the two red plastic chairs. "Stay seated at all times. Do not approach the glass. Do not attempt to pass anything to the prisoner or take anything from the hatch. Do not attempt to converse with the other prisoners. We will monitor you, but if you feel threatened in any way, hit the panic button on the outside of the cell and someone will return immediately."

"Thanks." Zak must have already noticed the

security camera that panned directly on to them; he kept his head turned away. Had Rodarte managed to block the footage already? They didn't want the guards watching this encounter.

"Are you ready?" Zak asked as the man disappeared.

"I think so. Let's get on with this."

It was a mission like any other. Except it didn't feel like that. This was going to be one of the hardest things she'd ever done – confronting an old enemy who may have been involved in the conspiracy to murder her mum. She walked ahead, fixing her eyes on the chairs. She didn't want to see the prisoners in the other cells.

"Hey, pretty boy. Come over here and give me a kiss!"

Zak followed close behind, ignoring the catcalls and whistles from the female prisoners.

"Jessica Cole." The familiar voice rang out even though she hadn't reached Margaret's cell.

She took a deep breath and stepped in front of the glass. Margaret stood with her back turned, wearing regulation blue uniform.

"Only you would use my granddaughter's name to get in here. You knew I'd want to meet whoever dared to take her identity. But I have to admit, I'm still trying to guess who stole my grandson's name."

Margaret spun round. Her white hair was a little shorter and her face thinner than the last time Jessica had seen her in court, but her eyes were still cold. Margaret stared at Jessica for a few seconds before turning her attention to Zak. Her eyes flitted back and her lips curled into a smile.

"New boyfriend? I thought you were with Jamie. Or has there been trouble in paradise?"

Jessica's cheeks flushed. Margaret had mentioned Jamie's name to make the point that she was keeping tabs on her from behind bars.

"This is Zak. And he's not my boyfriend."

Margaret chuckled. "Not yet."

Jessica could feel her blush deepening as Margaret looked Zak up and down.

"You must admit, you'd make a very attractive couple. You have good looks in common. With those razor-sharp cheekbones, Zak, I'm guessing you're a model too?"

"That's correct," he said coolly. "Calvin Klein, among other contracts."

"So you're an American model who's gained last-minute clearance to see a high-risk prisoner like myself. Let me guess. That must make you a member of Rodarte. Am I right?"

It was Zak's turn to redden now. "Yes, you are. Now maybe—"

"Where are my manners? Won't you both take a seat, since you've taken the trouble to drive all the way from London to visit me?"

Jessica glanced at Zak as she arranged her coat on the back of the chair. They had to tread carefully. Margaret was deliberately making them feel at a disadvantage.

"Nice coat, Jessica," Margaret said. "Is it Ossa Cosway, by any chance? I recognise the unique ribbing around the collar and sleeves."

"Yes, it is."

"How can I forget? You're Ossa Cosway's new muse, aren't you? I think I remember reading about it the other day."

"You seem remarkably well informed for someone

who's been in solitary confinement for the last six months," Zak said.

"I still have access to newspapers and books." Margaret gestured around her cell. "I like to keep my brain active."

Jessica leant forward. "What about computers?"

According to the file Zak had let her study, Margaret had supervised access only once a week in the prison library. A guard sat next to her while she browsed BBC Online as well as Egyptology websites, which she'd developed an interest in. Margaret couldn't log on to emails or any social networking site. The firewalls were so strong that supposedly she couldn't click away on to sites that weren't approved by the prison authorities. Had she found a way around the rules to contact the leader of The Collective?

Margaret ignored Jessica and turned her attention to Zak. "It's interesting that Rodarte and Westwood have joined forces. In my experience, the agencies don't work so well together. Egos tend to get in the way and the jobs become complicated and messy. Rodarte always tries to ride in at the last minute and steal the glory or whatever else it can get its hands on."

Margaret smoothed her hair behind her ears. "You should be careful, Jessica. Male Rodarte agents have a reputation for breaking hearts, you know. They see pretty, young Westwood agents as quite the conquest. I'm guessing that will upset Jamie."

Jessica kept her face perfectly still as Margaret scrutinized it. She couldn't afford to betray any emotion, otherwise Margaret would realize she'd hit a nerve and continue to push her buttons.

"To be honest, I'm not totally sure this is an official MI6-sanctioned partnership, judging by the way you both sneaked in here," Margaret continued. "MI6 would have sent more senior agents, not a slip of a girl from Westwood who helped convict me. It'd be too much of a risk to bring us face-to-face again. Does your beloved godfather even know you've come to visit me? What about your school? Are you playing truant today?"

Jessica looked away. This was classic Margaret. She was fishing for information.

"Look—" Zak began.

"No, you look!" Margaret snarled. She pressed her palms against the glass. "Come here, boy."

Zak looked up the corridor and got out of his seat. He approached the glass even though it was against the guard's orders.

"I presume you had the foresight to take out the cameras back there?" She jerked her head. "And the listening devices. They have those here too, naturally."

Zak touched his hidden earpiece. "We're good for three minutes."

"Excellent," Margaret said, smiling. "This shouldn't take long. So tell me, what is Rodarte offering me in exchange for information on The Collective?"

Jessica's heart quickened. So she was right. Margaret *did* know something. If only Nathan had listened to her.

"We can move you out of this high-risk wing into another, more private, larger single cell," Zak explained. "You will be given extra privileges – as many books and newspapers as you want, a job in the library and access to online distance-learning courses. You've expressed an interest in studying for a PhD in Egyptology, haven't you? We can make that happen."

"Wow." Margaret smirked. "Let me consider this for all of two seconds. The answer's no. What else are we going to talk about for two minutes? Correction, one minute and forty seconds?"

"Why?" Zak frowned. "What else were you thinking? Name it and I can take it back to my bosses."

"Transfer me to a prison in the United States, where I'll tell you everything I know. Once that's happened, you'll release me under a new identity and allow me to live out my days somewhere in America under the witness protection programme."

"That's never going to happen," Jessica said, rising to her feet. "Is it, Zak? Tell her. She's going to die behind bars."

Zak relayed the message to his handler through a microphone embedded in his jacket. He listened to the voice in his earpiece. Jessica guessed he was being told to stall.

"I don't have the authority to discuss those terms with you," he said finally. "That would require sign-off from the director of the CIA, who's uncontactable at present. So let's discuss—"

"The truth is, Zak, you don't have the authority to clean my shoes," Margaret barked. "So I suggest you find someone from the CIA that I can do business with.

Remember, the clock's counting down. I wouldn't like to be in the shoes of those MI6 agents at three p.m. Tricky. Very tricky."

Jessica caught her breath. Margaret knew about LibertyCrossing's plan to publish the list. She glanced at Zak. He couldn't hide his shock.

"You're wasting time, Zak. Tick-tock, tick-tock. Don't you get it yet? I won't make a deal with teenage models. I want to speak to someone far higher up the CIA food chain than you." Margaret pounded her fist on the glass. "Guard? Is anyone there? Hello? We're done here."

Jessica glared at her. Margaret knew the guards couldn't hear; it was all for show. But there wasn't much time before they did become suspicious about the glitch in the CCTV footage and came to investigate.

"How do we know that you've got any information on The Collective?" Jessica said. "You can't expect to deal with anyone else from the CIA until we know what you've got. Give us something to take back to Zak's bosses."

Margaret folded her arms and shook her head.

"She's bluffing," Jessica said, turning towards Zak. "She's got nothing. Let's go."

"Really?" Margaret said. "You want to take that risk? The truth is, you both came here today because you followed the trail. I'm guessing members of The Collective hacked MI6 and left behind a clue."

Jessica spun around. "Lily. You told LibertyCrossing my mum's name."

Margaret chuckled. "I *sold* LibertyCrossing a lot more than that while I was still with MI6, long before I was arrested – background details about your crippled ex-MI6 agent father, your ex-Westwood grandmother, your boyfriend, Jamie – or is he an ex already? Your best friend, Becky. The list goes on and on."

"Jessica was right about you," Zak breathed. "You are a total psychopath."

Jessica clenched her fists. Margaret had mentioned everyone in her life, apart from her mum. There had to be a reason for that.

"You told the leader of The Collective about my mum's murder and its connection to Sargasso, didn't you? LibertyCrossing guessed that if I found the firewalls down in the MI6 computer, I'd search for confidential files. He used it as a trap to incriminate me and get me kicked out of Westwood."

Margaret smiled. "Your late mother's your weak spot. It always has been. That's your downfall. Now it's beginning."

She approached the glass. "What do you mean?"

"LibertyCrossing's going to rip you apart, piece by piece, until there's nothing left. I suggested his followers target Westwood and your school first. Your modelling career's next. A few abusive emails sent from your account to the editors of *Vogue*, *Tatler* and *Elle* and you'll be blacklisted for ever. Then maybe they should start on your friends, sabotaging your relationships with Becky and Jamie until your life as you know it is over and you'll wish you were dead."

"Back off her!" Zak shouted.

He lowered his voice as he pulled Jessica away from the glass. "We have to go. Rodarte can't keep the camera offline much longer."

Margaret burst out laughing. "The Rodarte knight in shining armour, riding to rescue the poor little Westwood girl in distress. How boringly predictable."

"I don't need help," Jessica retorted. "But you do, Margaret. I'm going to ring Nathan as soon as I leave here and tell him that my hunch was right, that you are connected to The Collective. That you sold information about me to LibertyCrossing and in return his army of hackers was supposed to bust you out of here. Except they failed on Saturday and now you're stuck here. MI6 will interrogate you and get the information it needs before three p.m., without any deal on the table."

"You silly little girl," Margaret hissed. "Believe me when I tell you that you'll never make that call to Nathan."

"Of course I will." Jessica frowned. What did Margaret mean? What was she missing?

"You'd both better scoot," she said, chuckling. "I'm guessing a guard will return in approximately thirty seconds. Security must be wondering what we've been talking about in private for so long."

Jessica scooped up her coat from the seat and threw it on.

"I must get myself one of those coats," Margaret continued. "I think black would suit me better. But maybe I'll opt for light blue too."

"You don't need a new coat. You're never getting out of here."

"Don't be so sure of that."

Jessica caught her breath. Was The Collective planning another strike on the prison?

A guard appeared at the end of the corridor, as Margaret had predicted. "Is everything all right down there?"

"Yes," Zak called back. "We're good, thanks."

"Either sit back down or leave." The man hovered, watching them closely.

Jessica hesitated. She wouldn't get another chance like this to confront Margaret. "Tell me what really happened to my mum. Who ordered the hit on her? Was it Vectra?"

"Come on, Jessica," Zak hissed. "We have to go."

Margaret walked to the back of the cell.

"Did you sabotage her helicopter?" she pressed.

"Stop it," Zak pleaded. "Margaret's messing with your head. She's never going to tell you what you want to know."

She ignored him. "What's Sargasso? I know it's

198

connected to Mum and the death of a former KGB officer. Why were they killed?"

Margaret picked up a book and flicked through it. To Jessica's surprise, she threw it down on her bed and returned to the glass. "They joined the dots and found Sargasso. Come closer."

"Get back from there!" the guard shouted as she approached Margaret. They were separated by a few inches of glass.

"Knowledge is dangerous, Jessica. I'll be sure to let Sargasso know that you've been enquiring about the organization. You'll end up the same way as your interfering mother."

Zak pulled her away. "That's enough. The cameras are going live again."

She ducked her head down and ran towards the guard. She'd got more from Margaret than she'd bargained for today.

"We're done here. Can you let us out?"

The guard glared at her. "Don't ever pull a stunt like that again. Follow me."

Zak caught up with them, gripping Jessica's arm.

"Are you OK?" he whispered.

"I'm fine." She pulled her arm free and followed the guard.

He pressed his thumbprint and entered his code at the first set of security doors.

"You don't look fine to me," Zak said as they walked through the next door. "Do you want to talk about it?"

That was the last thing she wanted to do. Thoughts of her mum's death, Sargasso and Margaret were swirling around her head. Zak could never understand what she was going through. She wished she could talk to her dad about what had happened.

"Tell me that Margaret's not going to get what she asked for back there," she said under her breath. "Promise me that your director won't cut a deal to release her."

"Not in a million years. Her request was instantly vetoed. I couldn't tell her that, of course. We had to play along and see what we could get from her."

A few more tantalizing clues about Sargasso, but nothing that would scupper LibertyCrossing's plan to release the list of agents this afternoon.

The guard stopped at the next set of doors. "That's

strange." A frown mark deepened between his eyes as he pushed open the door.

"What?" Zak asked.

"The door's unlocked. It doesn't need my thumbprint." He whipped out his walkie-talkie. "We have a security breach in corridor 243. Please investigate. Over. Hello?"

Silence.

Zak and Jessica exchanged glances as the guard strode ahead.

"Is this something to do with Rodarte?" she said quietly.

Zak relayed what had happened into his hidden microphone and listened to the reply. "Negative. We targeted the cameras, definitely not the locks. This is something different."

The guard was already examining the keypad at the end of the corridor when they reached him. This door was also unlocked. Jessica shivered. Margaret had insinuated something could happen.

"This is bad, really bad," Zak muttered.

"Follow me quickly," the guard ordered.

"What's going on?" Jessica asked. "Why are the

doors all unlocked?"

"I don't know. Something's wrong."

Suddenly, his walkie-talkie buzzed with static and a voice blared out. "This is a code six situation. This is not a drill. Repeat, this is not a drill."

Almost immediately, an alarm screeched.

"Let's go. Move it!" The guard broke into a run as shouts and screams echoed from deep within the prison.

Jessica sprinted after him. "What's happening?"

"We have a massive security breach. I need to get you both to safety."

"What does code six mean exactly?" Zak gasped.

"All the doors are open – internal, external. Everything."

Jessica skidded to a halt. The Collective was breaking out Margaret. "We have to go back."

"I can't allow that, ma'am," the guard snapped. "I can't guarantee your safety back there." He nodded down the corridor. "We need to put as much distance as possible between us and the maximum security wing."

Jessica didn't move. She couldn't.

"Didn't you hear me? There are murderers back there, child killers and arsonists. Believe me when I tell you, they'll do anything to get out of here. They won't hesitate to use whatever makeshift weapons they can get their hands on if you and your friend stand in between them and freedom."

"Zak?" Jessica appealed.

"We're leaving. The guard's right. We have to get out of here. That's an *order*."

She glared at him. That must be the directive he'd received from his handler. Hadn't Zak ever heard of challenging orders?

The sound of doors banging open and pounding footsteps echoed up the corridor. A look of panic crossed the guard's face. "Prisoners are heading this way. Go! We can't be caught here. We're too far away from help."

He roughly shoved them towards the door and kicked it open. Jessica's heart thumped madly as they burst through. What was she going to do? Margaret had probably got out of her cell by now. She had to be stopped before she managed to breach the prison walls. As they reached the east wing, the guard ordered them to help barricade the doors with chairs and tables.

"It should hold, at least for now," he said, mopping his brow. "Follow me, this way." He led them deeper into the east wing. After a few minutes, he stopped abruptly. "This is where I'll leave you. I need to regroup with the others in the comms room over there and assess the situation." He nodded towards a door on the right. "Take that corridor. It'll lead you back to where you registered this morning. You'll be able to find your way out. Just follow the emergency exit signs."

Zak pulled Jessica away as she started after him.

"No way. If they manage to get the security working again and go into clampdown, we'll end up trapped. We have to keep moving. We can't be found in here."

He grabbed her hand and pulled her down the corridor. After a few minutes, they reached an evacuation point and joined a queue of visitors waiting to be escorted out. Guards ticked off their names from their clipboards and hurriedly shepherded them through the door.

"Keep your head down and don't look at the cameras," he ordered. "Rodarte's already pulled out. It couldn't risk being exposed by the hackers."

They crossed the courtyard and filed through the gate with the other visitors. Racing to the car park, they jumped into Zak's blue Mini as police sirens wailed in the distance. He revved up and reversed out of the space. Jessica grabbed his arm.

"We can't go, Zak. We have to find Margaret."

"If we stay, we could be identified. This could all come back on us. It looks terrible that we were here when this went down."

Zak carefully navigated his way out of the car park. He slammed his foot down hard on the accelerator as soon as he hit the street, tyres screeching.

"Is this our fault?" Jessica asked. "Is this connected to the Rodarte hacks?"

He pulled out his earpiece and threw it on to his lap. "I have no idea. Rodarte's panicking. It's possible members of The Collective used our hacks as a smokescreen for their own. They could have piggybacked in via the loophole Rodarte exploited and unleashed a virus into the security system."

"Oh dear God. So we *did* help Margaret escape."

"Not intentionally."

"That doesn't make it any better. We're fools." She groaned as the realization dawned on her. "We've been set up."

Zak took a sharp intake of breath and eased off the accelerator as more police cars screeched past, followed by fire engines and ambulances.

"What if The Collective deliberately planted my mum's name, Lily, in the MI6 computer system to make me suspect Margaret's involvement?" she continued. "That could have been part of the plan. LibertyCrossing wanted us to follow up the clue and visit Margaret."

Zak tightened his grip on the steering wheel. "But he didn't know for certain that we would go, certainly not today."

"What if he took the chance? His followers could have assessed the prison's firewalls through the hack on Saturday and worked out a way for our visit to trigger Margaret's escape. Perhaps the hackers had guessed Rodarte would demobilize the cameras, which would help them get in, or maybe they deliberately timed a breakout to incriminate us. Either way, Margaret was right."

"What do you mean?" His brow was furrowed.

"She said I'd never call Nathan when I left here today. She's right. I can't. It looks like I've helped The Collective bust her out. Margaret knew this was going to happen and that it'd look really bad for me when it did."

He paused. "I agree Margaret must have known in advance. But how? She couldn't have contacted The Collective through BBC Online or whatever internet site she usually goes on. It's totally supervised. You read her file."

"I don't know how she's doing it, but she's found a way round the system. She knew about the MI6 list going up online. Someone on the outside's definitely been communicating with Margaret. Now she's on the outside too."

"Let's not jump the gun here. We don't know if any prisoners have breached the walls yet, let alone Margaret. She could have been apprehended by the prison guards by now and be back in her cell."

"She's gone" Jessica said, staring out of the window.

"How do you know?"

Zak wouldn't understand. She could hardly comprehend it herself. It was as if she had a sixth sense for danger. She *knew* that Margaret was free.

CHAPTER
TWELVE

The long car journey back to London was tense; neither Jessica nor Zak were in the mood for conversation, particularly as the three p.m. deadline approached. Now and then, Zak flicked on the radio for news updates on the Durham prison; a hundred prisoners were on the loose. Jessica wondered what Margaret's next move would be. Hooking up with The Collective? Leaving the country? Or coming after her? Any of those scenarios had to be a serious possibility.

By the time they pulled into a motorway service station at 2.50 p.m., her hands ached from clenching her fists so hard. She left Zak in the car park, speaking to his boss on his mobile, while she queued to buy drinks and sandwiches. She wasn't particularly hungry or thirsty, but needed to do something other than keep checking her watch and refreshing the news updates on her mobile.

She found a seat at the back of the café, close to a TV, which was tuned to a news channel, and took a sip of coffee. It tasted burnt and bitter, but at least it was hot. Her hands trembled as she put the cup down and glanced at her watch again. It was three p.m. The presenter had given an update on the Durham prison breakout and was now droning on about interest rates. No breaking news alerts about MI6 agents flashed up on the TV screen. It was odd. She'd expected the leader of The Collective to release the list with a massive fanfare of publicity.

For the next ten minutes, she scanned Twitter, BBC online and every other major news channel website on her mobile. Zero. Absolutely nothing about MI6 agents being outed. Had Westwood managed to stop The Collective? It was starting to look that way. She felt more confident as every minute passed. How had Nathan done it? Quickly, she scanned the hacking websites. None of them mentioned MI6 agents either, but hundreds more angry people had posted messages to LibertyCrossing, demanding the jackpot for the best hacks. Some were calling the competition a scam, as no winner had been announced.

By the time Zak returned, it was thirty minutes past the deadline. Still nothing had appeared on the news or online. He slumped down into the seat opposite and took a swig of cold coffee.

"Coffee frappé?" He raised an eyebrow. "Delicious."

"So what happened? Did Rodarte stop the leak or Westwood?"

"Neither," he admitted. "Both agencies are baffled. The Collective simply missed the deadline. LibertyCrossing hasn't published the list – either fully or in part – and hasn't contacted MI6. We're still monitoring online but there's no sign of The Collective since the prison breakout this morning."

She frowned. "That doesn't make any sense. Why has LibertyCrossing suddenly lost interest in Lee Caplin?"

"I've no idea. But that's one thing less to worry about."

"So? Hit me with it. The thing you don't want to tell me."

His green eyes bored into hers. "You were right about Margaret. She's among the prisoners who are missing."

Jessica bit her lip, nodding. It was hardly a surprise. Margaret had probably spent months planning this breakout with The Collective. The hack on Saturday, obscured by the attacks on all the other prisons, had been a fact-finding mission.

"What else?"

"They're investigating your theory that we were set up to visit the prison, to somehow trigger the escape. Rodarte agrees The Collective could have taken a punt that we'd visit at some point. But what worries them is the fact they knew it was happening today and were prepared. Rodarte's done a full security check of its own computer systems. It hasn't been hacked. The Collective didn't find out from us."

"Well, it can't have come from hacking into Westwood either. No one knows we were there today."

Zak flinched slightly as he took another slurp of coffee.

"Please tell me Westwood doesn't know we were there." Her heart almost skipped a beat. "Does it?"

"Not yet, but Rodarte doesn't know if any footage identifying us remains. It had to pull out of the CCTV system as soon as the prison went into meltdown. It couldn't wipe any film. I'm not even sure it managed to cover its own tracks."

"Great. So you're basically saying that Agent Hatfield could launch a dawn raid on my home to arrest me if she recognizes us from the security tapes?"

"Rodarte's doing its best to avoid that." He pushed his cup to one side.

"Oh, gee, thanks. That makes me feel a lot better. I mean, it's not like you dragged me into this mess or anything."

Zak's phone vibrated with a message. "Oh God."

"What is it?"

He stared dumbly at his phone. "Lee Caplin."

"What about him?"

Zak jerked his head as a newsflash appeared on the TV screen.

"We're receiving reports of a major US prison breakout at Leavenworth Federal Penitentiary in

Kansas thirty minutes ago," the blonde-haired presenter began. "We'll keep you posted on developments as they happen."

Jessica gasped. "Lee Caplin's prison."

"It sure is." Zak snatched up his phone and bolted out of the restaurant, colliding into a woman balancing plates and cups on a tray. They slipped and smashed on the floor. She watched him disappear, stunned.

This could not be happening.

For the next half hour, she flicked between news websites, devouring every scrap of info she could find about the Kansas prison breakout. She clicked on an updated CNN story on her phone.

MAJOR PRISON BREAKOUT IN US – LEE CAPLIN ON THE RUN

Federal agents are hunting at least two hundred prisoners who escaped from the Leavenworth Federal Penitentiary in Kansas this morning.

Insiders report a total security breakdown that enabled all doors in the high-security prison to open shortly after visiting hours began at nine a.m.

At least two dozen prison guards were seriously injured, along with eight visitors, as inmates went on the rampage.

Among the prisoners on the loose are sixty-year-old Victor Enrique, who was jailed for forty years for tax evasion, and British cyberterrorist Lee Caplin, who recently began a thirty-year sentence for computer crimes.

The teenager almost started World War 3 after hacking into the Pentagon's computer system and has been declared highly dangerous by the FBI.

The Foreign Office said it had been informed of the situation but had no further comment to make about Caplin.

American authorities say they are confident all prisoners will be accounted for within forty-eight hours.

Jessica glanced up as Zak returned, white-faced. He sat down, shoulders sagging.

"I don't get it," she said, scanning the details online again. "Why would the leader of The Collective show his hand to MI6, demanding the release of Lee Caplin on Saturday, if he'd already planned to break him out today? Surely it would have been better to keep a low profile and then strike without warning?"

"Rodarte thinks it's all been smoke and mirrors. Everything that's happened up until today, including the hacking competition, has been a distraction to keep MI6 and the CIA busy while Lee's breakout was planned."

"It's certainly worked," she said, biting a nail. "The fact that LibertyCrossing hasn't bothered to publish the agents' list suggests that's not what he was really after."

"Exactly. Rodarte doesn't believe the leader of The Collective gives two hoots about freedom of information across the web, given his history for using hacking as a way to make millions. That was a ruse to take everyone's eye off the ball. The target all along was Lee Caplin. LibertyCrossing knew the US would never release someone as dangerous as him, so he devised an elaborate, prolonged smokescreen to disguise the breakout."

"After carrying out a successful test run at Margaret's prison first," she noted. "There was a four-hour lapse between the two attacks, and they used an identical modus operandi; a total breakdown in security timed to coincide with visiting hours. That has to be significant."

Zak nodded. "The CIA's analysing the security footage from the US prison. We're checking every visitor that came in to see if there's any connection with The Collective. So far, it's drawn a blank."

"Do you know yet if Lee Caplin received any visitors?"

"Funny you should say that." He fished out an iPad from his rucksack and entered his password before handing it to her. "Lee had agreed to be interviewed by this journalist from the *Wichita Eagle*."

"Helen Hamlyn," she read. "A feature writer and mother of three who's worked for the *Wichita Eagle* for the last twenty years. She now edits the women's page. Helen was due to interview Lee about his mother's death and the impact of his lengthy extradition process on her health."

She frowned as she stared at the photo of the middle-aged woman. Had Helen Hamlyn helped engineer the breakout for The Collective? It didn't quite ring true.

"I know what you're thinking," Zak said. "Helen doesn't fit the profile of The Collective's hackers, who are male and aged sixteen to twenty-five."

"Exactly."

"Helen's work and home computers are being analysed remotely. So far, there's no evidence of contact with LibertyCrossing or any hackers connected to The Collective. In fact, she only appears to use the internet for researching women's health articles and uploading family photos on Facebook. Her editor says she received an anonymous phone call at work, offering an exclusive interview with Lee. He said it was short notice and Helen jumped at the chance to go."

"Where's Helen now? Has she been interviewed? She may have seen something useful without even realizing it."

"Unfortunately, she was injured during the breakout. Prisoners ripped up their cells and used the debris as missiles. We've got agents waiting on standby at the hospital to talk to her when she regains consciousness."

Zak's phone buzzed. He raised an eyebrow as he checked the message. "We've retrieved some visuals from Helen's visit as she waited to see Lee. The rest is corrupted."

He tapped at his iPad. Jessica leant over and stared at the black-and-white footage. Helen looked nervous, fiddling with her tape recorder and notebook at a security check. She wore a raincoat and carried a large black handbag.

"It's not supposed to be very interesting," Zak said, trying to grab the iPad back. "She goes through after that."

"Hold on. Isn't that an Ossa Cosway raincoat?" She paused the footage and enlarged the picture. "You see the piping around the collar and sleeves? Margaret commented on *this* earlier." She held up her own trench coat. "She recognized Ossa's distinctive detail. It's the same on all his coats and jackets."

"Big deal," Zak snorted. "What does that have to do with anything?"

"Probably nothing," she admitted. "But it might be worth a look. You could get your agents to ask Helen how she can afford a five-thousand-dollar coat. I got mine for free. How did she get hers?"

Zak shrugged. "Maybe she got a discount or saved up her hard-earned pennies. Who cares?"

"I thought you were supposed to work for Rodarte? Isn't that kinda your field, you know, working a fashion angle?"

"Not this time. Do you have any idea how stupid it'll make me look to create a big deal out of the fashion label on a coat when the biggest prison breakout in US has just happened? It'd be career suicide."

Her phone buzzed.

"Anything important? Or is Jamie telling you he misses you?"

Jessica couldn't be bothered to retaliate. She showed him the single-word text message: *Tulips*.

"So what? I don't get it."

"It's the code word my *Big Issue* contact said she'd use if she found Henry Murray."

"What are we waiting for?" he said, rising to his feet. "Let's go."

Paranoia was the best policy. Zak and Jessica

didn't want to take any chances. It was possible LibertyCrossing had disappeared back into cyberworld now he'd released Lee Caplin, but they couldn't presume this was all over. The only safe option was to visit Lucy in person – rather than text or call – to find out what she knew. Henry Murray was a loose end that The Collective might still plan to tie up.

Once they arrived back in London, they agreed to return home to dump their ID passes and credit cards before hooking up again at Earl's Court tube station at six thirty p.m., with only cash to get them through the evening. Rodarte hadn't ruled out the possibility that one or both of them had been carrying electronic bugs, planted in their belongings, which allowed The Collective to listen in and discover their plans to visit the prison this morning. They needed to get to Lucy's spot at High Street Kensington and onwards without detection by The Collective or MI6.

Thankfully, the house was empty when Jessica arrived. Her dad had left a note saying he was out on a job and Mattie was meeting up with her book club friends tonight. Even better. She scribbled a note, saying she was staying over at Becky's, and left it on the hall dresser. To be doubly safe, she texted Becky saying she'd gone down with flu. She didn't want her friend dropping by unexpectedly and ruining her cover story. Next, she checked the landline for messages. Nothing. Nathan wasn't exactly beating her door down to invite her to return to Westwood. Neither was her school. Her dad had rung Nathan and begged him to analyse their home computer as well as the school's IT system. She was confident that Sam would give an unbiased assessment, but that could take time; other things were higher on his agenda, like investigating the two prison breakouts. Would he discover her and Zak's faces on the footage at Margaret's jail?

Jessica went upstairs and flicked through the bulging wardrobe in her bedroom. It'd grown considerably since she'd been signed as the face of Ossa Cosway – designer day dresses, skirts, blouses, jumpers and trousers arrived every few weeks, together with cocktail dresses and evening gowns in an array of colours, coats and accessories. She'd packed as much as she could in among her day-to-day New Look and Topshop staples and vintage items she'd discovered in markets and second-hand clothes shops. The rest, she'd had to squeeze into the wardrobes in the spare bedroom as well as her dad's.

Ignoring her designer clothes, she pulled on her favourite grey cashmere sweater and jeans. It felt good to be in her normal clothes again. So what if she got into trouble for breaking the clause in her contract? She had absolutely no intention of being photographed by any lurking paps; they wouldn't be hanging out anywhere near where she was going tonight.

The doorbell rang. Had her dad finished his job early and forgotten his key? She flew down the stairs and opened the door, excuse ready.

Her mouth fell open. "What are you doing here?"

Jamie frowned. "That's a nice welcome. Aren't I allowed to visit my girlfriend? I thought I'd swing by and see how you're doing."

"Sorry. It's great to see you. I was surprised, that's all. I wasn't expecting you."

Jessica reached forward to give him a kiss, but he turned his cheek.

"Clearly," he said drily, noticing her coat and rucksack lying on the floor. "Going somewhere interesting?"

"No. Not really."

"So can I come in or not?"

She quickly checked her watch. She was supposed to meet Zak in thirty minutes.

He sighed. "I'll try not to take up too much of your valuable time."

"Don't be daft." She held open the door. "I'll put the kettle on."

He followed her into the kitchen. "So is there any news?"

Jessica frowned. "About what?"

"Duh. Returning to school, of course." Jamie rolled his eyes impatiently. "Or have you got something more important on your mind right now?"

She had, actually, like trying to find Henry before he ended up dead.

"Last time we spoke, you seemed to think your dad would be able to help clear your name," he prompted. "He was getting the computer software checked."

"Yes, about that—" The doorbell rang.

"Saved by the bell," Jamie said. "You get that and I'll make some herbal tea. Do you want your usual?"

"Please." The last thing she wanted was a cup of camomile, but she didn't want Jamie to take offence again. She walked back into the hallway and flung open the door.

"Oh God. It's you."

"Thanks for the Hollywood welcome." Zak stepped inside without waiting for an invitation. He'd changed into a navy sweater, jeans and a black anorak. "We need to talk. I couldn't ring or text you, so I thought it'd be easier to swing by here first." He tossed his rucksack on to the floor, next to hers.

"Get out!" she whispered.

"Why? Is someone here?"

Jamie appeared in the hallway.

"Oh," Zak said, shooting a worried look at Jessica.

Jamie strode angrily towards them. "This is why you were so anxious to get rid of me, because *he* was coming round? Again?"

"It's not like that."

"So you're not going off somewhere with *him*? Behind my back?"

"I am. I mean, it's not behind your back. It's nothing like that."

"Brill, Jess. You know, you could at least have had the decency to break up with me before seeing someone else. I didn't think you were the kind of girl who'd cheat. I see I was wrong."

Zak walked towards him. "There's absolutely nothing going on between Jessica and me. I promise you. We're just friends."

Quick as a flash, Jamie leapt forward, fist flying. Zak stepped neatly aside and grabbed his arm, twisting it behind his back.

"Stop it! Let him go, Zak."

"Not until he calms down."

Jamie struggled against him harder. "I'll give you calm!"

"You're going to break his arm," Jessica yelled. "Let go of him."

Zak obeyed and Jamie staggered forward, clutching his wrist. She reached out to touch him but he pulled away, glaring furiously.

"You have to stop this, Jamie. You have to trust me."

"Why? How can I possibly do that when you continually lie to me?"

She caught her breath. "I'm not lying to you now. I love you, Jamie. Honestly, I do."

"If that's the case, why do you keep cancelling whenever we arrange to meet? Why are you spending so much time with Zak?"

"I've told you about London Fashion Week already." Why had she brought that up again? Even she thought it sounded like a lame excuse.

"Yeah, right. Like he needs regular meetups to discuss, er, clothes. I'm not that stupid." He paused. "I know you're lying about where you were on Saturday when we were supposed to meet at the café."

Jessica froze. "What do you mean?"

"You said you were helping Becky learn her lines but you weren't. Becky said she hasn't met up with you since your girls' night in. You're too busy to see her even though she needed help with a French essay. You haven't returned her calls, or mine, these last few days. She doesn't know what's going on either. Where were you? This time tell me the truth."

She opened her mouth, but no words came out. What could she say? She couldn't possibly admit that she'd been called to an emergency meeting at

Westwood. But there wasn't an alternative, plausible explanation he'd actually believe.

"Jessica was with me on Saturday," Zak said finally.

"What?" she mouthed.

Jamie clenched his fists again. "I knew it."

She shook her head vigorously. What was Zak thinking, or wasn't he? She should have found something to say quicker. If only he hadn't opened his big mouth. He was making things a lot, lot worse. Was he deliberately trying to make trouble with Jamie again? He'd enjoyed winding him up the first time they'd met.

"I wanted her to help me practise my walk ahead of the shows," Zak continued. "She didn't want to tell you because she knew you'd freak out. But that's all that happened that day, I swear."

Her stomach clenched. She'd never seen Jamie gaze at her with such contempt before. She couldn't bear the look in his eyes.

"I don't know who you are any more," he said quietly. "It's like you've been replaced by a stranger. The old Jessica Cole would never have lied to me. That's what I always used to like about you. You were totally upfront. You never misled anyone."

She winced. He was talking about her, about their relationship in the past tense. Tears welled in her eyes. "That's still me. I promise you, it is. I love you, Jamie. It's always been you. Not anyone else. Not Zak."

A tear slipped down Jamie's cheek. He brushed it away brusquely. "So tell me, Jess. If you had to choose between stepping out that door with me or Zak, what would you do?"

She tried to grab hold of Jamie's hand again but he backed away.

"I need an answer."

Couldn't he see this was breaking her heart? She had to leave with Zak right away if they had any chance of finding Henry, but it would rip her relationship with Jamie in two.

"This is crazy," she said finally. "Why do I have to choose?"

Jamie shook his head sadly. "Because I need you to. Months ago, you wouldn't have hesitated. You'd have come with me. I know you would. You were a different person back then."

"You don't understand."

"You're right, I don't. I don't get you at all any more. We're finished."

"Don't do this. Please, don't, Jamie."

He shrugged her off as she tried to embrace him and strode out the door without looking back.

"Jamie!" She followed him to the gate, but he was too fast. He was already running down the street.

This was all her fault. Why hadn't she broken the rules and told him about Westwood? She was no longer a member; she couldn't be disciplined for blabbing about the secret organization. But deep down, she knew why. She wanted back in and hated herself for it.

"I'm sorry," Zak said quietly. "But it was the only explanation I knew he'd actually believe, however much he wouldn't want to."

Jessica closed the door and leant against it, eyes closed. She didn't want Zak to see her cry. "It was *the* worst possible thing you could have come up with, in case you hadn't noticed."

"But it meant you didn't blurt about Westwood. I had to stop that."

"I wasn't going to, thanks very much! And I didn't need you to say anything at all. Why can't you just butt out of my business?"

"OK, OK. Calm down. I'm sorry. Whatever you said would probably have had the same outcome."

She glared at him. "I guess we'll never know now, will we?"

"You did the right thing," he continued. "You couldn't go with Jamie. We have to save Henry. That's the most important thing. Hopefully you can find a way to patch things up with Jamie later. He might come around."

Seriously? She'd allowed the love of her life to walk out, suspecting the worst of her – that she was a lying cheat, thanks to Zak's helpful intervention. There was no way he'd come around. Nathan had warned her right from the start that leading a double life would put a strain on personal relationships. That was undoubtedly why he didn't have someone special in his life. She'd still signed up to Westwood, but back then she hadn't realized it would break her heart, and Jamie's.

She blinked away her tears. "What's so important that you had to come over here? We'd agreed to meet at the station."

"Gadgets." He pointed at his rucksack. "I've gathered what I could from home. I wanted to check whether MI6 left anything when they confiscated your stuff."

She nodded slowly. "Nathan didn't give Agent Hatfield a full list. He left off some things, like my taser trainers. It was probably an accident."

"Maybe a part of him still wants to help you."

She stared at the gold bracelet on her wrist. Nathan had given it to her shortly after she joined Westwood. She'd used a similar one to rescue him and Mattie back in Monaco, by blowing a hole in the side of a sinking boat they were all trapped in. Perhaps the bracelet had sentimental value for him.

"Maybe. I don't know." She shrugged. "Anyway, I've got a few things upstairs."

"Good. Gather up whatever you have. We don't know what to expect tonight, so we'll need protection. I've brought a debugging device for our phones. I'll check everything we take to make sure we're clean. We can't afford to leave anything to chance tonight. Not this time."

Jessica turned away before he could see fresh tears

forming. Gripping the banister, she slowly climbed the stairs.

"It's going to work out OK," he called after her.

How did he know that? Hadn't he seen the hurt in Jamie's eyes? Hadn't he heard what he'd said? It was all over. There was no going back even if she finally told him the truth. Zak had seen to that.

CHAPTER
THIRTEEN

Sheets of rain bounced off the pavement as they reached the arches near Charing Cross station. An injured boy matching Henry's description had been dossing down among other rough sleepers. He'd shunned the help of volunteers from a homeless charity, bolting when anyone approached him, according to Lucy. She'd also warned Zak and Jessica that other *Big Issue* vendors had been approached days earlier by two teenage boys, waving large wads of cash in exchange for info on Henry's whereabouts. They claimed to be school friends, but there was no doubt in Jessica's mind that they were members of The Collective, tasked by LibertyCrossing with finding the missing hacker.

The pair had swapped between buses, taxis and

the tube after leaving Lucy at High Street Kensington. Zak claimed it'd have taken a team of at least twenty to keep tabs on them as they looped across central London, trying to avoid surveillance cameras. Teenage hackers weren't highly trained like MI6 and CIA operatives; they wouldn't have been able to keep up as the pair jumped from one mode of transport to another en route to Charing Cross. But they could be attempting to trace them through CCTV.

"It's impossible to tell if Henry's been here today," Zak said, scanning his torch across the cardboard city. A few old men rubbed their eyes and hurled abuse before rolling over again and attempting to get comfortable.

"He might have moved on already," Jessica said. "If he's heard that people are looking for him, he'll find somewhere else to hide."

"We'll have to scope this place out. I hope you didn't have any plans for tonight. It could be a long one."

Jessica flinched. She had no plans whatsoever after what had happened with Jamie. Was Zak's short-term memory that bad?

"That was insensitive, sorry." He hesitated. "Honestly, I didn't set out to cause a confrontation between you and Jamie back there or in the café. I concentrate on the job, and other things…" His voice trailed off. "Well, sometimes they suffer and I don't mean them to."

"It's been building up for a while, I suppose," she said quietly. "It's been tough keeping secrets from him."

"This job isn't exactly great for personal lives, is it? I do know what you're going through. I had my heart broken. My girlfriend dumped me a while back. But you do start to feel better. Eventually."

What? She'd expected Zak to be the heartbreaker, not the other way round.

His eyes misted over. "I guess we both knew what we were signing up for, didn't we?"

Did they? Would she have joined Westwood if she'd known back then that it'd ruin her relationship with Jamie? Would Zak have signed up to Rodarte?

He squeezed her shoulder. "You'll pull through this the way I did. You're tough, like me."

She didn't feel tough; far from it.

*

For the next couple of hours, they huddled together for warmth against a wall, far enough from the camp not to be detected. An overhanging tree protected them from the worst of the rain, but the damp had already penetrated Jessica's trainers and anorak.

"How are you holding up?" Zak didn't take his eyes off the makeshift camp.

"I'm fine," she replied, stamping her feet. She took a sip from her bottle of water and shoved it back into her coat pocket. What wouldn't she give for a hot chocolate?

"I'm going back to try and speak to the men over there again." She jerked her head towards the cardboard boxes and stepped out from the shadows. "They might open up to a girl after I've explained we're here to help Henry."

Zak threw her back against the wall, his body pressed against hers.

"What the—?"

"We've got company."

She couldn't see anything in the dark. "Where?"

"Approaching from the west. A dark van, registration plate SR42 YMK. Check database. Start now."

She stared down the street and glanced back up at him. She couldn't see a van but could make out the shape of a contact lens in his right eye. "You've got bionic vision, right?"

"Latest technology from the CIA. The van's using stolen number plates."

Not bad. He'd been able to instruct the eye gadget to search vehicle records, receiving info via the small plug in his right ear. His lens was far more advanced than the one she'd worn that night at the Shard. No way would she have been able to see all the way down the street and perform a number plate check within seconds.

The van parked adjacent to the camp and killed its lights and engine. They'd been right to be paranoid. The Collective had found Henry Murray's last suspected location.

"Shouldn't you call for backup?" Jessica urged.

"We can handle this."

"Don't be stupid! We don't know how many people are inside the van. We'll probably be outnumbered, plus they could be armed."

"We don't have time," Zak said. "Henry's already here."

238

A tall figure with a baseball cap pulled low approached, keeping to the shadows on the opposite side of the path.

"Are you sure it's him?"

"The facial recognition check's come up positive. Henry's walking straight into a trap."

Jessica held her breath. Henry was almost upon them. She glanced back at the van. The doors remained closed. The darkness and driving rain worked in their favour; visibility was terrible. But within seconds, he'd be spotted and the doors would fly open.

Zak darted out.

Henry froze. "Get back! I'm armed."

"Keep your voice down," Zak hissed. "We're here to help."

"Who are you? What do you want?"

Jessica removed her hood. "We met before at your school. You need to come with us."

"I told you to leave me alone," Henry said, falling back a pace. "The Collective will find me."

"They already have," Zak said, throwing a glance over his shoulder. The van doors were open and dark figures streaked towards them. "Come with us if you want to live."

Before Henry could speak, the arches lit up with an almighty explosion. Frightened shouts rang out from the cardboard boxes. Jessica heard a dull thud as something landed close to their feet. Almost immediately, there was a flash of piercing whiteness. She closed her eyes. This was a more powerful version of the device used that night at the boarding school, designed to obliterate night vision.

"Help me!"

Coloured shapes danced in front of her eyelids. She blinked again and saw Zak fall to his knees, clutching his right eye.

"It's burning! I can't see!"

She grabbed her bottle and thrust Zak's head back, pouring water over his face. As the water rinsed his eye, she flicked the lens out with her little finger. By then, four masked black figures had already surrounded them. They weren't here to negotiate Henry's handover. They moved in, attacking. Jessica lunged in front of Henry, kicking the first man in the stomach. She aimed again at his jaw and heard a loud crack. He fell to his knees, screaming.

The second attacker wrestled Zak to the ground while two more dragged Henry towards the van.

"Help! Help me!" Henry hollered.

Jessica started to run after him, but the man closest to her stood up again, clutching something in his hand. She managed to block his arm as he charged, but her hand grazed whatever he was holding. A searing heat rocketed up to her shoulder. The pain almost took her breath away. No way could she risk being zapped by that again. Lifting up her foot, she flicked open the sole of her trainer and fired a taser. The man screeched, dropping the gadget, and convulsed on the ground. She snatched up the device and ran over to Zak. He was on his back, grappling with a large man. Zak was fighting him off with one hand while trying to grab his rucksack with the other. He hadn't had time to pull out a single gadget before they were ambushed. She slammed the device into the side of the man's neck. He bellowed with pain and slumped to one side, unconscious.

"Thanks." Zak clasped his throat, coughing.

She helped him to his feet. "Can you see OK?"

"My vision's fuzzy in this eye, but it's getting better."

"They've got Henry," she breathed. "Over there!"

The men had almost reached the van, half carrying, half dragging Henry past the rough sleepers. Jessica ran towards them, ripping off the book charm from her bracelet. She aimed at the van. A dart rocketed out, piercing a tyre. Within seconds, there was a loud bang as it exploded.

Bullseye! Even if the men managed to get Henry inside, the van wasn't going anywhere. She tried aiming a taser from her other trainer at one of the men, but he managed to dodge it. She wasn't close enough. Zak passed her and grabbed the closest guy, managing to karate kick him in the shin and then the kneecap. He collapsed in agony. Zak spun round, kicking the other man hard on the chin. Jessica zapped him in the chest as he came at Zak again, this time armed with a knife.

Both attackers lay on the ground, but one of the men further up the path was already on his knees, attempting to stand.

"What now?" Henry cried.

Jessica grabbed his arm. "We run."

They flew past the row of terrified homeless men, not stopping until they'd crossed the main road and reached civilization: shops and people. There was definitely safety in numbers here, despite the CCTV camera that Jessica had already clocked across the street. The men wouldn't dare attack them in public; there were far too many witnesses.

Henry gripped his side. "I can't go on. I have to rest."

Zak leant against a doorway, panting. "We should be OK for a few minutes."

Jessica handed him a tissue. He dabbed at his lip, which was split and bleeding.

"How did they track me down?" Henry also accepted her offer of a tissue. His face was bloodied and smeared with dirt.

"Members of The Collective asked street people if they'd seen you. We think they've also been hacking into surveillance cameras to look for you." She jerked her head towards the camera.

Henry shuddered. "I told you they'd find me."

"Why are they after you?" she asked. "We know you were The Collective's best hacker. You were responsible for most of the stuff on Saturday. What made LibertyCrossing turn against you?"

Henry bit his lip. "How much trouble am I in exactly?"

"*A lot* if your hacking's made public," Zak admitted. "It'll destroy your dad's career and you could end up in court. Zero trouble if you help us track down the leader of The Collective. That's our priority."

A look of panic crossed Henry's face.

"MI6 isn't looking to prosecute you," Jessica insisted. "That's what I was trying to explain to you the other night. We can keep your identity secret in return for you giving up everything you know about LibertyCrossing."

"I didn't expect it to end up like this," Henry admitted. "It was a bit of fun. I wanted to see what I could hack into, like Lee Caplin. He was a hero of mine."

"Did you ever meet him?" Jessica said. "Online, I mean."

Henry shook his head. "I only got into this about a year ago and Lee had been forced offline by then. But he had lots of fans, people like me who wanted to carry on where he left off. We met in forums and discussed what we'd done. It's a competitive world, you know. Everyone wants to be better than the next hacker."

"This way." Zak gestured for them to start walking again. He was getting jumpy about staying in one place too long. "How did you meet LibertyCrossing?"

"I blogged about how I'd managed to get into the computers at the National Grid and the Metropolitan Police. Someone called LibertyCrossing started regularly posting comments to me. We started to correspond via a hacking website and eventually, when he trusted me enough, through a protected email address. LibertyCrossing became a kind of mentor; it was obvious he was far more experienced than me. Sometimes I showed off what I could do hacking-wise, and other times LibertyCrossing asked me to target something."

"Like what?" Jessica demanded.

"A few months back, he wanted me to test the firewalls in the security system at the Leavenworth Federal Penitentiary in Kansas."

Her eyes widened. That was Lee's prison.

"I didn't actually release any prisoners," Henry said hastily. "I looked for glitches and found a few, which I reported back. I'd helped LibertyCrossing organize the hacking competition and thought it'd help me win the million dollars if I did exactly as he said."

He'd fallen for that too? LibertyCrossing probably had no intention of paying the jackpot to anyone; he was dangling a lucrative carrot and getting hackers to do all his dirty work. It was time to cut to the chase.

"Do you know the identity of LibertyCrossing?" Jessica said.

Henry shook his head. "He always encrypted his identity and didn't give away personal details. But he knew all about me. He must have traced my IP address and checked me out because he deliberately let slip towards the end that he knew where I went to school, what my dad did and how bad this would look for everyone if I ever talked about what I'd done." He shivered. "I was naive to get involved, but you have to understand, it was exciting to begin with."

"So what went wrong?" Zak asked.

"I'd helped LibertyCrossing launch the hacks on Saturday. I posted suggestions for places to be targeted on hacking websites, different challenges that LibertyCrossing believed would cause maximum disruption across this country and in the United States."

Zak ignored the sign for the Underground and hailed a black cab. He had to give the driver a wad of cash to persuade him to take them; Henry stunk to high heaven and they all looked rough. Zak checked that the light was turned off in the back, indicating that the driver couldn't listen in, before nodding to Henry that it was safe to continue.

"I guess on the day, it all went to my head. I felt in control for once in my life, instead of being known as the son of someone powerful." Henry stared out of the window, his eyes vacant. "I hacked the emergency services, the traffic-light systems and virtually every prison in the UK. LibertyCrossing had been quite specific about targeting the prisons and filing a full diagnostics on the firewalls at each. He wanted to discover any flaws in the computer systems. That's when I asked LibertyCrossing for my million dollars."

"You thought you were the best?" Zak asked. "Even after the hack on the federal bank in the US?"

"That was my idea," Henry snapped. "Sorry. I mean, it was obvious I was the most useful person.

LibertyCrossing had said so in an email, how I'd inspired other hackers to do things they'd never even dreamt of. I knew no one could beat me, even by deadline day. I was the best."

Jessica coughed. The sense of pride in his voice was nauseating. Didn't he feel any remorse for the mayhem he'd caused that day? People could have died in car crashes or been killed in the prisons because of his hacks. She took a deep breath. It was pointless laying into him; he'd only clam up.

"LibertyCrossing wouldn't talk money?" she persisted.

"He fobbed me off repeatedly, saying he had to wait to see how successful the hack had been on MI6. That really grated. I mean, what hack? We'd never discussed targeting security services before. LibertyCrossing wouldn't tell me who'd done it or how. I was his right-hand man and suddenly I was frozen out and replaced."

So it was wounded pride, not money, that had made Henry turn against the leader of The Collective.

"What did you do?" Zak asked.

"I lost my temper. I uploaded a new virus I'd

constructed that collects personal passwords on to an email attachment and sent it to LibertyCrossing. He was distracted that day, I guess. He clicked it open and immediately tried to close it down, but it was too late. I'd found his IP address – something he'd always managed to disguise before. A bit more digging around the internet and I'd called up the geo-location of the computer. From the traces I ran, it seemed to be the one he used most frequently."

"You have the actual address of the leader of The Collective?" Zak sat bolt upright in his seat. "That's why you were attacked at school? LibertyCrossing realized you'd discovered where he was based?"

"It was stupid. I should never have gone after him like that."

"It's good you did because now we can find him and stop him from hurting you again, or anyone else," Jessica said. "What's the address?"

Henry reeled off coordinates while Zak wrote them on his hand with a biro.

"What's there?" he asked.

"No idea. I was too afraid to look it up and find out. Dumb, I know. Like that could protect me.

LibertyCrossing emailed me a message with two words afterwards – 'Big mistake' – and then cut off all contact. I emailed again and again, apologizing for what I'd done, but heard nothing back. I planned to go into hiding that night when someone came for me. They hit me over the head as I was leaving my room. I didn't get to see their face, before you ask. It all happened quickly."

"You were lucky," Jessica said. "You could have been killed."

"Yes." Henry paused. "Thanks to you, I wasn't. But my laptop was destroyed, which gave me nothing to bargain with. I knew that LibertyCrossing would set other hackers on me. I thought I could keep them at bay, you know, by threatening to hand my laptop over to the authorities. When that was destroyed, I had nothing. I had to disappear."

Henry looked from Zak to Jessica. "What happens now?"

She knew what Zak was thinking; he wanted to go to the mystery location straight away.

"We need to get Henry off the street first," she reasoned. "He can't go back to sleeping rough again.

It's below zero tonight."

"Where will you take me?" Henry asked. "LibertyCrossing has eyes everywhere, believe me."

"Not everywhere," she said, thinking fast. "I know a place we can go."

They'd switched taxis to be on the safe side. Jessica had picked a blind spot to flag down another ride, away from the view of CCTV cameras. She handed over the remainder of their cash, in return for the driver taking a long, complicated route to the address she'd hastily scribbled down on a piece of paper.

She was confident they hadn't been tailed; she'd been watching out of the back window throughout the journey while Henry and Zak rested. They'd both refused medical treatment even though the taxi driver had suggested taking them to hospital. Zak's eye was bloodshot and weeping and the gash on Henry's forehead was still bleeding. The driver had dropped them off a short distance away from Everley Road. They walked slowly down the street. Every bone in Jessica's body ached; Zak and Henry had to feel as bad. It'd been one hell of a night.

"Wait here." Her hand hovered on the gate.

Zak and Henry leant against the wall with their backs to the house as she hammered on the door. The hall light flickered on and she heard the *tap tap* of footsteps.

"Who's there?"

"It's me, Jessica. Let me in?"

The door flew open and Becky peered out, make-up-less and wearing glasses. "Ohmigod. You look awful! Aren't you supposed to be in bed with flu? I thought you must be really ill. You didn't return my texts tonight."

Jessica fell into Becky's arms. She choked back tears as she inhaled her familiar Katy Perry perfume. She needed a hug. The house was quiet apart from the drone of a TV from the sitting room.

"What's wrong? You're scaring me!"

Jessica stepped back. "Are your mum and dad here?"

"No. They've got theatre tickets and an after-show party. Why?" Becky tucked her black bob behind her ears. "What's going on? You look terrible and I don't mean because of flu. Seriously, you're freaking me out." She stared down at the large, angry welt on

252

Jessica's hand. "Has someone hurt you?"

Quickly, she shoved her hand into her pocket. "Can we come in? I wouldn't ask unless we were really desperate."

"We?" Becky raised an eyebrow as Zak and Henry limped down the path. "I'm not exactly dressed for guests, particularly of the hot male model variety." She glanced down at her blue onesie despairingly. "Seriously? Zak has to see me looking like this?"

"It doesn't matter what you're wearing. We need your help. Please let us in."

Becky stepped to one side, Her eyes widened as she took in Henry and Zak's wounds. Jessica double-checked no one had seen them enter as she closed the door.

"Hi," Zak said, planting a kiss on Becky's cheek. "It's good to see you again."

She blushed furiously. "Erm ... hello. You too."

Henry hung back, unsure what to do. He smiled shyly at Becky.

"Are you sure this is going to be OK?" Zak turned to Jessica, wincing. "We can't afford to take any chances."

She handed him another tissue for his bloody lip.

"Becky's my best friend. I'd trust her with my life."

Zak nodded. "Then I do too."

Becky turned an even deeper crimson colour. "Why don't you and your silent friend go into the kitchen? I'll make some coffee. It looks like we could all do with a pick-me-up."

Henry beamed gratefully. Jessica doubted he'd had anything hot to eat or drink for days. Zak followed him into the kitchen, but Becky stepped in front of Jessica, blocking her path. She waited until the door closed.

"I wish you'd given me a bit of warning. I'd have changed."

"I'm sorry. It was kind of last-minute."

"So I heard. Jamie was here earlier," she said, frowning. "He told me you'd gone out with Zak. He was in bits."

"It was hardly a date," Jessica pointed out. "I can't believe we've broken up because of tonight." The words didn't feel real. She and Jamie were no longer an item; they wouldn't text each other every night before they went to sleep or share Saturday brunch again. She doubted whether he even wanted to stay friends. When he left, he looked like he hated her guts.

Becky jerked her head towards the kitchen. "You can't blame him being paranoid when he's competing with Zak."

"He doesn't need to compete. I promise you, hand on heart, there's nothing going on between us."

"Not from your side."

Jessica shook her head vigorously. "No way."

"You must have noticed the way Zak looks at you," Becky pressed. "He likes you. Sure, he's charming and friendly when I meet him. I'm sure he's super nice to all the girls. But he doesn't look at me the way he looks at you. I could see it a mile off at our DVD evening. There was a spark between you. I bet you felt it too."

"No way. We're just friends. We..." Her voice trailed off. In truth, she wasn't sure what they were. They weren't exactly friends, yet she was spending more time with him than anyone else in her life right now. "We work together. Jamie couldn't get his head round the fact that we were hanging out."

Becky sighed. "It's hardly surprising, is it? You haven't made any of Jamie's gigs recently, you lie about where you go and Zak's hot, hot, hot. Plus, he's got that bad boy vibe going for him, with all those sexy battle scars. Girls go for that sort of thing. *I* go for that sort of thing."

"Not me," Jessica said firmly. "I model with him, that's all."

"That's not strictly true, though, is it?" Becky persisted. "There has to be more to it than that. You lied to me tonight. You don't look like you've got flu; you've all been involved in some kind of bust-up. Whatever happened tonight goes way beyond modelling."

Jessica stared down at her muddy trainers, figuring out how she could start to explain.

"I recognize the other boy. You do realize that his face is plastered all over the TV and newspapers?" Becky continued. "They're saying that Henry Murray ran away from his boarding school and the police are looking for him. His dad's some kind of high-powered diplomat, but you must know that already."

She was tired of lying to Becky. She had to come clean – up to a point. "You're right. I don't have flu and I'm sorry I lied to you and didn't return your texts. Mattie thinks I'm staying at yours tonight. I texted to say I was ill because I didn't want you to swing by and scupper my story. I had to help find Henry Murray."

Becky didn't flinch. "Why have you brought him here?"

"It's not safe for him to return to school. And he can't tell his family where he is for the moment. I know it's a massive thing to ask when I haven't been totally honest with you, but he needs to stay here for a while, without anyone knowing, including the police. Tonight, perhaps tomorrow, until I've figured out what to do."

"You do know what you're saying? Have you any idea how much trouble I'll be in if anyone finds out I'm hiding him here and didn't tell his school? What about his family? Don't his parents have the right to know he's safe? They must be worried sick."

"You're the only person I could think of who'd do it for me," Jessica admitted. "I wouldn't be asking unless there was a really good reason for not allowing him to return."

Becky didn't skip a beat. "Does this have something to do with your dad's job? Is that why you couldn't tell Jamie the truth about what's going on? You're working on some kind of case with your dad?"

That was the closest thing to the truth she could admit. Becky knew that her dad was a private investigator and that she sometimes helped him out on cases that involved surveillance and planting bugs. She had no idea about his MI6 background or Jessica's involvement with Westwood and that was the way it had to stay. But at least Becky's guesswork wasn't *too* far from the truth.

"His work has to be kept secret, to protect his clients. I can't betray that trust, even to Jamie, however much I may want to. Henry must be kept safe, away from anyone connected to him."

Becky studied her face for a few seconds. "But why rope in Zak if you can't confide in Jamie?"

"It's complicated to explain, but he has a connection to Henry."

"Which you can't go into?"

Jessica nodded. "I'm really sorry. I'd tell you if I could."

"OK," she said finally. "Henry can stay tonight. I've got some hair dye he can use to disguise his appearance if necessary. I'll tell Mum and Dad he's a friend from the National Youth Theatre who needs a bed. But that's all I can do. They'll become suspicious if he stays any longer than a night or two."

Jessica hugged her. "Thanks. I knew you'd come through for me."

"Haven't I always? You're hard to say no to, Jessica Cole. I'm going to change out of this wretched onesie, pretend that I've got a shot with Zak and then I'll help patch you up. You're a wreck, girl."

"Tell me about it."

CHAPTER FOURTEEN

"Are you sure this is right?"

Jessica stared up at the large warehouse situated in the heart of a deserted industrial estate in South London. They'd left Henry at Becky's house after a quick pasta supper and traced LibertyCrossing's coordinates using a map rather than the GPS app on their mobiles. Cutting through the wire fence that surrounded the unit had taken seconds with Zak's laser pen. It also contained a mini blowtorch, which they could use to seal up the fence on their way out.

The warehouse had no signage, but that wasn't particularly unusual. A few neighbouring ones didn't display business names either. Maybe the owners were very private. Was this The Collective's HQ?

It was possible that LibertyCrossing had bounced his IP address around different locations to prevent his permanent base from being discovered.

"The coordinates are correct." Zak slipped on a pair of thermal imaging glasses and scanned the building. He took them off again. "It looks empty. We could have a quick scout around while we're here even if it's just to rule it out. What do you think?"

He hadn't wanted to call the coordinates into Rodarte until he was sure the location was a goer.

"Yeah, let's do it."

They circuited the building to check for burglar alarms and decided to break in via the back entrance. Zak aimed a shaving foam can at the alarm and sprayed it; a liquid solution jetted out, expanded and covered the yellow box. Jessica's eyes narrowed. Rodarte and Westwood's technology was similar; she'd used a perfume bottle just like it in Paris. She pulled a grip out of her hair and stuck it in the lock, jiggling it about, along with some tweezers, the way her dad had taught her.

"Don't bother. I can laser it" Zak pulled out his pen again.

"No. Hold on. I can do it the old-fashioned way."
She fiddled with the grip and felt the lock spring
open. She pulled two torches from her rucksack
and opened the door. "Here goes."

She stepped into the darkness first, flashing her
torch around. The faint scent of a pine air freshener
filled the air. Zak followed her into the bare, white-
walled corridor, halting as the floorboard beneath his
feet creaked. Carefully, they moved forward, swishing
their feet skater-style instead of walking heel to toe to
try and reduce the noise. Zak had said it was empty,
but they couldn't afford to take chances. Within
seconds, they'd turned right into what looked like the
heart of the warehouse. Zak scanned the open space
with his torch, illuminating row upon row of sewing
machines and racks of fabrics.

"A clothing factory? This isn't the right place." He
didn't bother to lower his voice. "Do you think Henry
deliberately tricked us?"

"Why would he?" she said, walking down the
aisle. Her torch picked out patterns and trays of
multicoloured cotton spread out on the work counters.
"He needs our help."

"Then he must have gotten the coordinates wrong." His tone was exasperated. "Let's get out of here. It's a waste of time."

"No. Wait. Look over here!" She aimed her torch at the wall, revealing dozens of sketches of outfits.

"They're just clothes designs," Zak scoffed.

"They're Ossa Cosway's."

"Are you sure? How can you tell?" He was already at her side, peering at the drawings of dresses and evening gowns.

"Look at the edging around this jacket and that dress. I recognize Ossa's signature style." Jessica peered closer, moving along the row of pictures. She shone her torch on one print after another. "Each one is signed O.C. in small letters at the bottom right."

"So what?" Zak frowned. "What's the big deal?"

She tucked her hair behind her ears. "It's odd, don't you think? Ossa's name keeps cropping up in all this for some reason."

"Er, how, exactly?"

"Don't you remember? That American reporter, Helen Hamlyn, wore an Ossa Cosway raincoat to the prison when Lee Caplin escaped. The coat I wore to

Margaret's prison was also one of his; Margaret even made a point of admiring it and saying how much she wanted one when she was free. Plus LibertyCrossing has used a computer somewhere in this warehouse, which happens to make Ossa Cosway clothes. It all adds up to an awful lot of coincidences, don't you think? You need to call it in, Zak. This place needs a thorough going-over by Westwood – I mean, Rodarte."

Jessica flinched. It still felt odd not to be part of the Westwood team. Unfortunately, it also meant that Zak was ultimately calling the shots, not her, otherwise she'd be on the phone to Nathan ASAP.

"We don't have enough to go on yet," Zak countered. "Like you say, it could be an *awful* lot of coincidences. Open any fashion magazine and you'll find a star wearing one of Ossa's designs. That doesn't mean every A-list actress in Hollywood is embroiled in this hacking conspiracy. Unless that's a new theory you care to run past me."

She scowled. Was Zak being deliberately obstructive because he hadn't been the one to spot a possible link between Ossa Cosway and The Collective himself? He'd shot her down the first time she mentioned the possibility of looking into how Helen Hamlyn had acquired her expensive designer raincoat.

"Fine," she said through gritted teeth. "Let's find the computer that Henry traced."

Zak nodded curtly.

She brushed past him. Why did he have to be so annoying? There was only one way to go – straight down the aisle, in between the sewing machines. The far right-hand corner of the warehouse was sealed off in plastic sheeting. She made a beeline for it. It was probably designed to protect clothes from dust, but still worth a look. She ducked through the opening in the plastic.

Shining her light around, she could make out the table where dressmakers cut out patterns and fabric, together with a rack of different-coloured threads and a large, industrial sewing machine. A jacket with Ossa Cosway's trademark braiding around the collar hung nearby. A long piece of silver thread trailed down from the lapel, which was half stitched. She shone her torch on the rack of bobbins and pulled out a silver one. This was the thread being used on the unfinished jacket. She picked it up and examined it closer. It looked similar to the one she'd found stuck in the window frame at Henry's boarding house.

Jessica snipped off a sample with a pair of scissors, along with lengths from three more bobbins with near-identical colours. Had forensics examined the thread left behind at the International High School yet? Sure, MI6 had collected it from her house. But she could hardly ring Nathan to ask what they'd done with it. She slipped the threads into the small plastic bag she'd brought for gathering potential evidence and stuffed it into her back pocket. Carefully, she put each reel back in its place and went to find Zak.

He was in the office next to the toilets, his legs up on the desk as he stretched back in a leather chair. Was he deliberately trying to wind her up by appearing so relaxed in the dark? She ignored him and looked around. This was definitely Ossa Cosway's office. A three-piece suit covered in plastic hung from the coat stand, along with one of his hats. It was nothing like his stylish, minimalistic office at Ossa Cosway HQ in central London; this one was purely functional, with a scratched desk, a computer and a large grey filing cabinet. Her torch picked out a date planner taped to the wall, plastered with yellow Post-it notes. Paint peeled from the walls.

"Before you ask, I've flicked through the filing cabinet," Zak said. "It contains invoices, bills, spreadsheets and the sort of business stuff you'd expect to find. No trace of LibertyCrossing or The Collective, nothing worth reporting to Rodarte."

"What about the computer?"

"Yeah, right," he drawled. "It shouldn't be a problem hacking into it, if it belongs to the leader of The Collective, as you seem to think it does. I expect LibertyCrossing – I mean, superhacker Ossa Cosway – left the password on one of these Post-it notes." Zak flicked on the switch and the computer whirred to life. "Now which one is it?" He glanced at the wall and drew his finger along the yellow notes.

"Ha ha, very funny. You're right. The computer *could* be massively protected if it's the one LibertyCrossing's been using. Alternatively, he could have plugged a laptop in over there to coordinate the hacks." She nodded at the modem. "Don't you think?"

He rolled his eyes. "You really think that Ossa Cosway could be the leader of The Collective?"

"I don't know what I think exactly. But I've a hunch that something's not right here."

"Well, I'll come straight out with it. I don't buy it. Why would Ossa Cosway give two hoots about a teenage hacker like Lee Caplin? I've met loads of designers and they only care about one thing – fashion. You're hard-pressed to get them to talk about anything else. World events? What's that? I bet Ossa Cosway's no different. He's probably never even heard of Lee."

"Maybe. Or fashion could be a good front. I did a shoot for him this week and he was big into the latest digital technology. He'd created a hashtag dress that you could text with messages, which was beyond cool. If he can do that, what else can he do with computers? After all, who'd suspect a fashion designer of being a superhacker? Maybe he feels protective towards a teenage hacker who's landed himself in big trouble."

"That's a lot of maybes."

Wow. She'd love to wipe that supercilious smirk off his annoying face by proving him wrong. She swiped his feet off the desk as she strode over to the filing cabinets.

Zak glared at her. "What are you doing now? I told

you I've checked them."

Ignoring him, she put her torch down and went through the drawers until she found the files containing lists of freebies that Ossa's PR department had given away to various celebrities. Her name was one of the few under "C". Her eyes widened. The document stated she'd received £257,000 worth of clothes as part of her contract with Ossa Cosway Ltd. She flicked through the documents until she got to "H" for Hamlyn.

"Aha. Explain this." She pointed her torch at a white piece of paper. "Why was Helen Hamlyn, the American reporter, given a free size fourteen raincoat from Ossa's latest collection? She's not exactly going to be featured wearing it in *Hello!* magazine, is she?"

"Let me see that." Zak jumped up and snatched the paper off her. He studied it for a few seconds before finally speaking. "It's odd. I'll give you that. Helen's a total nobody in celeb land."

She stared at him as an idea started to dawn. "Do you still have the names of the wealthy people in the US who were targeted by The Collective?"

"Why?" Zak tapped at his iPhone.

"Cut me some slack, why don't you?" She looked at his phone and read out details under the first name on the list. "Victoria Alton, a wealthy, married Hollywood actress, blackmailed for ten million dollars last August. She was trying to prevent details of her affair with an entertainment lawyer being made public." She leafed through the data and pulled out two pieces of paper, itemizing outfits ranging from trousers to cocktail dresses. "Victoria's a regular customer of Ossa's and buys from each collection he launches. She was also given a hundred thousand dollars' worth of couture gowns to wear on the red carpet at the worldwide launches of her latest movie. Two months later, she was hacked."

Zak's eyes widened. "Let's try another." He stared at his phone. "How about this one? Tyler Harper, a dot-com millionaire whose bank account was raided. He lost twenty million."

Jessica's fingers lingered on the document. A shiver of excitement passed down her spine. Her intuition was right. There *was* some kind of connection between Ossa Cosway and The Collective.

"Tyler Harper's here." She showed him the itemized

list. "His wife, Jo, is also a regular Ossa Cosway customer. She received a gift of free dresses to wear at dot-com conferences four months before her husband's bank account was drained."

The pair methodically made their way down the list, mentally ticking off the names one by one. Within minutes, they'd discovered every single person on the hacked list was a customer of Ossa Cosway Ltd who'd received a free gift.

"You're right," Zak said finally. "It's way too much of a coincidence that everyone who gets free Ossa Cosway clothes ends up being hacked, but what's the connection?"

"Ossa could be LibertyCrossing, hacking wealthy people on his customer database. Alternatively, he's working with the leader of The Collective and identifying targets for him to hack through the clothes deliveries."

"The clothes could be a ruse to get into people's houses," he admitted. "Ossa or an accomplice could hand-deliver them to a target and then hack the computers once they're inside."

Jessica rubbed her forehead, trying to make sense of

what was unravelling. "When I got all my deliveries, it was just a bloke in a van. He made me sign for the clothes and left them on a rack in the hallway. He wasn't out of my sight for the few minutes he was there and didn't go into the study where my dad's computer's kept."

"We should still check the transportation angle. It's the only thing that makes any sense – a delivery that coincides with a hack. I didn't notice anything in the filing cabinets about how the clothes were shipped." Zak sat down at the desk again, staring at the security box that had flashed up on the computer. "You're Ossa's muse. Can you think of the password he'd use?"

"Try Sunflower. It was the name of his first couture collection."

Zak tapped the word in and pressed return. He made the sound of a game-show buzzer. "Next."

"Shogun. It's the name of his pet cocker spaniel."

"Seriously?"

"Trust me. I'm not kidding. He's nuts about that dog."

He tried again and shook his head.

She racked her brain. "Belinda. It's his late mum's

name. They were really close."

The computer remained locked. "Wrong again." Zak pushed himself back in the chair. "Think, Jessica."

Suddenly, a timer appeared on the screen.

Ten, nine, eight...

"Whooaaa. That isn't good."

"We must have activated an alarm by getting the passwords wrong," she said quickly. "It could destroy everything on the computer's hard drive. Close it down."

Zak tried, but the computer wouldn't turn off.

They watched helplessly as the numbers counted down. Five, four, three, two, one.

Nothing happened.

"Maybe it's still OK?" Zak said.

Suddenly, a massive explosion racked the warehouse, followed by another and another and another.

CHAPTER
FIFTEEN

Zak flung open the door and they stumbled out into the dressmaking section. They watched in horror as a chain reaction of small explosions grew closer and closer, throwing out balls of fire across the warehouse. Within seconds, a wall of flames, fanned by rolls of fabric, had blocked their escape route. Heat smothered Jessica's face, making her lungs constrict and eyes sting. Why hadn't she figured out that it was dangerous to mess with the computer? LibertyCrossing had booby-trapped the warehouse to blow if someone attempted to gain unauthorized access online.

"This way." Zak ran back towards the emergency exit door, next to the office. He rattled the handle but it remained shut.

"It's jammed on the outside," he breathed. "But I can take out the hinges." He fumbled with his laser pen.

"No!" She dragged him back.

"What?"

"Down there!" She pointed her torch at a small air vent next to the door. It was ill-fitting and a wire poked out. It could be the site of another hidden explosive, ready to detonate if the door opened. The only way to go was forward, into the furnace. They fell to their knees in between the sewing benches; there was more oxygen closest to the floor. Frantically, they looked about for another exit with their torches, but couldn't find one. Jessica gazed at the nearest wall.

"We'll have to blast our way out," she said, coughing. "I've got a device on my bracelet, which should blow a big enough hole."

"It's too risky," Zak spluttered. "It could fan the flames even more."

"We don't have a choice." Crawling along the floor, Jessica could barely see through the smoke. She checked the wall and couldn't find any booby traps. Pulling a hedgehog charm from her bracelet, she stabbed the pin into the plaster. Quickly, she wriggled back to Zak. Had she done the right thing? This would be a far more powerful explosive than the ones LibertyCrossing had used to rig the building. *Those* had been directed inwards to destroy evidence inside the warehouse.

Ten, nine, eight, seven...

She counted down in her head.

BANG!

The blast hurled them both backwards. Jessica felt a rush of cold air as she staggered to her feet. Grabbing Zak's hand, she blindly lunged towards the wall. The smoke was too dense to see anything, but the hole *had* to be big enough to squeeze out. Flames crackled dangerously close as they made it to the jagged gap. Clambering through, they fell, panting, on to the cold, wet ground.

"We need to keep moving," Zak urged. "Come on." He pulled her up. They ducked down and ran, but a terrific explosion threw them to the ground again. The roof collapsed into the blazing warehouse, sending orange sparks flying. More explosions boomed and fire spurted through the windows, smashing the glass.

They scrambled up and sprinted, not stopping until they reached the neighbouring warehouse. Slumping down, they watched black smoke and flames billowing from the building. Neither needed to say it – if they'd been stuck inside a few seconds longer, they'd both have been killed.

"You were amazing back there," Zak panted. "I don't think I've ever met anyone like you." He hesitated. "There's something I need to tell you, Jessica."

"Not now," she said quickly. "Call it in."

Things moved fast over the next few hours. Henry Murray was picked up from Becky's house and taken into protective custody, where he received medical treatment; an arrest warrant was issued for Ossa Cosway and his London offices were raided. The agents debriefing Jessica at the American Embassy in London's Grosvenor Square popped in and out of the sparsely decorated room, as their phones vibrated frequently. The constant interruptions were a relief. Whenever Hal, the taller agent, spoke, she got a whiff of old, stale cigarettes that he'd failed to mask beneath his overpowering aftershave. Was Zak holding up any better? She hadn't seen him since they'd arrived. He was being grilled in a room further down the hall. What was he saying about tonight?

She sipped a lukewarm cup of sweet, milky coffee as Hal and Robert scuttled off again. They were desperately trying to build their case against Ossa. It didn't seem to be going well, judging from what she'd managed to glean from eavesdropping on the agents' conversations outside the door. They hadn't managed to locate Ossa yet; he wasn't at his exclusive Knightsbridge flat. The raid on his offices was proving problematic too. Something was up with the computers.

Jessica darted back to her chair as a third, louder voice rang out. It sounded like her interrogators were getting a dose of their own medicine from someone more senior. The door banged open again. She stared hard into her drink, willing them all to go away. Surely that was it? She couldn't think of anything else to say. Apart from *leave me alone and let me go home*.

"Jessica!"

She glanced up, shocked. Rising to her feet, she

clutched the blanket tighter around her shoulders. "Nathan!"

This was bad, really bad. She was in for *the* tongue-lashing of her life or even worse. Had he come to arrest her for alleged involvement in Margaret's prison breakout?

Nathan crossed the room in a few paces with a determined look on his face. Holy smoke. Was he actually going to hit her? To her surprise, he enveloped her in a tight hug.

"Are you hurt?"

"I'm OK." She stared up at his lined, worried face. "What are you doing here?"

"Rodarte called. They finally came clean and explained what's been happening today."

Jessica gulped. "Er, they told you everything?"

Nathan's grey eyes narrowed. "You mean how you and Zak were almost killed in Ossa Cosway's booby-trapped warehouse? And how hours earlier, you both secretly confronted Margaret in prison – a profoundly reckless action that may have inadvertently resulted in her escaping? Yes, Rodarte filled me in. They had to after we traced a CCTV hack at the prison back to their London unit. Unfortunately for Rodarte, it didn't have time to fully cover its tracks before The Collective uploaded a virus, disabling all the locks."

What a disaster. The whole mission had been doomed. The Collective had deliberately left Rodarte exposed.

"I'm sorry, Nathan. I'd never have gone to the prison if I'd known there was a chance it could lead to Margaret's escape. I wanted to prove she was linked to The Collective."

"I don't blame *you*. I blame myself for not listening to you earlier about Margaret and I blame Rodarte for green-lighting such a foolhardy mission. Our American colleagues are still trying to figure out how The Collective used you and Zak to perform the hacks today. But what bothers me most is their total disregard for your and Zak's safety. What do you think would have happened if you'd both been trapped inside that prison with inmates on the loose?"

Jessica shook her head. She couldn't think about that now. There were more important things to worry about. "Have you found Margaret or Lee Caplin yet?"

"You're still officially suspended, remember?"

"You know I'm innocent, and whether you like it or not, I've been working the case with Zak."

Nathan cracked the knuckles of his left hand. "I know, and that's partly my fault for not protecting you from Agent Hatfield." He paused. "No doubt Zak will tell you later that the CIA's heading the hunt for Lee in the US and MI6 has sent agents to South America, where Margaret has extensive contacts. All our agents are secured now in case LibertyCrossing decides to finally follow through with his threat to publish everyone's names."

Was that likely? Zak had said Rodarte didn't believe that releasing the agents' names was ever on LibertyCrossing's agenda. It was only about freeing Lee Caplin. Or perhaps it wasn't. She couldn't think straight. Her head pounded and her body was shaking with tiredness.

"You should get some rest, Jessica. I've already told Rodarte you're done here. They'll need to go through me if they want to talk to you again. I'll drop you home."

"That would be great," she said, rising to her feet. "And Zak?"

"He's still in debriefing. He could be a while."

She followed Nathan out, steadying herself against the door frame. The agents had vanished and the men standing guard on the front door didn't attempt to stop them as they walked out. Every part of her body ached and a vein in her right temple throbbed as she walked slowly down the street. Despite feeling rotten, she had to know where she stood.

"Are you going to lift my suspension? You know I'm not working with The Collective. I was almost killed exposing their operation tonight."

Nathan took a sharp intake of breath but didn't ease up his pace. "It's not as simple as that, unfortunately." He guided her towards a black Mercedes, parked illegally on double yellow lines. "Sam's proved that your dad's home computer was hacked with a virus, which also attacked your school's IT system. It had similar coding to the virus that launched the assault on MI6 via your phone, which was also hacked."

"Which proves my innocence," she said, climbing into the passenger seat. "I had nothing to do with the hack on MI6, so what's the problem?"

"There's still the whole accessing Sargasso files

business to deal with. That isn't going away. Your prison visit hasn't helped matters either – you arrive and suddenly Margaret escapes. Agent Hatfield has her claws into you, but even worse than that, she's coming after Westwood. She thinks the whole division needs to be closed down. She's using you as a scapegoat for a much bigger agenda."

Jessica gaped at him as he started up the engine. "What?"

"She doesn't believe that teenagers should be trusted with state secrets. She's finding evidence to fit her theory that Westwood agents aren't up to the job; that the division isn't needed and shouldn't even exist."

"Does she have the power to close us down?" The words caught in her throat.

"She's whispering in the ears of some very important people in government, people who have the power to pull the plug on our funding. If that money goes, so does Westwood. Mrs T has privately confirmed that MI6 can't afford to siphon off resources from other departments to keep us going."

"We have to stop that from happening. Surely tonight has helped to prove that Westwood is needed?

That I'm up to the job? I discovered Ossa Cosway's link to The Collective, something that MI6 hadn't established yet."

Nathan tapped his fingers on the steering wheel impatiently. "Rodarte's already taken the credit for that. Zak said he suspected a link between Ossa Cosway's clothes and The Collective and saved your life in the warehouse."

"No way!" She stared at him, aghast. Zak was seriously unbelievable. One minute he was telling her how amazing she was and the next, he was stitching her up in spectacular fashion. Hadn't Margaret warned her that Rodarte always swooped in at the last moment to claim the glory? She hated to think Margaret had been right. Quickly, she reeled off what had *really* happened.

"I did wonder about Zak's version of events..." Nathan's voice trailed off. "He's obviously trying to impress his bosses after the disaster at Margaret's prison. It worked. He's flavour of the month."

Not with her. She'd kill him when she saw him next. "*We* need to start impressing people big time. We can't let Rodarte take the credit for everything. *We* need to find Ossa Cosway, Margaret Becker and Lee Caplin."

She had to prove to Agent Hatfield – and everyone else, for that matter – that she was up to the job. If she secured a big success, it'd help Mrs T persuade the men in suits that MI6 needed their division.

"It's going to be tricky," Nathan said. "You know that, don't you? Agent Hatfield's mind's already made up. Plus, we're already hitting a brick wall where Ossa's concerned. We've got Sam trawling through his HQ, but it doesn't look good. A virus has been downloaded, corrupting every single computer and iPad in the building. It's destroyed anything potentially incriminating. It could be a long, drawn-out process, piecing together Ossa's involvement in this unless he confesses to everything when he's finally arrested. We don't have any hard proof of his involvement in any of this, just a lot of circumstantial evidence."

"When has it ever been easy? You have to take me back, Nathan. I can help, truly I can, particularly when it comes to Ossa. I know him better than anyone at Westwood or Rodarte. I'm supposed to have a fitting tomorrow ahead of London Fashion Week. I can keep my ear to the ground and find out whether his employees have heard from him or know anything. They're more likely to talk to me. They've seen me around a lot over the last few months."

He hesitated. "I'm guessing the catwalk show will go ahead even without Ossa. We can't close down Ossa Cosway Ltd even after what happened tonight; it's far bigger than one man. It's become a billion-dollar worldwide industry, with what appears to be quite a complicated financial structure. It's going to take us some time to get to the bottom of what's been happening there."

"So use me. Let me see if I can dig up anything."

Nathan's eyes narrowed as he weighed up her offer. "Agent Hatfield must never know. This has to be completely off the books until we manage to turn up something concrete."

"Of course. As far as she's concerned, I'm just Ossa Cosway's muse, but I'll be quietly picking up clues along the way. Talking of which, I have this." She delved into her back pocket and pulled out the bag containing threads she'd taken from the warehouse. "I held off giving this to Rodarte. I was trying to think of a way to get it to MI6 so you could compare these samples against the thread I found at Henry Murray's boarding house."

"Smart move. I'll get this over to forensics and see if they've got an early readout from the evidence at the school. You're friendly with Lucas over there, aren't you?"

"Yeah. I spent a few days shadowing him during my training. He's cool. Why?"

"He was asking about you the other day. He doesn't know you've been suspended. I'll tell him to copy you in on the results since you found both leads. He'll do as he's told and keep Agent Hatfield out of the loop, without asking questions."

"Brilliant." This was a good start. Hopefully she'd managed to salvage something from the warehouse that was helpful to Westwood; Rodarte didn't have a sniff about this clue. She hadn't mentioned it to Zak earlier.

She sank back in the seat and closed her eyes. She couldn't waste this chance. Westwood had to fight back. Failure was not an option.

CHAPTER SIXTEEN

"Keep still, please. This won't take much longer." Christine Cooper spoke through a mouthful of pins. The head dressmaker knelt at Jessica's feet, doing some last-minute adjustments to the shimmering gold evening gown. It featured intricate beading and gold embroidery around the cleavage and hem, which had come undone. A few threads hung loose and needed tidying up.

Nathan was right; the Ossa Cosway show was going ahead at London Fashion Week. The issuing of Ossa's arrest warrant hadn't been made public; Westwood and Rodarte didn't want to prematurely alert hackers across the UK and the States that they were rapidly closing in on them. Miranda Heartley, chief executive of Ossa Cosway Ltd, was only too happy to keep quiet about the impending scandal. She'd been cleared of involvement in The Collective, after remote checks on her home computers, iPads and phones. But she couldn't shed any light on the designer's whereabouts. Nathan had said she was terrified about the allegations around Ossa being made public and had agreed to all of MI6's demands, including signing the Official Secrets Act to prevent her from discussing the investigation with anyone else. She'd also given full access to company documents.

The secret clampdown meant that agents had been able to seal off the designer's HQ before employees arrived for work, blaming an investigation by the fire brigade into possible faulty electrical wiring, which they claimed was also behind the warehouse blaze. It enabled agents to forensically examine the computers at the scene without removing them, and check through all the paper personnel files for links to The Collective. Miranda was allowed to make a public statement, announcing that the runway show had been unaffected by the warehouse blaze; most of the couture collection was being stored at another site owned by Ossa Cosway Ltd in West London. Only one jacket, which was undergoing further work, had been destroyed in the fire. In agreement with MI6, Miranda had moved their main London office to this temporary base. It was where Jessica and the rest of the Ossa team had been redirected by email and text early this morning. Others steadily drifted in after failing to get the message and reading the sign on the door of the closed HQ.

"Sorry I'm late. The traffic was unbelievable." A young man wearing biker shorts and a helmet strode across the room towards them.

"Don't worry, Mark." Christine flashed him a quick smile. "It's been a funny old morning for everyone. I don't think you'll be the last of the stragglers. We're still missing a few of our team, including Ossa. He's not coming in today or tomorrow."

"Seriously?" Mark mopped the sweat from his brow with a handkerchief. "He's going to miss his own show? Is he gravely ill or even dead? Those are the only possible explanations I can think of."

Christine continued to stitch the hem of Jessica's dress. "I've no idea what's going on. We're always the last to know. Miranda's not saying a word. She told me to step into Ossa's shoes and do absolutely everything to ensure the show's a huge success tomorrow."

"No pressure, then!" Mark replied.

Jessica opened her mouth to speak, but the junior dressmaker was getting into his stride.

"I swear something fishy's going on. Ossa's gone AWOL at the same time that our HQ's been closed due to faulty wiring." Mark removed his cycling helmet. "I didn't see any fire engines outside the building when I swung by this morning, just lots of guys in suits. It's suspicious, don't you think?"

"They're probably from the health and safety executive," Jessica said quickly. "I mean, I guess they're the sort of people who'd be involved in something like this, aren't they?"

"Hmm." Mark sniffed. "It still seems odd to me. Why would the fire brigade assume that the same wiring was used at the warehouse that burnt down and at our HQ? Seems like a big leap to me. I didn't believe the note on the door at all."

That was a good spot, which Nathan may not have anticipated. He'd only had a few hours to come up with a plausible cover story. Had anyone else at Ossa Cosway Ltd begun to smell a rat?

"Oh no," Christine said, laughing. "Are we about to hear another one of your mad conspiracy theories? Which one is it today?"

"Laugh all you want," Mark replied. "But I'm telling you, Ossa Cosway's got a secret life."

Jessica's ears immediately pricked up. "What do you mean?"

Mark dropped his voice. "I think he's some kind of weird time traveller. Either that, or he's a really good magician."

Now that *was* a mad conspiracy theory. For a moment, she thought Mark might come out with something interesting.

Christine rolled her eyes.

"I'm telling you, Ossa's some kind of illusionist," protested Mark.

"Why? Can he make spoons disappear?" Jessica asked.

"Ha ha. Not that. But he can stop time."

"For goodness' sake, stop with this nonsense," Christine said abruptly. She stood up, dropping her box of pins, and jerked her head across the room. "Those dresses aren't going to steam iron themselves."

Mark jumped at her abrasive tone. Red-faced, he bent down to help pick up the multicoloured pins.

"What are you talking about?"

Christine tutted loudly. "Don't encourage him, Jessica!"

Mark stood up, clutching a handful of pins. "I've noticed it for a while now, particularly since we started work on this ready-to-wear collection a few months back. It's as if time stands still when you're around Ossa. I double-check my watch and mobile when I arrive at work and they're exactly on time. Yet when I leave at the end of the day, I've always lost at least five minutes, maybe ten, on both. That's if my phone's still working. Often the battery's completely drained even though I've charged it that morning."

"That *is* strange," Jessica said. "I wonder—"

"It really isn't odd," Christine interrupted. "It means that Mark's a cheapskate and needs to buy a new watch and phone." She fixed him with a cool, hard stare. "Can you start to do some work? I don't think it's asking too much when we've got a major runway show tomorrow afternoon."

"Right away," he said stiffly.

"Good." Christine frowned, suddenly distracted. "What are you doing with that dress, Amanda? Leave that flower alone!"

The spikey-haired twenty-something blonde jumped guiltily. She clutched an exquisitely beaded white chiffon gown, studded with large gold embroidered flowers, from the rail. It was the showstopper dress that Jessica was scheduled to wear to close the runway show. She hadn't had a fitting for it yet. That was next up after Christine had finished altering the hem of this dress.

Amanda stared at the flower. It was a theme of the show, featuring in different shapes and sizes across the collection. "Something . . . something's wrong with this." The junior dressmaker picked at it with her index finger. "It's not right. I mean it's not lying on the fabric as it should, and I've noticed there's. . ."

"Put it back on the rack!" Christine stormed towards her, bracelets jangling and eyes sparking with anger. "You don't get to touch that dress unless I tell you. Do you understand? Have you any idea how long it took me to individually embroider hundreds of flowers? I won't have them ripped off by some idiot who's fresh out of college and has no idea what they're doing. Now back off!"

Amanda's bottom lip quivered as she choked back tears. Christine's reaction was totally over the top; everyone else in the room clearly thought so too. The other dressmakers and models stared, wide-eyed, and then quickly turned away. They didn't want to get caught in the crossfire. Within seconds, the temperature of the room felt like it had dropped by a degree or two.

"Is Christine usually that fiery?" Jessica whispered. She meant "bad-tempered", but figured it was best to be careful. She didn't know how close a relationship Mark had with her.

"She's a creative, like Ossa, and expects things to be perfect," he replied equally carefully. "If things aren't perfect, she gets slightly irritated."

Mark was talking in code too. Christine had a nasty temper. Jessica remembered the argument between the dressmaker and Ossa at the *Teen Vogue* shoot; that clearly hadn't been a one-off. Back then, she'd assumed that Ossa was being unreasonable, but was it the other way round?

"I guess Christine's stressed out," Mark said hastily. "Miranda will blame her if the show isn't its usual huge success. *Vogue* magazine editors from Italy, America, Paris, Brazil and Russia will be flying in specially. From what I've heard on the grapevine, there will be other important guests in the front row too. It'll be a disaster for the brand if it goes badly."

"Of course," she said, straightening her dress. She could see why Ossa's no-show had become a big problem for Christine, but was it necessary to reduce a member of her team to tears?

"It wasn't only me," Mark said suddenly.

"What?" Jessica's eyes followed Amanda across the room as she sneaked off, teary-eyed. Presumably, she was going to compose herself in the toilets. Christine stood at the clothes rail, examining the gown.

"You know, what I was saying about time stopping. Christine thinks I'm barking mad. But believe me, I've asked around and it's happened to other people; their watches always slowed down and their mobile phone batteries ran flat back at HQ. I guess it'll be OK today since Ossa's not here."

"I believe you. I don't think you're mad, by the way."

"Thanks. The conspiracy theorist in me thinks that maybe Ossa found a way to mess with our watches. That way he squeezed an extra five or ten minutes' work out of us each day." He winked at her. "It's all smoke and mirrors in fashion."

He picked up an iron, saluted Jessica with it, and waltzed a bemused male dressmaker over to another rail of dresses, a safe distance away from their boss.

OK, so she took that back. Mark was a *tiny* bit mad. She pursed her lips as two more latecomers slipped into the room. Zak was clad in biker leathers, clutching his rucksack and chatting to a smitten-looking Bree. Great. Her nemesis had also been picked for the Ossa Cosway show. Bree looked horrified when she caught a glimpse of Jessica in a mirror. She studiously avoided making eye contact as she scooted off towards the changing area. Did she fear a public showdown?

Jessica waited until Zak had finished greeting almost *every* woman in the room with a kiss on either cheek before she walked up behind him and tapped his shoulder.

"Jessica!" Zak's eyes lit up as he spun around. "I hoped I'd have chance to catch up with you here."

"So you could show off about being Superman who rescued little old me, Lois Lane? You really are a piece of work."

Zak's face flushed. "Let's talk over here, *Lois*." He steered her into the corner of the room, watched by one of the pretty, young dressmakers.

"I know what you're thinking," he said quietly.

"I seriously doubt that," Jessica retorted. "You've got some nerve swanning in here, pretending nothing's wrong." She glanced over her shoulder and lowered her voice. "You lied in your briefing. I had to convince you to stay in the warehouse last night. If you'd had your way, we'd have left straight away and never discovered the connection to Ossa. You totally dissed my theory about his clothes right from the start. You never saw the importance of Helen Hamlyn's raincoat."

Zak took a deep breath and held up his hands. "I admit I bent the truth a little bit."

"A little bit?"

Zak's cheeks were aflame. "Look, I'm sorry. OK? I didn't set out to stitch you up, honestly I didn't."

"So why didn't you tell Rodarte that it was my hunch? Or at least say we came up with it together?"

"Because I didn't think it was a big deal."

"Yeah, right." She folded her arms. "Not to you. God, you're selfish. You were looking out for number one as usual."

Zak opened his mouth. He looked as if he was about to say something, but changed his mind. "You're right. I apologize. I needed this hit."

"What do you mean?"

"My bosses have been breathing down my neck ever since I suggested you come on board. They thought it was too risky after you were suspended from Westwood. They'd started to question my judgement, particularly after Margaret's jail breakout. I needed a success after I'd taken such a punt on you."

Jessica paused. She hadn't considered the risk Zak was taking with his own career by fighting her corner. "I guess I can see that. To a certain extent, anyway."

Zak's cheeks flushed to a deep crimson colour as

the penny dropped. "I was selfish. I was thinking about saving my own career with Rodarte. I forgot what a hit could mean for your reinstatement into Westwood."

"Exactly!"

He squeezed her shoulder. "I was wrong. I won't do it again. I'll include you in everything and give you full credit. Cross my heart."

And hope to die.

Did he mean that? Or was he telling her what he thought she wanted to hear? She glanced across the room as Bree emerged from the fitting room wearing a short gold cocktail dress studded with hundreds of tiny, shimmering flowers. She looked totally stunning. Zak followed her gaze.

"I asked Rodarte to check her out, you know, along with the other Westwood girls."

"And?"

"They were clean, apart from Bree. She *is* hiding something."

She knew it! "What have you got on her?"

"Rodarte forensically checked her computers, bank balances – everything. She's not dirty, but she does have a secret boyfriend that she hasn't declared to Westwood."

Jessica raised an eyebrow. It was hugely embarrassing, but Westwood agents had to submit the name of the person they were dating, or planned to hook up with, for a full background check. That helped protect spies from getting romantically attached to "unsuitables" – people who could damage their cover or Westwood's.

"Who's Bree's boyfriend?"

"He's called Chris and works in a bookshop. It looks like they might be moving in together. They've signed up together at a rental agency in South London, looking for one-bedroom apartments. We haven't had a chance to dig any further with everything that's been going on."

Jessica frowned. Was working in a bookshop a front for his real job? Could he have turned Bree and persuaded her to steal the blueprint that night at the Shard? It would explain why she hadn't submitted his name for vetting to Nathan if she knew he was dodgy. Failing to declare a boyfriend or girlfriend – let alone moving in with them – was a disciplinary offence and led to immediate suspension from Westwood.

She stared at Bree as Christine inspected the seams of her dress. What else was the model hiding that Rodarte hadn't managed to find? Christine glanced up and beckoned to Zak.

"It looks like Christine needs you for a fitting."

"Great. Just what I need after a night of no sleep: standing still for hours on end while I'm prodded and poked."

"Ditto."

"So are we good, Jessica? After, you know, what I did or rather didn't do. I'd hate for there to be bad blood between us."

She glanced down. "You're vibrating."

"Sorry?"

She pointed at his rucksack; the fabric was shuddering slightly. Zak fished around inside and dug out his Nintendo. Flipping open the lid, he scrutinized the screen.

"What is it?" she asked.

"My software's gone haywire again." He showed her the games console; random messages flashed up intermittently and she caught sight of the word

"Rodarte". It was a CIA gadget. She used to have a similar mini computer, except hers was hidden inside an eyeshadow palette.

"Something electrical's interfering with it," he said, looking around the room.

"Doubtful. There aren't any computers here. MI6 checked it over before we arrived today. I haven't seen any iPads lying around either, unless one of the dressmakers has a tablet in their bag."

"It's been playing up recently. I need to get it repaired." He examined the gadget once more before turning it off and tossing it back into his rucksack. "Rodarte spends millions on the latest technology and it really sucks sometimes."

Jessica watched him stride over to Christine. The dressmaker broke into a broad smile as Zak worked his charm.

"I need you too, Jessica," Christine shouted across the room. She pointed to the flower dress that had sparked the argument with Amanda. "You're in this next. Hurry up."

Yikes. Something told her she shouldn't mess with Christine's embroidered flowers. Why were they so precious to her? It didn't make sense.

Four hours later, Jessica was finally free from the endless fittings. All her gowns were hanging on the rail, marked up with her photo and a number indicating the order for the show, together with the rest of the models' outfits. She'd also managed to squeeze in a quick runway rehearsal with the other girls; Bree had mustered a brief hello and then continued to avoid her like the plague.

Zak sighed as Jessica walked past. He was stuck in fitting hell, fidgeting as Christine lowered the hem of his trousers. She dug around in her Victoria Beckham handbag for her mobile. She was desperate to know if MI6 had got anywhere with Ossa. Nathan could have texted or emailed a coded update. She stared down at the phone in disbelief. It was dead. The battery had run down even though it had been freshly charged. Heart beating rapidly, she checked her Omega watch; it had been specially adapted by MI6 with secret functions, including a telescopic lens, and could withstand explosions and water as deep as fifty metres. She gripped it tightly in her fist as she shouted her goodbyes to the dressmaking team and walked briskly out.

She scanned the street for passers-by and ran to catch up with a young woman, who confirmed it was four ten p.m. She uncurled her fist and stared at her watch. It was running exactly six minutes late. Zak's mini computer had also been affected. Mark wasn't crazy. The problems he'd described back at HQ were continuing here, even when Ossa wasn't around.

How was that possible? What was going on?

CHAPTER
SEVENTEEN

"I wanted to see you in person to tell you the news," Zak said, beaming. "You know – the way I promised to keep you in the loop. It's Rodarte's success, obviously, but we couldn't have done it without Westwood's help."

Jessica gritted her teeth as she sat down next to him on the bench. His gloating was hard to take. A pigeon brazenly strutted up to her feet and snatched a discarded bit of sandwich. It was tempting to wrestle the mouldy scrap off the bird and hurl it at Zak. He'd texted her an hour ago and asked to hook up for an early morning meeting in the park close to her home.

"If this is about Ossa Cosway and Lee Caplin, I've already heard," she said flatly.

"You have?" Zak was temporarily thrown. "How?"

"Nathan had a change of heart and decided to keep me in the loop. I had a brief chat with him shortly before you texted."

"That's brilliant! So it's win-win all round?"

Not exactly. It was 2–0 to the Yanks. Not only had Lee Caplin been apprehended at a police roadblock in a western suburb of Kansas City, but Rodarte had also managed to swoop in and arrest Ossa attempting to board an American Airlines flight from Heathrow Airport to Washington. Both were now in custody and being questioned. Jessica tried hard to be glad, she really did. The main thing was that they'd been caught. However, Westwood had *really* needed those arrests to prove that the unit shouldn't be axed.

"You are pleased, aren't you? This is a good thing, Jessica."

"I know that. Tell me everything."

Zak outlined how Lee was pleading the Fifth Amendment and refusing to answer any questions from the police about how he'd managed to escape from prison and who had helped him. Ossa was a lot more forthcoming, but Zak said Rodarte was highly sceptical of his story.

"Ossa denies being LibertyCrossing and claims to know nothing about The Collective. He says he tried to leave the country when he realized his financial affairs were about to come to light following the warehouse blaze."

"What's up with his finances?"

"A hell of a lot. Ossa says he was contacted by email in his final year of college by an unnamed person, offering millions of dollars to help launch and support his fashion empire. The investment was on a number of conditions: that he never attempted to trace the identity of the backer and turned a blind eye to any suspicious activity in the company, particularly on computers. He also had to agree to all appointments that were put forward anonymously, including the employment of a very specific accountant who looked after the books. Needless to say, the bookkeeper's been arrested. Ossa claims cash regularly enters company accounts and he never checks its source."

Jessica raised an eyebrow, remembering the interview for *Teen Vogue*. Ossa had said his mystery investor was publicity-shy, but there was obviously far more to it than that. The anonymous backer sounded like he was using Ossa Cosway Ltd to launder money – taking advantage of the front of a legitimate business to conceal the source of money obtained illegally. It must have been lucrative; Ossa charged tens of thousands of pounds for haute couture dresses, which had been made using dirty money. How could Ossa have been stupid enough to take part in this scheme? He was hugely ambitious, but she couldn't believe he'd agreed to break the law to get to the top faster. He either didn't realize the legal implications or simply didn't care.

"If he's telling the truth, LibertyCrossing could be the silent investor for Ossa Cosway Ltd," Jessica pointed out. "That person had already made millions from hacking in the States and could have invested in Ossa's business as a way to carry out further hacks on wealthy fashion clients. It'd explain why LibertyCrossing's modus operandi changed suddenly. He'd found a way to look legitimate while targeting more affluent people."

"Ossa's made that suggestion too," Zak admitted.

"But another possibility is that he's come up with this story in a bid to save himself some jail time. Ossa could be LibertyCrossing, which means he invested all the millions he scammed from hacking into the start-up of his own company. He made up the story about a mystery backer to cover up how he obtained so much investment. We've carried out a preliminary analysis of the laptop he was carrying in hand luggage on to the plane; it's the only gadget that survived the virus that wiped out every single computer at Ossa Cosway Ltd."

"And?"

"We found exchanges of emails between LibertyCrossing and Henry Murray as well as other teenage hackers, plus downloaded data from MI6. We discovered the entire agent database that LibertyCrossing was threatening to leak."

"That evidence could have been planted," Jessica said. "Plus your theory doesn't explain the connection between Ossa and Lee Caplin and how he managed to hack the couture clients."

Zak stared at her. "Are you having a sudden change of heart?" His tone was sharp. "I seem to remember that back in the warehouse you argued the case *for*

Ossa Cosway being LibertyCrossing. If my memory's accurate, I recall you saying the designer could have acted because he had sympathy for a teenage hacker."

Jessica flushed. "I know what I said back then, but—"

"But what?"

"Something's not right. Hating to sound like *you* back in the warehouse, I don't buy that Ossa is LibertyCrossing any more. I think he's telling the truth about the money laundering and that he turned a blind eye to odd things happening at Ossa Cosway Ltd, because *really* odd things are happening there."

She described how watches were routinely losing time, mobiles were running out of batteries and how Zak's own gadget had been affected by something inside the temporary premises while Ossa was absent.

Zak shook his head. "You know what I think, Jessica? You're annoyed that Westwood didn't make these arrests, so you're deliberately casting doubt on everything I say. You don't want to believe it."

"Sure, I wish Westwood had got there first, but it's not about that. This is your *theory* about Ossa. That doesn't make it fact. I'm being objective and assessing the *facts*. I'm just saying I'm not sure you've got the right man."

Zak stood up, glaring. "Don't worry. We'll find enough *facts* to keep even you happy. This was only the first interview. There's plenty of time to draw out more incriminating info from Ossa. We're not done with him by a long shot."

Jessica got up too. She wondered what Nathan made of it all. They hadn't had a chance to discuss the arrests; he'd only given her the barest of details before he prepared for a briefing with the prime minister.

"Thanks for filling me in."

"No worries," Zak said stiffly.

"So..."

"Needless to say, Ossa won't make the show this afternoon and you can't discuss his arrest with anyone there," he snapped.

Like she'd been planning to announce it on loudspeaker. "It's definitely going ahead?"

She'd received a text earlier that morning from the chief exec, giving details of the time she needed to be in make-up and hair backstage at the BFC Courtyard

Show Space at Somerset House. It was the official venue for London Fashion Week.

"We don't have the power to pull the show, particularly at such short notice. Details of Lee Caplin's capture will make the news bulletins shortly, but we're planning to sit on news of Ossa's arrest for the moment. We can't stop Ossa Cosway Ltd from trading until we've got a forensic accountant to thoroughly investigate the company's finances, which will take weeks."

Jessica nodded. Nathan had intimated the same. "So I guess I'll see you at two p.m."

The tension in his face melted a little. "I'll be there hours earlier to do a recon of the site, you know, before the president arrives."

She'd forgotten about Zak's main reason for being in the country. "His daughter's still walking for Burberry? It's at BFC too?"

"Lydia's show is on right after ours, so it fits my cover," he replied. "I won't have to dash between venues. The president and the National Security Council have been fully briefed on the latest developments. The Collective's no longer seen as a high risk with Ossa and Lee in custody, so the president's itinerary for this week will continue as planned."

"I'll see you later, then."

"Yep," Zak said, swinging his rucksack over his shoulder. "I guess."

She watched him walk out the park. Yikes. That had been the most awkward goodbye. Ever.

CHAPTER
EIGHTEEN

Jessica's phone beeped as she sat alongside the other models in make-up, backstage at BFC. She snatched it up while Marie began painting her eyes with a sparkly silver colour.

"Jessica? It's Lucas."

"Lucas?"

"You know, from forensics?"

"Sorry. How's it going?"

"Great. Look, I couldn't get hold of Nathan so I thought I'd give you a heads-up about the threads you gave us."

"Can you give me one minute?" Jessica mouthed to Marie. She scuttled over to the corner of the room. "Go on."

"There was a match between the thread you discovered at Henry Murray's boarding house and one of the silver samples you took from Ossa Cosway's warehouse."

"Brill. Thanks, Lucas. I need to scoot." She walked back towards make-up again.

"Hold on, that's not the interesting bit."

"Go on."

"Neither piece of thread was normal. They weren't what you'd expect to find in clothing or in a fashion warehouse."

She stopped, ignoring Marie, who was waving a scarlet lipstick at her.

"Go on."

"They're both superconductive, but far more advanced than anything I've ever seen before."

"Come again?"

"Conductive threads are a way to connect electronics on to clothing. They make electronics wearable when they're woven or stitched into a garment. The thread carries current for power and signals and conducts electricity. It's usually at quite low levels. Some people stitch the thread into the fingers of their gloves, as it enables them to work a touchscreen."

She glanced around the room at the models. They all had mobiles glued to their ears. "Could this thread drain the batteries of phones and affect watches?"

"Undoubtedly, if the watches are battery-powered. I've never come across a thread as powerful as this. It can create small electromagnetic pulses that would affect non-battery-powered watches too, but not only that. It could interfere with other electronics from a short distance away – computers, iPads, laptops, public announcement systems. That's why it's so strange to find something like this linked with fashion."

Jessica felt the hair on the back of her neck prickle. She dodged past the make-up station and headed straight for the rack of Ossa Cosway clothes. A few models who had finished in make-up were already getting dressed. She snatched her dress from the rack: the white chiffon one studded with gold flowers.

"Tell me, is superconductive thread always silver?"

"It doesn't have to be."

Her fingers trembled as she touched the gold flower.

"Could the thread be stitched into clothes and used to hack into computers?"

Lucas paused. "Yes, given the complexity and sophistication of this kind of thread, you could get into virtually anything you wanted. The thread could hack in and download a virus into any surrounding programmable electronics, such as laptops and phones. It'd provide unlimited access to a remote user."

Jessica gripped the phone hard. "You need to pull Nathan out of his meeting."

"I can't. His secretary says he's in with the prime minister and mustn't be disturbed."

"Do it now. Tell him that LibertyCrossing has been hacking through Ossa Cosway's clothes. The superconductive threads have been stitched into the designer garments and sent to wealthy clients."

"I'm on to it now." He hung up.

This was scarily brilliant; the work of a genius. Ossa Cosway Ltd *was* a front for hacking; that must be how all those celebrities and affluent people in the US had been targeted, through deliveries of clothes, which were secretly stitched with superconductive thread. The garments had hacked into the home computers or iPads of the victims, leaving their security exposed. LibertyCrossing then found his way into the computers through the back door, draining online bank accounts and finding damaging online material that could be used for blackmail purposes.

She caught her breath, remembering *her* wardrobes back at home, stuffed full of Ossa Cosway clothes, and the clause in her contract that demanded she wore his designs at all times outside school. The clothes had probably hacked everything – her phone, iPad and dad's computer – months before LibertyCrossing revealed himself to MI6. She *had* hacked into MI6, but not deliberately. She'd worn an Ossa Cosway coat the day MI6 came under attack; it had hacked into her phone and then Nathan's laptop in the briefing room. Then the designer coat had hacked again, enabling a virus to be downloaded into the mainframe when she was in the comms room with the other agents.

What about her visit to Margaret's prison? Again, she'd worn an Ossa Cosway coat. That was how the security system had been brought down. LibertyCrossing had used Henry Murray to find glitches on the day of the major hacks. He'd then lured Jessica to the prison by planting evidence that made her suspect Margaret's involvement with The Collective. LibertyCrossing had banked on the fact she'd be wearing an Ossa Cosway coat and used it to hack in and open the locks on all the doors. The method was replicated in Lee's prison – the ultimate objective all along. The American reporter, Helen Hamlyn, had been sent a freebie coat, stitched with the thread, and was also persuaded to visit the prison by being offered an exclusive interview. She had no idea that she'd become Lee's get out of jail free card, just as Jessica had been with Margaret.

Her heart thumped madly. Had she been set up from day one? It had to be a possibility. She could have been put forward to become Ossa Cosway's muse not because she was the best model but because Margaret had sold info about her to LibertyCrossing. That person knew she was also a Westwood spy who'd provide vital access to MI6. So who was LibertyCrossing? Was it really Ossa Cosway?

She picked at a flower on her dress; Amanda had been doing the same when Christine Cooper blew her top yesterday. The junior dressmaker was right. The flower didn't sit right because the threading was heavily stitched. Jessica skimmed through the other garments left on the rail. Christine said she'd hand sewn every single flower in the collection. Up close, all the flowers looked quite ugly; they too were embroidered with lots of gold thread. No wonder a fellow dressmaker had spotted the poor finish, especially when Christine was such a perfectionist.

Someone had used too much superconductive thread.

Had Christine known about the high-tech thread and not wanted Amanda to draw attention to it? Jessica remembered the fashion shoot for *Teen Vogue* earlier in the week when Ossa had lost his temper because Christine had brought the wrong dresses. Back then, the dressmaker had claimed that someone must have switched the outfits at the last minute. But what if she had deliberately replaced the gowns herself because she daren't risk dresses stitched with electronic currents coming into contact with water?

If that were correct, Ossa was probably telling the truth. He had no idea what was really going on at his business. He didn't know his garments were being stitched with electronic thread, or perhaps he simply ignored anything suspicious. Ossa concentrated on rising to the top of the fashion world, enabling Christine, his ever-helpful personal assistant and dressmaker, to have a free rein.

She was LibertyCrossing, not Ossa.

The dressmaker had access to the computer in the warehouse and to all the garments that were used for hacking. Christine could easily have disguised her voice when she broadcasted her message to MI6. She helped with model castings and could have persuaded Ossa to give her the modelling job. But why did Christine want Lee Caplin released from prison and how had she discovered a way to hack using superconductive threads? She'd been a dressmaker all her life after leaving school. Jessica couldn't see the connection.

She scanned the room but couldn't see Christine anywhere. She glanced back at the clothes on the rail. She'd never noticed the superconductive thread on the clothes she'd been given before. It must have been a lot more subtle, possibly stitched into Ossa's distinctive ribbing around the collars and hems. Christine had deliberately overdone the high-tech thread for this show, but why? Was she planning to drain the bank accounts of celebs sitting in the front row? Jessica rang Nathan and left a message, relaying her suspicion that Christine was the superhacker, not Ossa.

She skirted around the room, trying to find Zak. Where was he when she needed him? She spotted Bree being helped into her dress by an assistant. Most of the other models were now dressed. No way was she putting *her* hacking dress on. The show would start any minute. It couldn't be allowed to go ahead. How was she going to stop it? Bree looked up, her eyes narrowing. She raised an eyebrow quizzically.

Jessica couldn't confide in *her*. Zak was the only person who could help, but he must still be doing security checks. She hadn't seen him backstage at all. She tried his phone, but it went straight to voicemail. Doubling back, she headed towards the front, where she could hear the rumble of voices and scraping of chairs. She peeked out from the wings; most of the guests had already been shown to their seats. The front row was still vacant; the VIPs were always the last to arrive. She caught a glimpse of Zak near three men in dark suits at the back. They scanned the crowd, looking for potential troublemakers ahead of the president's arrival at the next show. She'd already checked the timetable. There was a twenty-five-minute break between Ossa Cossway's collection and Burberry. Christine had to be arrested before the president got here. Jessica edged through the gap, trying to get Zak's attention.

Suddenly, a hand grabbed her arm and pulled her back.

"What are you doing here? Why isn't your face done yet?" The stage manager glared, taking in her jeans and blue-and-white starred sweatshirt. "We're about to open and you're not even dressed!"

"You need to cancel the show."

"Come again?" The middle-aged man's tiny grey moustache quivered.

"I'm telling you, it's not safe for the show to go ahead."

"I've no idea what you're talking about and I don't want to hear it." He dragged her back towards the dressing area. "Get ready or I'll make sure you're never booked for London Fashion Week again!"

She opened her mouth to try again, but stopped.

What was the point in arguing? It was wasting time. She couldn't tell him exactly what was wrong with the dresses; MI6 would definitely want that kept secret.

"Have you seen Christine? I wanted to check she's happy with my dress."

"She's out front, waiting for the show to begin, and I'm sure she'll be ecstatic when she sees you're finally wearing it. Now scoot!"

Jessica turned around. The Ossa Cosway models were already lined up in the order they were walking. What was she going to do? She no longer had the gadget she'd used at the Shard, which could take out the music system using an electromagnetic pulse. The models' wired-up dresses could probably interfere with that anyway. But the secret service had the power to close down the whole event due to the security risk. She had to get to them.

"What's going on?" Bree tottered over in gold stilettos and a short gold rose-studded dress. "You're not ready and you're acting really strange." She paused. "Even for you."

Jessica sucked in her breath. She slid her mobile into her pocket; it was probably a futile exercise. No doubt the dresses on the rail had hacked into her phone already, which meant that Christine could have heard the voicemail message she'd left for Nathan. Had she managed to delete the warning?

"I get that you don't trust me," Bree said.

"Can you blame me? I know your secret. And you're right; I don't trust you an inch. I haven't since the Shard."

Bree flinched. "I don't know—"

"You have precisely ten seconds to get dressed, Jessica Cole," the stage manager interrupted. "Or you'll be replaced in the line-up and Hanna will close the show, wearing *your* dress."

She took a deep breath. "So fire me."

"What?" Bree looked startled.

Jessica fled, dodging past stylists and PRs, and made her way towards the audience area. Beyonce's distinctive vocals boomed down the corridor. She wriggled past latecomers, through the door and into the standing-room-only section. The white runway stretched the length of the room, with rows of chairs on either side. Her jaw dropped as she took in the front row.

No way.

Sitting directly opposite was Robert Eastwood, the president of the United States, and his daughter, Lydia. They'd arrived early to watch Ossa Cosway's show. The lights dimmed. This was bad. Christine had deliberately ramped up the superconductive thread, which would come into range of the most powerful man in the world. Was the dressmaker planning to hack into his phone and download top-secret data right under the nose of secret service agents?

She pushed through the crowd, ignoring the glares and loud tutting. She had to get to the security detail before it was too late. But Bree was already striding down the runway, a vision in gold. Within seconds, she'd reached the end and tipped her head back as cameras flashed. Another model had reached the halfway point on the catwalk while a second emerged, striking a pose.

A loud scream rang out. "Dad!"

"Help the president!" someone shouted.

Bree hesitated slightly and then sashayed back up the runway as another female model emerged, followed by Zak. Jessica elbowed her way to the front. The president was slumped back in his chair, his face a horrible grey colour.

"Dad, Dad!" Lydia shook his shoulder while a secret service agent felt the president's neck for a pulse. A photographer shifted position and Jessica noticed Christine standing at the end of the runway. Her eyes were locked on the president, her mouth curled into a smile.

What had she done?

Jessica hurled herself on to the catwalk. "Get away from him!" she yelled at the models.

Bree tottered on her high heels and almost fell over, but the other girls froze to the spot.

Zak sprinted towards Jessica. "What's happening?"

"Get back!" she cried. "Keep away from the president!"

"What?" he faltered.

She glanced at the president. Secret service agents were easing him on to the floor to perform CPR while others created a human shield.

"The clothes are attacking the president somehow. You have to keep your distance and get the others off the runway."

He fell back a step. "Tell me. Quickly."

"Christine, the dressmaker." Jessica pointed at the throng of snappers, but she'd vanished. "She's sewn the clothes with high-tech thread that hacks computers and phones. Somehow she's using it to hurt the president."

Zak's face paled as he walked backwards. "Check his insulin pump. The hacks could have affected the dosage. I'll find Christine." He shouted over to the secret service agents. "Jessica's good. She's with me. Let her help."

He ran back up the runway, shouting at the models to follow him. Jessica jumped off the stage and pushed through the agents. She knelt down by the president, next to Lydia.

"Your dad's insulin pump could be malfunctioning. Do you know how to work it?"

"I think so."

The secret service agents had swelled in number, preventing anyone from taking photos as Lydia ripped open her dad's shirt. The insulin pump was attached to his belt; a soft plastic tube ran from it to a needle that was inserted into the skin close to his belly button. Jessica remembered the interview Lydia had given about the condition; the pump fed insulin into the body to control the blood glucose levels.

Lydia studied the monitor. "Dad's overdosing. Way too much insulin is being pumped into his body."

"Can you fix it?" Jessica said urgently.

"I think so."

Lydia fiddled with the monitor. "It's back to normal levels, but it's too late. He's had a massive dose. He has to get to a hospital."

The secret service agents swung into action, heaving up the president and carrying him to the nearest exit.

"Thank you." Lydia brushed away her tears and ran after them.

Jessica stood up. Where was Christine?

CHAPTER
NINETEEN

Hundreds of people had spilled out into the courtyard. Jessica frantically looked about, but it was impossible to spot Zak or Christine. She had to calm down and think logically. Christine must have hatched an escape plan after attacking the president. How would she get away? She'd have known she couldn't have got very far on foot if secret service agents were in pursuit. Relying on hailing a passing taxi was too risky, as was using the Underground.

Jessica turned around. She'd walked along the river to get here a few hours ago. Christine had to be escaping by boat along the River Thames. She ran out on to the river terrace and made her way down the steps to Victoria Embankment. She darted across the road, dodging traffic, and made it to the pavement. Christine couldn't be far; she must have moored a boat nearby. Her eyes were drawn to an abandoned jetty, which used to belong to a river cruise. As she pelted towards it, she spotted Zak lying sprawled on the gangway next to a docked speedboat. Christine stood over him, an arm raised above her head.

"Stop!" She clambered over the railings.

Christine sprang away, dropping a metal pipe, as Jessica sprinted towards them. The dressmaker untied the rope fastening the boat to the jetty and jumped aboard. Jessica reached Zak and knelt down. He was mumbling incoherently as he drifted in and out of consciousness. Blood pooled around his head. She stood up, fists clenched.

"Keep back!" Christine shouted as she attempted to start the engine. "That's what happened to your boyfriend when he tried to stop me."

"He's not my boyfriend." She leapt aboard. Before her feet had touched the bottom of the boat, a hot, agonizing pain ripped through her body. She crumpled into a heap, her limbs like jelly.

Christine loomed over her, holding a small device

that fitted into her cupped hand. "Bad choice. Have you forgotten what this can do?"

Jessica tasted blood in her mouth. She'd bitten her lip as the electric current poleaxed her. She couldn't fight back, not yet anyway. The only option was to keep Christine talking long enough for them to be discovered by the secret service. They'd have to come looking for Zak when he didn't check in and would figure out Christine's escape route the way she had.

"That was you at Henry Murray's boarding house?" she said, panting. "You attacked Henry and knocked out Natalia with that device?"

Christine gave a curt nod. "She received a higher dose, poor girl, but she shouldn't have got in my way. Sometimes if you need something doing, you have to do it yourself. Other times it pays to have hired help."

"You mean the thugs that attacked us at Charing Cross?"

She tried to start the engine again, but it spluttered and failed. "I'd like to say they were the best money could buy, but clearly they weren't."

"And you've made a lot of money from all those hacks in the US, haven't you?" Jessica attempted to sit up. "You ploughed millions into the launch of Ossa Cosway Ltd as a front for your hacking business."

"Get down!" Christine pushed her back as a lifeboat powered past. She waved at the crew, her ornate gold necklace swinging from side to side.

"Nice pendant," Jessica breathed. "Is that a phoenix engraved on it? As in a phoenix rising from the ashes?"

Christine ignored her as she fiddled with the boat's controls.

"You recorded that message for MI6 using a voice disguiser so you'd sound like a man, didn't you? All that stuff about wanting to bring about total freedom of information on the internet was rubbish. You don't believe it for a minute. You needed a distraction, which is why you incited all those hackers to cause mayhem. It all came down to this, didn't it? Releasing Lee Caplin and killing the president of the United States who'd refused to give clemency to a dangerous cybercriminal."

"He is not a danger to anyone," Christine snapped. "He's just a teenage boy. A sweet but misguided boy who didn't think through what he was doing." Her voice wavered as she tried the key again and again. "I had to do something. Lee didn't deserve to be jailed."

"What do you mean?" Jessica's fingers trembled as she felt in her pocket. Blast. Her key ring was in her handbag. For once, she had no gadgets on her. She'd changed out of her taser trainers into ballet pumps when she arrived at the venue, and removed her watch. Personal jewellery had been banned for today's show.

Christine's fingers slipped from the controls as she turned around.

Yes! Lee was her weak spot. Jessica had to continue to distract her. She stared at the device in Christine's left hand and back to her necklace again.

"I think I've seen that pendant before. It's quite unusual. It was in a photo. Lee Caplin's mum was wearing it."

Christine took a deep breath. "Louise Caplin was my half-sister."

So that was the connection! "You were doing all this for your family?"

Christine's grip on the electrical device loosened as tears filled her eyes. "I had to do whatever it took to free Lee, even if it meant setting up Ossa and hurting people who got in the way. I owed Louise that much."

"Why? I bet she'd never have wanted you to hurt Henry Murray, another teenage boy, even younger than Lee."

Christine brushed her tears away with the back of her hand. Jessica's eyes remained glued on the gadget. She couldn't defend herself properly in this position. She needed to get back on her feet, but her legs were too shaky to move.

"Don't you see?" Christine said fiercely. "I was responsible for *everything* that happened."

"That can't be right," Jessica said gently. "It's not your fault that Lee got himself arrested for serious computer crimes and Louise died."

"But it was," Christine sobbed.

"I don't believe you."

"Four years ago my husband, Harry, was dying of cancer. He worked in IT for the civil service, earning a pittance. He was good at what he did in the office, but he was brilliant at something else out of hours."

That could only mean one thing. "As in hacking?"

"It began as a hobby, but he'd found a way to send

out phishing emails and obtain personal passwords. I was shocked when I first found out, but then he became too ill to return to his IT job and was fired. My dressmaking wasn't paying enough to cover the mortgage. Harry trained me up and hacking became our main source of income. It paid for his cutting-edge private cancer treatment in the States. When he died months later..." Her voice broke. "When Harry passed away, I wasn't going to carry on, but then Louise's husband had a heart attack and died. I was financially supporting her and Lee through hacking as well as carrying on with my dressmaking. It was regular hours and allowed me to spend more time with Lee after school. He was massively into computers, but Louise wouldn't let him have his own. Lee used to come over to my house to go online."

Jessica caught her breath. "You taught Lee how to hack, didn't you? The family business continued after your husband died."

Christine nodded. "Lee wanted to learn and was good at it. Eventually, I confessed how I was making so much money. He wanted to help. Together, we made a good team – not that we ever told his mum.

Louise would never have approved. Before long, we were making crazy amounts of cash."

"That's when you started money laundering?"

"I couldn't exactly pay hundreds of thousands of pounds each month into my current account or Louise's. The bank would have reported me to the authorities. I had to find a way to recycle the cash. Investing in a fashion business seemed like a logical step. I could continue dressmaking and get a return on my investment as a silent backer."

"Why Ossa?"

"I worked with him in his final year at college and genuinely liked and respected him. That wasn't a pretence. He's a true fashion genius, but I realized he'd do absolutely anything to get to the top. He was also totally useless with money, preferring to focus on his designs rather than the nuts and bolts of how he'd actually get a business off the ground. I guessed he'd take millions unquestioningly if it meant he became a superstar. I was right. It all worked out very well."

"Except Lee got caught."

"He didn't stick to my rules and became careless. He bought his own computer to use at home. He stopped targeting people for money and performed ever more risky hacks to show off to his cyberfriends. He hacked into the Pentagon and downloaded files about new weapons and spy technology: superconductive thread that could be sewn into soldiers' uniforms to allow them to download information on the battlefield without the need for devices; high-tech electrical stun guns and grapnels that were far superior to anything ever created before.

"He also deleted files on other warfare techniques he found abhorrent and hacked into the missile system to show how easy it was to manipulate, how close countries could come to war by the push of a button. He never had any intention of firing those missiles. He was just making a point. A really silly, life-changing one."

Jessica managed to ease herself into a sitting position. "Which led to his arrest? The authorities had evidence of those hacks, but not the ones where you scammed people and targeted their bank accounts. Those were performed on *your* computer, which meant you could let Lee take the fall."

"I didn't want to but I had no choice. Don't you see?

I was far more useful on the outside than locked up. I recruited an army of hackers that I knew could help me wreak havoc when the time was right. Plus I thought, because of Lee's age, that the president would take pity on him and intervene, especially if they looked into his background and saw that he was strongly anti-war. He'd never have started World War 3. Instead, the president did nothing and the Americans built a case around him being a dangerous cybercriminal. His extradition killed Louise. The president killed Louise."

"You could have come forward and confessed to your involvement. Lee would have got a lighter sentence if you'd explained what you'd done and provided a character testimony."

"But I'd have been behind bars. I remembered some of the documents Lee had downloaded and realized there was another way. If the military could use superconductive thread in uniforms, why couldn't I stitch it into couture clothing? I had a list of military suppliers I could secretly buy it from. I experimented using Ossa's US clients, and it worked. It helped fund the legal costs to fight Lee's extradition. When that failed, I knew I could use the same method to get him out of prison – using superconductive thread stitched into clothing to hack into the jail's security system. I just had to pick a journalist at random who'd be thrilled about receiving an expensive freebie and then entice them to the prison with the offer of an interview. It worked."

"You failed. Lee's been recaptured and he's probably going to serve an even longer jail term, thanks to you. Your assassination attempt on the president didn't work either. Give yourself up, Christine, and help free Lee another way, by coming clean about your involvement. You could help reduce his sentence if you take the blame. He shouldn't have to do this alone, not when he's lost his mum."

"Why would I volunteer to be jailed when I can do this my way? I have the technology. I can break Lee out again and we can start a new life together, far away from the US and here." Christine tried the engine again. This time it started.

Jessica felt a scorching pain in her chest and fell on to her back. Christine knelt over her, waving the gadget.

"You should never have followed Zak. This device

was designed by the US government to fire electrical pulses. It can take out the glass in any window from a range of a hundred metres. When it's ramped up to full power, as it is now, it can also stop hearts. I'd estimate you have about thirty seconds left before the blood stops pumping around your body."

Waves of excruciating pain washed over Jessica. It felt as though someone was sitting on her chest, crushing the air out of her lungs. Christine stared down, smiling. Then a look of confusion flickered over her face. The dressmaker's mouth opened into a scream and she fell sideways as blackness flooded behind Jessica's eyelids.

A sharp pain stabbed Jessica's forehead. She tried to open her eyes but a flashing light made her swiftly shut them again.

"Jessica? Jessica Cole? Can you hear me?"

Her tongue felt too heavy to reply.

"She's with us again."

She opened her eyes. This time they managed to stay open longer. Faces stared down at her. She didn't recognize any of them. Then it went dark again.

She realized she must have blacked out again because when she woke up for the second time, she was lying in a bed. The stiff sheets scratched her bare arms and legs. A bright light seared through her eyelids and she could smell disinfectant. She opened her eyes slowly.

"She's coming round. You need to give her some space," an unfamiliar voice said. "Move back a minute while I make her more comfortable."

A woman leant over and plumped her pillow. She squinted and the woman came into focus. She had red hair and a blue uniform.

"There, that's better, isn't it?"

"I think so," she said groggily.

She looked about the hospital ward. The last thing she remembered was Christine screaming. Had she fallen? What had happened?

A tall, raven-haired figure stepped out from behind the curtain.

"Bree!"

The model hovered by her bedside. "You're going to be OK. I called for an ambulance."

"You did? Z-Zak." She stumbled over the word.

"What about...? I mean, he's...?"

"Zak suffered a deep head wound and is still unconscious, but the doctors say he'll pull through. You were in a far worse state. Your heart stopped. The paramedics had to bring you back twice in the ambulance. If they hadn't arrived when they did, you probably wouldn't have made it."

Jessica tried to think through the pea-soup fog in her head. She'd almost died and Bree had saved her life. Probably Zak's too. Why would she do that if she were a double agent? It didn't make sense.

"The secret service agents were looking for Zak and Christine," Bree continued. "I figured they must have gone to the river; it was the only logical getaway. I saw Christine attack you. I knocked her out with a stun dart in my watch and dragged you off the boat."

"You did all that?" Jessica breathed. "For me?"

"Astonishing, I know, that someone who routinely freezes on assignments didn't screw up this time. I helped apprehend Christine and saved the lives of two government agents."

"I'm sorry. I didn't mean it like that."

Bree shrugged. "I know you judge me."

"You judge me," she whispered back. "You think I only got into Westwood because of my godfather; that I haven't earned my place."

"I did think that at first. It all seemed to come so easy to you."

"That's not—"

"Let me finish. I was wrong about you, I admit that. I've seen you in action and can understand why you're here, which has nothing at all to do with Nathan. You're a natural at this, something else that got under my skin."

"I don't get it. I irritate you now because I've proved I can actually do the job?"

Bree took a deep breath. "I'm not explaining this well. You were right backstage. I have been hiding a secret and I don't want to any more."

"Go on." She eased herself up the bed. Was Bree about to confess to betraying MI6 and attacking her at the Shard?

"I'm not cut out for Westwood. I know it. I hated the fact that you knew it too. I've pretended it's OK for a while, but it isn't. I loathe the lies and deception, and the truth is that I'm not very good at what I do.

I panic in the field and people end up getting hurt – you, Natalia. You doubted me and you had reason to. I didn't betray you the way you seem to think I did. But I know I let you down. I'm sorry for how horrible I've been to you. I'm sorry for everything."

Jessica stared at her, stunned. Of all the things she thought Bree would say, she hadn't expected *this*.

"You see, I've started seeing someone," Bree continued. "A normal person who doesn't have to tell lies every single day of his life. It's hard to believe there are people like that when you do a job like this, but it's true. His name is Chris and he works in a bookshop and he has absolutely no idea what I do. I think he's the one and I never want him to find out about Westwood."

Jessica's mouth fell open. "That's why you didn't get him vetted?"

Bree bit her bottom lip.

"Zak told me. Rodarte ran checks on you. There was no record of vetting under his name at Westwood, yet you're looking at flats together."

"I didn't see the point in getting him checked out when I never had any intention of telling him about my work. Meeting him has helped make up my mind. I can't live this double life."

"It's tough for everyone," Jessica murmured, thinking of Jamie. What wouldn't she give to see him now?

"I know that, but some people, like you, can cope better with that secret life than me."

Really? Look how she'd screwed things up with her ex.

"I wanted you to be the first to hear that I'm quitting Westwood. I'm handing my notice in to Nathan today."

"Seriously?"

"I've never been more serious about anything in my life. You're Westwood through and through. I'm not. I never have been. I had doubts right from the start."

Jessica shook her head. "I'm not Westwood either. I'm still suspended and will probably stay that way thanks to Agent Hatfield."

"Westwood will have to reinstate you after today. You saved the life of the president of the United States. He's going to pull through, thanks to you. You'll probably even get a medal or something."

"I doubt it." If she had a choice, she'd much prefer to get back with Jamie and have her suspension lifted at school.

"We'll see." Bree stared at Jessica. "Despite *everything*, it's been kind of fun working with you." She turned to walk away.

"I'm sorry."

Bree stopped, her hand resting on the curtain. "Don't be. Good luck with everything. I mean it."

"You too. And thank you for saving my life."

Bree winked. "It was the least I could do."

Jessica sank back into her pillow. She believed Bree; she wasn't a double agent, just someone who wasn't cut out to be a spy. She probably shouldn't have been recruited in the first place. But if Bree hadn't attacked her and stolen the USB device that night at the Shard, who had?

CHAPTER
TWENTY

The doctor had discharged Jessica; she hadn't suffered any long-term effects. But that hadn't stopped Mattie from launching a campaign to drive her slowly mad by moving into their spare bedroom at home and treating Jessica like an invalid again. She'd been back from hospital for two days and even though she was still getting splitting headaches, she was seriously thinking about returning to school so she could escape from Mattie. Her head teacher had cleared her of any wrongdoing and lifted her suspension, as had Westwood.

Maybe she should beg Nathan to give her a foreign assignment? Saving the president's life had also protected Westwood, silencing Agent Hatfield's whispering campaign. She'd been quietly reassigned to another department and Jessica was *the* golden girl of the division. She reckoned she could ask for almost anything and she'd get it. Things were good; Christine had confessed to everything, including inciting Lee to commit his crimes. He was being released from prison in the US and allowed to return to the UK, to serve out a substantially reduced sentence on probation. Henry Murray had escaped prosecution in return for his evidence against Christine. But the dressmaker faced a lengthy jail sentence, as did Ossa Cosway, for participating in money laundering.

"I've got that," Jessica called as the doorbell rang. She slowly climbed down the stairs. With any luck it'd be her guardian angel, Becky, arriving, armed with a plan to drag her off to Café Panorama for a hot chocolate and blueberry muffin.

She flung open the door. "Zak!"

He broke into a grin. "Hello. Can I come in?"

"Of course." They hadn't caught up properly; he'd been discharged from hospital before her. She nodded at the bandage on his forehead. "I see you're rocking the 'injured member of a boy band' look."

"Thanks. You don't look so bad yourself. Or aren't I allowed to say that?"

She smiled. "You've never asked my permission to say whatever you like, so why change now?"

"Touché."

"Hi, Zak." Mattie peered over the banister. "It's lovely to see you again. Is Jessica going to ask you if you want a coffee or should I come down and make it?"

Jessica scowled up at Mattie, willing her to vanish. She had an uncanny ability of appearing at *the* most awkward times.

"It's fine, thanks. I'm not staying. My taxi's waiting outside. I've got a flight to catch back to the States."

"I'm sorry to hear that, Zak," Mattie replied. "But come back and visit us soon. Bon voyage."

Jessica waited until she heard the door of the spare room close. "You're going back?"

"Rodarte's got another assignment lined up for me. Plus I've got exams to cram for and my family's expecting me back from my art history trip."

"That's how you'd describe this last week?" she said, laughing.

"I'm not sure how I'd define it, but meeting *you* has certainly been an experience."

Jessica blushed. "We made a good team. In the end, anyway."

"We did, didn't we?" Zak's green eyes bored into hers. He thrust his hand into his pocket and pulled out a small black box. "This is for you."

"You're not proposing, are you?" she joked.

"Don't worry. You're not *that* lucky."

Rolling her eyes, she opened the box and pulled out a silver compact.

"It's to replace yours," Zak said. "It's far better than MI6 technology. This has Rodarte's added functions. It can run facial recognition checks as well as the usual paralysing powder, X-ray vision and photographic functions."

"Thanks. That's really thoughtful."

She flicked open the lid.

"I engraved it for you with your favourite quotation."

Her eyes widened as she stared at the words. *I am no bird; and no net ensnares me; I am a free human being with an independent will.*

"How did you know about this?" Her voice faltered. "Who told you?"

Zak frowned. "I remember you said you liked *Jane Eyre*. I can't remember when, but I guess it stuck with me. The quotation reminds me of you; how independent and free-spirited you are. Jessica, I—"

He reached out to embrace her, but she stepped back. "I never told you anything about this."

"I'm sorry. Don't you like it?" He frowned. "I guess I should have stuck with something safe like flowers. Anyway, I should go. The taxi's on meter. Goodbye, Jessica." He walked back towards the door.

Jessica darted forward and caught his arm. "Look at me, Zak."

He glanced away for a few seconds before meeting her gaze.

"It was you." Her hand dropped limply to her side.

"What are you talking about?"

"It was you that night at the Shard. You knocked me out with my own compact. That's the only way you could have known about the quotation. You read the engraving when I was unconscious."

He shook his head vigorously. "You're wrong. Dead wrong."

"Ohmigod." Her hand flew to her mouth. "You attacked me and stole the USB device. Then you came round to my house to check on me. You wanted to see if I could remember anything about my attacker from that night; if I could identify you. You deliberately made me suspicious of Bree."

"Jessica." Tears glistened in his eyes. "You don't understand."

"You're right, I don't understand." Her voice wobbled. "You said I was amazing and you pretended to like me. Everything we've been through together this week has been a lie. All of it."

"That's not true." Zak gripped her arms tightly. "I wasn't lying when I said I thought you were amazing. You are. I'm not lying when I tell you that I'm falling for you, that I couldn't take my eyes off you the first time I saw you. I thought Jamie was the luckiest guy alive to be your boyfriend."

Jessica shrank away. "I have no idea who you are."

"I'm the same as I always was."

"A big-headed arrogant liar? I should have stuck

with my gut instinct, but you reeled me in. I believed you." She took a breath. "There's no point denying it. I know it was you. At least have the decency to admit it."

He paused. "You're right. I owe you that."

Jessica felt her knees weaken. "Why?"

He brushed the tears from his eyes and jutted his chin out. "Because it was an order. And we follow orders, remember? That's what we do. The CIA had heard that the MoD had a major problem – its employee Drew Hopkins was selling the driverless truck blueprint to the Chinese. We had to stop that. We intercepted internal correspondence at MI6 and discovered when the meet was happening, how Westwood planned to intercept the buyer and retrieve the USB device at the Shard fashion show."

"You mean you hacked into MI6?"

"Governments do that all the time. You must know that."

"You're no better than Christine and her army of teenage hackers," she spat out. "I don't get it. Why were you so anxious to intercept the meet? Didn't you think Westwood could stop the deal from going ahead?

Rodarte had to fly in and save the day, taking all the glory, because you didn't think we were up to the job?"

Zak didn't answer.

"It's not that, is it? You came to London to *steal* the blueprint. That was your intention all along."

He nodded slowly. "You know as well as I do how valuable a driverless truck will be to a country in the future. It could change the face of modern warfare; an army would no longer have to invade a city. The driverless trucks or tanks would do it for them. Thousands of soldiers' lives would be saved. The United States is dangerously far behind the Chinese when it comes to this kind of technology. We couldn't afford for that situation to continue. We have to catch up."

Jessica could hardly process what he was saying. "At any price? It didn't matter who got in the way or who you hurt as long as the US government got what it wanted?"

"I'm sorry you got hurt, I really am. I wanted to come clean and tell you what had happened. I tried to tell you the night of the warehouse blaze, but you wouldn't let me."

"You don't know the meaning of the word sorry. I trusted you, Zak."

"I know you did," he said softly. "This isn't personal. Yes, I fancied you when we first met, but we're spies first and everything else comes after that. You'd do the same if Nathan gave the order."

She shook her head vigorously. "I'm not like you. My family and friends come first. I'm a spy second. This is what I do. It's not who I am."

"Then you won't get very far with Westwood. I did what I had to for my country so I could get that USB device. This was just another job."

"Was it? You claimed to like me and knew I was a Westwood agent, yet you still attacked me."

"I didn't expect to encounter *you* at the top of the Shard." His voice wavered. "You were one of the most junior operatives on the team. It should have been Bree or Sasha going after Drew, not you. I took your compact because it was the closest to hand in the dressing room, but I never wanted it to be you."

"So that made it OK to attack Bree or Sasha? You're unbelievable."

"I'm just saying they were the most experienced

operatives, according to the files. Except they both messed up. They didn't have the guts to go after Drew, but you did. I couldn't have anticipated that. I underestimated you."

"Ditto. You're a world-class jerk. I hate you."

"No, you don't. Deep down, you like me back and that scares you. It frightens you that I know you better than Jamie."

"No way. You're wrong."

Zak tried to take her hand, but she snatched it away.

"Don't you see? Jamie will never be right for you. He doesn't understand you, because he can't. He doesn't know who you really are. Only another spy can understand what it's like, the things you have to do. I get all of that. You know I do."

"Jamie understands me far better than you. He's decent, really decent." She let out a sob. "And it's ruined, all because of you. You came along and destroyed us."

"No. The moment you signed the Official Secrets Act, your relationship with Jamie was doomed. Deep down, I think you knew that."

"How could I?"

"Because you made a choice. You can't have relationships outside this job. You chose joining Westwood and discovering what happened to your mum over your boyfriend. Now you have to deal with the consequences. That's on you, not me."

"Is it really?"

"I get that you're angry, but we can work this through. You said we made a good team and we still can."

"Never. Not in a million years."

"We're good together. You know that. I think you have feelings for me too; you just don't want to admit it. Call me when you've had time to process all this; when you've calmed down."

"Get out."

Zak paused at the door. "Think about it, Jessica. Do that for me."

"I don't need time to think. I never want to see you again."

She waited for him to walk out and slammed the door.

‹ CHAPTER ›
TWENTY ONE

A week later

It seemed to take an age before Jessica heard the light tap of footsteps cross the hall. The front door finally swung open.

She took a deep breath. "I know I'm the last person you want to see, but please hear me out."

Jamie ran a hand through his hair and stared. Shifting position, he shoved his hands into the pockets of his jeans. At least he hadn't slammed the door in her face, which she'd been half expecting.

"All you have to do is listen to what I have to say."

Jamie gave a brusque nod. He still hadn't invited her

inside, so they'd have to thrash it out on the doorstep. Not ideal, but better than nothing.

"Go on. I'm listening."

"You were right," she began. "I have been lying to you for months, but not for the reasons you think. I want to tell you everything, about who I really am. What I belong to."

Jamie frowned. "Do you mean about Westwood? I know that you're a member of an MI6 division that recruits models, particularly ones that it can mould from a young age."

"That's impossible. You can't... How long...? Why...?" Her words barely made sense. How could Jamie know about Westwood? It was top secret. She hadn't told anyone she was going to come clean to her ex today; he certainly hadn't been OK'd by Nathan or anyone else at MI6. They hadn't been going out long enough before their split for him to be cleared. He'd be classed as a "compliant civilian", someone who could inadvertently blurt out secrets to a third party.

"You'd better come in." He stepped aside, smiling encouragingly.

She followed him into the sitting room, her mind racing. None of this made any sense.

Jamie sat next to her on the sofa and tentatively took her hand. "I want to apologize for the way I treated you. I had no idea how important your job was. What you were doing to help Henry Murray and your country."

She stared back, shell-shocked.

"I'll never doubt you again if we get back together. I know it's a big 'if' after what a jerk I've been. I promise you that from now on I'll understand when you have to go off on your next Westwood mission." He squeezed her hand. "And I won't get all weirded out if you have to work alongside another male agent, like I did with Zak. I get that you sometimes have to work with other agencies such as Rodarte."

Rodarte was classified, like Westwood. No way should he know about it.

"Who told you about all of this?" Her voice cracked.

"Your handler."

Nathan? Not in a million years. He wouldn't allow such a blatant security lapse. If he had his way, she wouldn't even have a boyfriend or an ex or whatever. He believed things like that got in the way of the job. He'd prefer Westwood's agents to be robots without love lives, which got icky and complicated.

"She stopped by this morning for a chat," he continued. "She even brought red velvet cupcakes, because she knew they were my favourite as well as yours." He flashed a grin at her. "I guess you told her that about me. Anyway, she spent quite a long time helping me to understand things you haven't been able to speak about before. She said that I'd been thoroughly vetted and that I'd been given clearance to be told everything."

That couldn't be right. Who'd told him that? She couldn't picture Celia ever doing something so rash. Had Bree thrown caution to the wind now she was officially "retired" and decided to stage an intervention on Jessica's disastrous love life? But how could she have known about Jamie? Jessica had never discussed him with Bree.

"Did she give you a name? I mean, I have a few handlers for different missions." A lie slipped out. So much for deciding to tell Jamie the whole truth and nothing but the truth. Her good intentions hadn't lasted very long. About three minutes, to be precise, since she'd stepped through the door.

"Anne, I think she said her name was. But you spies always use different aliases, don't you?" Jamie grinned. "Can you tell me any of yours? I bet they're really cool."

"Honestly, they're not very interesting. Can you describe my handler? As you say, I don't think she was using the name I'd know her by."

"Oldish, you know, in her sixties, with dark brown hair."

Her face must have looked blank because Jamie's brow furrowed. "She told me a lot about your mum, how she used to be a spy, like you. How you think she was murdered by an MI6 traitor called Margaret Becker and a terrorist who had a name beginning with V, which I can't quite remember."

"Vespa?" Jessica hated it, but she had to test him.

"No, not that. I've got it now. It was Vectra. She said that you'd worked out it was all linked to something called Sargasso and that you were in great personal danger. She said I should impress upon you to be very, *very* careful from now on, and for your dad and Mattie to do the same."

Jessica caught her breath. Margaret Becker.

But it couldn't be. Why would she take the risk of breaking cover to visit Jamie in disguise? Was she banking on the fact that MI6 was searching for her off-grid and hadn't made public her escape from prison? They'd arrested the guard she'd bribed to carry messages between her and LibertyCrossing. Nathan had said that many of Margaret's old haunts were under surveillance. They hadn't thought to check here. Why would they? What were the chances she'd turn up at Jessica's ex's house?

"What else did *Anne* say?" she persisted.

"She told me to give you this." Jamie sprang up and grabbed an envelope from the mantelpiece.

She tore it open. Her fingers trembled as she pulled out a photo. It was taken years ago, but there was no mistaking who was in the picture. A much younger Margaret with bobbed blonde hair sat to the left, in what looked like a bar. Her mum was in the centre. Her strawberry blonde hair tumbled over her shoulders and she sported her trademark gap-toothed grin. On her right was the man from the Sargasso file – Sergei Chekhova, who'd died in a car crash.

"Anne thought this picture would mean something to you. Does it?"

She nodded, not trusting herself to speak. Margaret was taunting her. She was proving what power she had over her life. Even when she was on the run and secretly being hunted by every police force and intelligence agency across Europe and America, she still had the time to visit Jamie and sit across the room from him. She could have killed him right there and then if she'd wanted. That was the real message she'd used Jamie to give. She could get to Jessica or anyone close to her at any time. They were all in danger. She'd spared Jamie's life – or had she? Margaret may actually have deliberately endangered him by telling him about Sargasso. He'd become another loose end that might need to be tied up later.

Who else had Margaret visited? She texted her dad, Mattie and Becky with the same message: *U OK?*

Her dad and Mattie messaged back saying they were fine. Becky didn't reply, but she did have a rehearsal for her new play today. She'd probably turned her phone on to mute while she ran through her lines.

"Is something the matter?" Jamie asked. "You've gone awfully pale."

"It's a shock, you knowing about all of this. No one had told me beforehand that this was going to happen, that MI6 was going to clear you."

"But it's good, isn't it? It means that we don't have any secrets. We can be completely honest with each other from now on. We can make things work between us. That's if you want to."

She smiled, but inside she was being torn to bits. Of course she wanted to get back with him. But would he be placed in even greater danger by becoming part of her life again? Or didn't it make any difference as far as Margaret was concerned? She could return to finish him off, whether they were together or apart. Her eyes rested on a series of digits, written in black ink, on the back of the photo. Was that the date the photo had been taken? It was five months before her mum's helicopter crash.

"Did Anne leave any other messages for me?" Jessica asked.

"She said the photo was taken the day your mum and the man in the picture joined."

"Joined what?"

"Sargasso. That's why they were celebrating."

She shook her head numbly. Jamie had misunderstood Margaret. Her mum and Sergei must have been investigating Sargasso, not joining it. Jamie made it sound like some kind of country club, except this organization killed people who even knew of its existence, according to Margaret's threat in prison.

Her phone vibrated, but she ignored it as she pondered the puzzle Margaret had left.

"Are you going to get this?" Jamie asked, picking up the phone from the sofa. "It's Becky."

Jessica snatched it up. "Becky! How's it going?"

There was a muffled sob on the end of the phone. "No, it's Marie. Becky's mum."

"Mrs Roberts? What's wrong?"

"Becky's been taken into the operating theatre for emergency surgery. We won't know anything for a couple of hours. We're waiting and praying. Oh God, Jessica. How could this happen?"

"What is it?" Jamie mouthed, putting his hand on her shoulder.

"What happened?" Her tongue felt too thick and

heavy for her mouth. She clenched her fist, screwing the photo of Margaret into a tight ball as Mrs Roberts continued breathlessly.

"Some maniac in a van mowed into Becky's bike as she was riding to her play rehearsals. They didn't stop. Can you believe that? Witnesses said the driver accelerated and deliberately aimed at her."

Margaret. She'd got to Becky before Jessica could warn her.

"Can we come to the hospital?" Tears streamed down Jessica's face. "I'm here with Jamie. We both want to be there when she comes out of surgery."

"Thank you. Text me when you get to reception and I'll give you directions to intensive care."

She hung up and staggered to her feet. "We need to go. Becky's hurt."

Jamie hugged her close as she sobbed out the bare details of what had happened.

"This is my fault," she said.

"How can it be? This has nothing to do with you."

It had everything to do with her. This was Margaret's revenge for giving evidence against her in court six months ago.

"Let's go," Jamie said. "We can hail a cab on the street. It'll be quicker."

Jessica nodded, brushing away her tears with the back of her hand. "Did Anne leave a mobile number, by any chance?" She rummaged in her handbag for a tissue. "I don't think I have her up-to-date one."

"No. But she did say she'd catch up with you soon."

She followed him into the hallway. Margaret was coming for her. The last time she'd hurt someone close to her – Nathan – Jessica had sworn that she'd join Westwood so she could use all of MI6's resources to bring her to justice. This time it'd be on her terms. She'd do whatever it took to catch Becky's attacker, even if it meant breaking all of Westwood's rules. She'd find Margaret herself.

This time Jessica would take her down for good.

ACKNOWLEDGEMENTS

I'd like to thank the wonderful team at Scholastic, particularly my lovely editor, Helen Thomas, the press team, Rachel Phillips and David Sanger, and my patient desk editor, Pete Matthews. I'm extremely grateful to my former agents, Suzy Jenvey and Ajda Vucicevic and current agent, Sallyanne Sweeney, who have all loved Jessica Cole.

Thank you to the brilliant book bloggers on Twitter including Faye Rogers, Jim Dean, Lucy Powrie, Michelle Toy and Vivienne Dacosta and supportive fellow authors including Lindsay Antonia, Gary Meehan, Eve Ainsworth, Rachel Hamilton, Rachel

Craw, Emma Haughton, Christina Banach, Lisa Glass and Helen Grant.

A special thank you to my mum who always reads my proofs, Darren who endlessly listens to my ideas for plot twists and a big hug for James and Luke. Finally a huge thank you to my wonderful readers who always make me want to come up with ever more exciting adventures for Jessica Cole.

Catwalk Criminal is Sarah Sky's third novel in the JESSICA COLE: MODEL SPY series. Sarah is a freelance education journalist and a fan of martial arts. She is currently training for her black belt in karate after getting her brown belt/two white stripes and has a green belt in kick-boxing. She lives in London with her husband and two young children. She would have loved to become a spy but was never recruited by MI6. Or was she…?

@sarahsky23